Training Horses and Hearts

NICOLE GUSTAFSON

About The Author

Who am I? Let's see. Butch, nonbinary lesbian. 4-H, baseball, and soccer mom. Criminal prosecuting attorney. Previous law enforcement officer for 16 years. Wiccan nature lover. Animal rescue volunteer. Artist in graphite and colored pencil. Extensive animal experience with cats, dogs, pigs, chickens, rabbits, horses, llamas, alpacas, donkeys, doves, iguanas, bearded dragons, hamsters, guinea pigs, and two Madagascar Hissing cockroaches. And now, a published author.

Training Horses and Hearts

NICOLE GUSTAFSON

BELLA
BOOKS
2023

Bella Books, Inc.
P.O. Box 10543
Tallahassee, FL 32302

Printed in the United States of America on acid-free paper.

First Edition - 2023

Editor: Heather Flournoy
Cover Designer: Kayla Mancuso

ISBN: 978-1-64247-472-5

PUBLISHER'S NOTE

Acknowledgments

I'd like to thank my family for supporting my insane idea to write a novel and for always encouraging me to be relentlessly and unapologetically myself, even when it's hard. Thank you to Amber, JC, and Jules for being my readers, laughing at my ridiculousness, and giving me feedback and support. And thank you to my son, Ethan, whose endless imagination inspires my own.

Dedication

To my son, Ethan: I hope you never read this book.

CHAPTER ONE

Sam

"Just think about it, okay? It'll do you some good."

Manz's words had echoed around in my head for a few hours before I made up my mind. Okay, fine. More like minutes. Either way, I now found myself sitting in the Denver International Airport, a bulging duffel bag under my feet, waiting for my flight to SFO.

It was irritating how well Manz knew me. No semblance of mystery or secrecy for me around that one. Amanda, my best friend since elementary school and adoptive sister, had given herself the nickname Manz when we were kids. She thought it was hilarious that being "Manz's Best Friend" sounded like I was her pet puppy, and the name had stuck. Only Manz could get away with so shamelessly nicknaming herself.

A large man—easily six foot four and quite obese—flopped down into the seat across from me, his enormous feet against my duffel. I discreetly pulled the duffel closer to me with my heels, which the large man took as an invitation to manspread a little farther. Two words: Moose knuckle. If I could get any more gay, that just might have done it.

Completely oblivious to my annoyed sigh, my new neighbor breathed heavily as he began unloading items from a greasy McDonald's takeout bag: two Big Macs, an enormous french fries, and what I could only assume was the largest size of Diet Coke—because, you know, too much sugar in regular Coke. Before he began to eat, his cell phone rang loudly.

"Yeeeellow. Jim Cambron here." Jim. It was the perfect name for him. No, actually, not quite. Jimbo. Yes, he was definitely a Jimbo.

"Oh, yeah, you betcha! I'm all done in Colorado, and I'll finish it up today. Don't worry. Everything will get done just like I promised." His voice was filled with forced cheerfulness. "Yup, I'm headed back to San Fran in a few minutes. I'll handle it first thing when I land."

Oh great. Good ol' Jimbo and I were going to be on the same flight. With my luck, we'd spend the three-hour flight sitting side by side.

My cell phone buzz-buzzed with a text notification from Manz.

So, are you coming?! Pleeeeease? Bitch, I know you have a ton of cash saved up. Take a week and come play in the California sun!

I typed out a reply.

Already on my way. My flight takes off in 30 mins.

Within seconds of hitting Send, a photo of Manz's cat—a handsome black-and-white boy named Tuxedo—filled the screen. Manz found it hysterical that I had "a picture of her pussy" on my phone, which showed up as her profile picture every time she called. Thank goodness her wife, Jen, was so patient and understanding of Manz's wildly inappropriate sense of humor.

I answered the call and, before I could say anything, Manz shrieked, "Really?" in my ear. I chuckled and said yes in my most indulgent parent voice. I could hear her phone clatter to the ground with the high-pitched scream of a gleefully excited child. My chuckle evolved into a full-blown laugh. I could hear the phone being picked up from where Manz had dropped it.

"Hello? Manz? Are you there?"

"Hey, Sam. It's me. Um, Manz is…uh…" Jen's low voice trailed off as Manz's shrieking continued in the background. "So, you're coming to visit, huh? What time can I pick you up at the airport?"

I tried to decline, but Jen's calm demeanor wouldn't be swayed. "You really think she's going to calmly wait here at the house for you to arrive?"

"Honestly, I'm surprised she hasn't already left."

"Can't. I've got the keys."

I stowed my duffel into the overhead compartment and settled into my window seat. Flipping idly through the in-flight magazine, I heard a commotion at the front of the plane. Ignoring it, I went back to reading about the best way to dry rub a barbecue roast.

"He stinks! I can smell him from here. I am not sitting here. Move me to first class *at once*."

A blonde with fake eyelashes was screaming at an unsettled young flight attendant. And Jimbo—poor, embarrassed Jimbo—stood in the aisle, awkwardly holding his carry-on bag.

"I'm sorry, ma'am, but—"

The blonde interrupted, "At once! Change my seat. I am not sharing an armrest with this…" She scanned Jimbo up and down. "This Jabba the Hutt!"

An older, calmer flight attendant approached the blonde. "Ma'am, the flight is fully booked. There're no other seats to move you to. We can give you a voucher for a later flight, or…" Now, nearly everyone on the plane was watching the scene unfold.

"Absolutely not!" she screamed. "I have an audition and I can't be late. I'm not missing my big break because I smell like"—the blonde waved her hand dismissively at Jimbo—"like dirty feet and body odor."

"She can have my seat." The words were past my lips before I even knew it. All heads turned to me. *Aww, crap. Me and my big mouth.* My face flushed as I stepped into the aisle. Not knowing what else to say, I repeated, "Go ahead. Come take my seat."

The blonde pushed past me in the aisle. "Well, at least someone on this goddamn plane has some sense."

The older flight attendant nodded to her subordinate and returned to first class. Jimbo still stood awkwardly in the aisle, holding his carry-on bag. A few moments of confusion followed as Jimbo gathered himself together enough to be able to tell me which seat was his and which was the blonde's. I sat in the window seat while Jimbo stuffed his bag into the overhead compartment. I checked my cell phone before switching it to airplane mode—two texts and three voice mails from Sophia. Delete. Delete. Delete, delete and delete. I shoved my phone back into my pocket as Jimbo flopped into the seat, sweat dripping from his face.

"Name's Jim." He extended a plump hand to me.

"Sam," I said as I shook his clammy palm.

" Thanks for that. For…you know." He looked down into his lap as my face blushed again.

Before I could reply, the young flight attendant interrupted, "I'd like to offer a free cocktail of your choice, as gratitude for helping us out with, um…" She quickly looked at Jimbo, then back to me. "With the seating arrangements."

I declined, but she persisted. I asked for red wine, which she promised to deliver once we were airborne.

When the flight attendant had moved away, Jimbo spoke up. "I'm a beer man, myself. Never got the taste for wine. Plus, it gives me a nasty headache in the morning."

"Only if you drink the cheap stuff," I replied with a chuckle.

"Is there any other kind? At least, not on my dime. Nope, good old Budweiser will do just fine for me." He settled deeper into his seat, his knee resting against mine and his elbow engulfing the armrest. He let out a deep sigh. "At least we got the evacuation row." He slid a little deeper into the seat. "More legroom."

The irony wasn't lost on me—this large man, who had effectively wedged me between himself and the wall of the plane, discussing the luxury of extra legroom.

"So, Sam, was it?" he said with his head resting back against the seat. I nodded. "What do you do for a living, Sam?"

I really didn't want to chat for our three-hour plane ride together, but the plane hadn't even taken off yet, so a few minutes wouldn't hurt. For a moment I considered lying but decided against it.

"I'm an animal trainer," I answered. I hated telling people what I do. If you say dental hygienist or receptionist, they say "Oh" politely and move on. Nothing interesting to discuss. But when you train animals for a living, suddenly everyone wants free advice for FiFi's potty training issues and Spot's anxious chewing of the couch while they're at work.

Jimbo's head lifted from the seat, and he turned to me with interest. "You don't say! What kinds of animals?"

"Horses and dogs, mostly. But the basics are pretty universal for any animal, really."

"Wow. Way more interesting than what I do all day." He settled his head back against the headrest. When I didn't ask, he continued, "I help manage nonprofits and not-for-profits. Boring as hell. It's all paperwork, paperwork, paperwork. Tax exemptions and declarations of finances. But..." He let out a deep sigh. "They're doing the good deeds, so the least I can do is help keep the lights on for them, you know? I'm basically an accountant, HR manager, tax adviser, and bill payer, all wrapped in one." He pulled a business card from his breast pocket and handed it to me. "Not to brag, but I'm damn good at it. But I admit, it's not nearly as fun as playing with animals all day."

Before I could indignantly say that training a half-ton animal with high intelligence and stubbornness to match is neither "fun" nor "playing," the flight attendants began the preflight safety instruction. I tucked the card into the butt pocket of my jeans and took the opportunity to immerse myself back into the in-flight magazine, in hopes to finish the flight in silence.

With my duffel slung over my shoulder, I stepped out into the cool, autumn air of San Francisco. I took a deep breath, catching a hint of the salty bay breeze hidden behind the exhaust fumes of the waiting taxis. As I looked to see if Manz and Jen had arrived yet, I caught a flash of blond hair incoming fast from my right. I braced myself just in time for Manz to launch through the air and grab on to me like a 120-pound flying squirrel. She hugged me tightly around my neck, my duffel awkwardly pinned to my side as her legs wound around my waist.

"Hi…Manz…Nice to…see you too," I struggled to say as she squeezed even tighter.

"What the hell, bitch? All I had to do is ask, and you come visit? Fuck, if I'd known that, I'd have asked sooner!" She gave me one last, joint-popping squeeze before hopping down to the sidewalk. "Come on. Jen's parked down here."

After dropping my bag into the open trunk, I gave Jen a quick hug. The polar opposite to Manz's spastic hyperactivity, Jen was always stoic and calm. She held the hug a little longer than our norm.

"You doing okay?" she asked, concern in her eyes.

"Yeah, I'm good," I said, smiling weakly.

"Liar." She released our hug.

"Oh my god. Get in the car! I want all the juicy deets too, you selfish bitches."

Jen shrugged as if to say, *You know how she is*, and we obediently got into the car.

I stared out of the car window as Highway 101 pushed northward, leaving behind the tall buildings of The City and into the rolling, straw-colored hills of the North Bay. My soul exhaled as I looked at the enormous old oak trees dotting the dry grasses of the hillsides. My quiet reflection was interrupted by Manz turning around in the front passenger seat to look at me.

"Okay, I'm sorry, honey," she said as she patted Jen quickly on the thigh. "I know you said, 'Don't bug her about it right away,'" she mimicked Jen's low, quiet voice. "But I can't wait anymore."

I sat quietly, not answering, the opportunity to torment Manz just too delicious to resist.

"So?" she insisted.

"So, what?" I feigned ignorance with the most angelic and innocent expression I could muster.

"This bitch," Manz mumbled. "So, what happened? Last we heard, she said she wanted 'some time apart.'" Manz made finger quotes in the air while rolling her eyes. "She wanted to see if she could 'fall in love' with you again."

"Mm-hmm."

"And?" she said impatiently.

"And what?" I cocked a cheeky eyebrow at her.

"And what happened next?"

I sighed. Time for games and playfully teasing Manz was over. My mood turned solemn, and Manz quickly reached over the back of the seat to take my hand.

"Oh, honey, no." She squeezed my fingers. "I hate when you're sad."

She unbuckled her seat belt and, with the agility only someone five-one could manage, she quickly climbed into the back seat beside me.

Manz took my hand again. "What happened?"

I took a deep breath. "She asked for time apart, and I agreed." Jen was quiet, but she watched from the driver's seat through the rearview mirror. "So I slept in the guest room, and she slept in our room."

Manz, quiet for once, nodded for me to continue.

"Hudson threw a shoe, so we had to cut our training short for the day." I was currently training the beautiful Arabian stallion for a movie role. His horseshoe had come loose, and we couldn't continue training until the farrier could come to reshoe him.

"I went home, but the front door was unlocked. I thought it was strange but didn't think much of it. Sophia can be absent-minded like that sometimes. I called out to let her know I was home, but there was no answer. So I went down the hall to the spare room—huh, my room now, I guess." I laughed sardonically. "And that's when I heard something. It was, like, a banging noise coming from our..." I cleared my throat. "Her room. And I could hear Sophia yelling in there. Screaming actually."

Manz's face dissolved from compassion to anger.

I continued, "My mind jumped back to the unlocked front door, and my first thought was Sophia was in our bedroom, being attacked by an intruder."

"Oh, Sammy, no." Manz said. Only Manz could get away with calling me Sammy.

"So I opened the door, and the whole world just froze. Sophia was bent over the end of the bed with some naked Italian-looking guy holding her hips from behind while the headboard of our bed—OUR BED!—banged against the wall. She was wearing her red lace bra—my favorite one. And she was wearing the shiny black stilettos I bought for her for our fifth anniversary last month."

Manz gasped. "She was banging a DUDE?" Jen's eyes were enormous in the rearview mirror.

"Yup."

"What the fuck did you do?" Manz asked.

"I stood there for a minute, just trying to make sense of what I was seeing. It was like my brain just kept spitting out error messages. None of it made sense. I did a sort of hiccuping-sob thing. She must have heard me because she looked up. We made eye contact, and the look on her face…" My words trailed off as my throat closed.

"Fucking whore." *Aww, Manz, you always know what to say.* It made me chuckle, and the moment's distraction helped me to speak again.

"Her face went from ecstasy to shock to fear. It was crazy. It was like a movie—like I was watching this scene, and my part in it, from the outside."

Jen chimed in from the front seat. "Did he see you too?"

I couldn't answer right away. "No."

Manz's face went blank. "Wait, hold the damn phone a minute. As you're standing there in the room with Sophia looking at you, Romeo is still back there just pounding away like a damn jackrabbit?"

"Yup." I stared at the calluses on my palm.

"Jesus fucking Christ, Sam!" Manz dropped my hand to rub her face briefly before taking my hand again.

"So…then what?" asked Jen.

I took a deep breath. "So, I closed the door and went outside to the driveway. I didn't know where to go or what to do. I couldn't think. I just kept seeing that look of pleasure—that look I used to give to her—on her face. It just…I don't know. It broke me." I took another deep breath. "After a minute or two, Sophia came running outside in a robe, still wearing those fucking heels." My eyes burned with tears threatening to fall. "And she said all the usual bullshit—he's just a friend, this is the first time, it doesn't mean anything, I love you, we were on a break, all that shit."

"WE WERE ON A BREAK!" Manz yelled out in her best Ross Geller impersonation. Jen and I both turned to her in shock. "Sorry," she said. "Go on."

"Not much else to say, really," I continued. "I told her to fuck off…"

"Good for you," Jen said quietly.

"And told her it's over. Like, really over. And I went back in and started packing. So when you texted for me to visit—"

"Wait," Manz interrupted again. "When did all this happen?"

"About…" I looked at my watch. "Five hours ago."

"Shut the fuck up!" she yelled. "This all happened today?"

"Yup."

"No shit," she said, shaking her head.

"So I threw everything into a duffel—well, everything worth keeping anyway—found the earliest flight, and got the fuck out of Dodge. I told her to get her shit out and be gone by the time I come back."

"Holy fuck," Manz whispered.

"Sam, I'm so sorry," Jen said.

It was quiet in the car for several minutes—just the sounds of the freeway as we continued driving toward their house. One big, hot, angry teardrop silently began to fall down my face. Manz stayed silent, holding my hand and rubbing her thumb over my knuckles. Hearing me sniffle, she leaned toward me and hugged my head to her shoulder. Tears flowed more freely, and for several moments, I cried against her shoulder. She gently stroked my hair until my crying eased.

Once I'd composed myself, I lifted my head and said, "Did you call him 'Romeo'?"

She shrugged. "It was the only Italian name I could think of."

All three of us burst into laughter.

Jen and Manz lived in an old farmhouse on two acres of land. They had bought it when they first married and had spent years renovating it, piece by piece. Now, seven years later, the house was country chic and comfortable—as warm and inviting as a country home should be.

We arrived after dark, and Bailey the black Lab greeted us in the driveway. I got out and immediately began giving him overdue Aunt Sam love—belly scratches and ear rubs.

"You know where your room is. I'll start dinner," Manz yelled over her shoulder as she walked into the house.

"More like, she'll order Thai food from Grubhub," Jen said in a stage whisper to me.

"I heard that, Jen," she yelled back.

"Love you, babe," Jen said with a smile.

"Love you too, Snookiebear," Manz yelled back and walked into the house.

"Snookiebear?" I smirked.

"Listen, I gotta take that shit from her. But I don't have to take it from you," she said playfully. "Keep it up and you'll share a bed with Bailey."

I pulled my duffel from the trunk, closing the lid. "Don't threaten me with a good time," I replied. "Huh, Bails? We could snuggle! Huh, big guy? Yes, we can! Who's a good boy?" I gently pulled his ears while we walked into the house.

CHAPTER TWO

Sam

Jen and I were sitting around the kitchen table, talking about nothing in particular, when Manz entered carrying two takeout bags.

"Told you so." Jen smirked at me.

"Shut up, Jennifer Marie," Manz said, opening the bags of food. "Besides, you weren't right, anyway. It's not Thai—it's Chinese food." She planted a flirty kiss on Jen's lips.

As cartons of pork fried rice and broccoli beef were passed between us, conversation moved comfortably from topic to topic. Manz poured three generous glasses of wine and handed them around the table.

"Does rosé go with Chinese food?" I asked, doubting it.

"Fuck if I know," Manz said after finishing a long sip from her glass. "I don't care, 'cause this shit is delicious."

I chuckled and shook my head as Jen switched topics to my work.

"Hudson wasn't hurt, was he?" she asked. "Was anyone riding him when his horseshoe came off?"

"Thankfully, no," I replied between bites of lemon chicken. "It'll be an easy fix, once the farrier arrives. But he was, I don't know…" I gestured vaguely with my chopsticks. "Traveling, or something, so we had to wait."

"He won't lose the training you've started, will he?" Manz asked.

"Hudson? No way. He's feisty as hell, but also incredibly smart. He'll pick right back up where we left off. My only concern is being able to finish on schedule." I popped another bite of chicken into my mouth.

"Oh, really?" Jen asked.

"Yeah," I continued after I finished chewing. "He's very close—just polishing up the final details now. A couple days at most." I sat thinking for a moment while I took another bite. "Actually, he's probably ready now. I think I'll just text my agent and let him know that I was called out of town for a week but that Hudson is screen-ready. I just want to make sure he's perfect, you know?"

"Perfect?" Manz scoffed. "No such thing. Well, except for you, honey." She playfully stroked Jen's cheek with her thumb.

"I know," I mused. "But my reputation as a trainer depends on making sure my clients are as screen-ready as possible. If not, they'll hire someone else for the next film, you know?"

Manz and Jen nodded quietly in agreement.

"But, if I'm here for a week, I might as well spend some time with Apricot. Make sure she hasn't forgotten her manners since my last visit." I chuckled as I snapped a fortune cookie in half. "How is she, by the way? I'll have to go say hello to the old girl in the morning."

Jen and Manz exchanged a look, but neither said anything. Jen pushed food around on her plate.

"What did I miss? Is she okay? What happened?" I quickly asked.

"No, nothing. Nothing like that. She's fine, I promise," Manz answered quietly. "She's just…not here anymore."

"Not here anymore?" I repeated, shocked. "What does that mean? You guys love that horse! Where is she? Is she okay?"

"Calm your tits, of course she is," said Manz. "She just… wasn't happy here after Conway passed. They were inseparable, you know, and she got so depressed. Didn't want to eat. Didn't want attention from us." Jen and Manz exchanged another look. "She got really thin, and her coat looked terrible. It happened so fast. It was heartbreaking to watch."

"Oh, man, I'm so sorry," I said. "They're such intelligent and loving creatures, I'm not surprised. Why didn't you guys tell me? Maybe I could have helped."

Jen and Manz looked at one another again. "We thought about it."

I shot Manz a look of skepticism.

"We really did, bitch," Manz exclaimed. Jen nodded in confirmation, and Manz continued, "But with the hectic training deadline for Hudson, and all the bullshit going on with Sophia…" I winced unconsciously at the sound of her name. "Besides, we didn't need your help anyway," she finished saucily. "We found our own solution."

I looked quickly between Jen and Manz. "Solution?"

"Yup," Manz said proudly. "A solution where she's happy and healthy, and where we can still visit whenever we want."

"And you can visit her too, while you're here. She's at a ranch just down the road," Jen added, a piece of broccoli balanced between her chopsticks.

"Great. I'd love to."

"Hey, I know! We'll invite the horse rancher whose property she's at to dinner tomorrow. You two can swap horse stories and plan a visit to the ranch to see Apricot." A flicker of mischief crossed Manz's face, so brief I doubted if I'd actually even seen it.

"Oh, she's with other horses? That's great." I flattened the paper fortune from my fortune cookie on the table. "That's probably what helped pull her out of the depression she was in."

"We think so too," Jen added.

After a moment's silence, I read my fortune aloud. "Your future is filled with excitement."

Jen and Manz looked at each other in confusion.

"What the hell you talking about?" Manz asked.

I chuckled, gesturing to my fortune. I read again, "Your future is filled with excitement…"

We looked around the table at each other and, in unison, yelled, "IN BED!" and dissolved into laughter.

CHAPTER THREE

Alyssa

"Back up." Hickory nudged me in the shoulder again. "Back up, you big ol' brute. I can't give you the oats if I can't get to your feeder." Hickory nudged me one more time and begrudgingly stepped back. I sprinkled the oats over his dinner as he nibbled on the collar of my shirt. His soft muzzle whiskers grazed the back of my neck.

"That tickles!" I said. I stepped aside and gave him a quick rub on the base of his ear.

"Who's next?" I yelled loudly down the main aisle of the barn. An answering nicker came from Apricot's stall.

"Hi, sweet girl." Her creamy nose reached for me over the door of the stall. I gave her a few quick scratches under the chin before unlatching the door. As I entered the stall, I gave her a quick once-over. She was still thin but getting better each day. I was so relieved to see her appetite blossoming. Already her coat was getting its shine back, and the sparkle was returning to her eyes.

Unlike her unruly neighbor Hickory, Apricot waited patiently for me to finish prepping her dinner. I gave her a quick kiss on the white diamond on her forehead.

"How you doing, sweet girl?" Apricot snorted out of her nose and pushed her soft muzzle into my hand. "What are you looking for, hmm?" I reached into my pocket and pulled out two apple slices. "Looking for these?" Her keen nose sniffed out the apples and delicately took them from my outstretched palm.

As she happily munched her snack, I smoothed her forelock of hair down over her forehead. "Any words of advice for Maddox?" Apricot looked at me inquisitively. "You seem to be the only one she likes around here. I wish you could tell me your secrets, girl." Apricot began nosing my pocket in search of more apples. "That's all for you tonight." One last chin scratch, and I left her stall.

"Here goes nothing," I said, steeling myself for Maddox's stall.

Two months ago, I had seen Maddox at the horse auction, which I had attended to assist a neighbor, Bette, with the purchase of her first horse. I was not in the market for another horse, but Maddox's obvious distress caught my eye. She was frothing at the mouth and sweat darkened her black-and-white coat. Her eyes rolled in fear as she pulled at the dual leads attaching her halter to opposite sides of the stall. She was labeled as "unsuitable for riding" and had a euthanasia date scheduled for shortly after the auction closed.

As I wandered the auction grounds, answering Bette's questions about different horses we saw, I kept gravitating back to Maddox's stall. She seemed exhausted from maintaining such a high level of anxiety for so long. Maddox's fear touched my heart. I ran through the pros and cons of having another horse—and a difficult one, at that—but ultimately, my compassion for this frightened creature prevailed.

Needless to say, my role as amateur horse consultant quickly transformed into auction participant, and Bette and I drove home with two horses in the trailer instead of one.

Tonight, like every night since I brought her to the ranch, I stood at her stall door, building the courage to enter. Inside,

Maddox snorted and neighed, stomping her hooves, and backed into a corner. She reminded me of a bull who's seen the red flag.

Thankfully, I'd learned she's more bluff than anything. If I filled her food and water trough and exited without any attempt to touch her, we could peacefully coexist. Staying as close to the farthest wall as I could, I gave Maddox her dinner. After retreating the way I'd come, I closed the stall door behind me. I stood at the door, my forearms folded on the top rail, and took the last two apple slices from my pocket and held them out to her. Her nostrils flared—I knew she could smell them—but her ears pinned back aggressively against her skull told me she wouldn't be accepting treats from me any time soon.

"Come on, girl. We can be friends. I promise." I jiggled the slices in my outstretched palm. She stared unblinking at me, refusing to move a muscle in my direction. After a few moments, I accepted defeat and tossed the slices into her feeder. "Maybe tomorrow, Maddox."

I shut off the stable lights and headed toward the house. The sun was setting, lighting the hills on fire with golds, reds, and oranges. In the far pasture, five white-tailed deer grazed quietly, the does' heads popping up occasionally to check for danger. The male's antlers were still small—only three points per antler—but he carried them as though he were king of the landscape. Two spotted fawns frolicked nearby, never straying far from the others.

Hickory nickered to me from the stable as I walked away.

"You've had enough treats today, bossy boy," I called to him over my shoulder. I could hear him snort and stamp a hoof in response. I lovingly rolled my eyes.

My cell phone rang in my pocket. Checking the caller ID, I saw it was Amanda, the owner of a nearby farm.

"Hello?" I answered.

"Hey, Alyssa! How are ya?" Amanda said brightly.

"I'm good. And you?"

"Same ol' bullshit, you know? How's Apricot?"

"She's great. Just checked on her, actually. Looking better every day."

"Excellent. But actually, Apricot isn't why I called."

A moment ticked by as I processed my confusion. "Oh? Well, how can I help you?" I mean, we waved on the road and stopped for a quick chat in the grocery store, but beyond that, our interactions were pretty strictly limited to Apricot's rehabilitation.

"You're coming to dinner at our house tomorrow night." It wasn't a request. My eyebrows rose in surprise. I could hear a scuffling noise and muffled voices as I presumed Amanda covered the phone mic.

"Ugh," Amanda continued. "Jen says I have to ask nicely instead of barking orders at you. So, fine..." She cleared her throat theatrically and continued in a terrible English accent, "Alyssa, please do us the esteemed honor of joining us for the evening meal on the morrow. We have a guest staying in the manor with us who seeks to inquire about the health and welfare of your newest equine, Madam Apricot. We'd love for you to make her acquaintance, so please say you'll join us."

I shook my head. *Is this Amanda chick for real?* "Sure," I said. "What can I bring?"

"Nothing, bitch." Amanda's normal sassy voice returned. "Just come over around six, okay?"

"Sounds great. See you then."

The call ended, and I stood staring at my darkened phone for several moments. What in the world was that? I knew "the lesbian couple," as people in town called them, but not well. And other than helping them relocate Apricot to my land, we hadn't had much interaction. I'd never been inside their house, let alone come to dinner. But if Amanda's wild personality was any indication, it was bound to be an interesting night.

CHAPTER FOUR

Sam

I woke early to the incessant buzz-buzz of my cell phone: Sophia on caller ID. I sent her call to voice mail but I couldn't fall back to sleep. Having her so close, just a button push away, made my adrenaline spike. Anger? Hurt? I couldn't tell. Tuxedo, Manz and Jen's black-and-white cat, had crawled into bed with me at some point in the night. I gave him a few scratches and pets, which initiated a loud, happy purr. But even snuggles from sweet Tux couldn't shake the anxiety of Sophia's call.

Still idly petting Tux, I summoned my courage to check my phone. Two other voice mails and one long text: Love you, miss you, sorry, he meant nothing, come home, take me back, we can make it work...all the predictable bullshit she had said in the driveway. Delete. I couldn't lie there anymore. I pulled on jeans and a faded Fleetwood Mac T-shirt and left the bedroom.

Manz and Jen's bedroom lights were still off. Bailey peeked his nose through the partially open door. Seeing me, he full-body wiggled his way down the hallway to me. After I gently roughed his ears and scratched his chest, Bailey leaned against my legs.

"Come on, Bails, let's go feed the chickens."

Quietly, we left the house and made our way to the animal pens. The chickens clucked nervously as we approached, and I threw the coop door wide to allow them to free range around the property. I scattered feed and grains for them to peck on the ground, and they began happily gobbling up their breakfast.

"Bailey, leave it. That's not for you." Bailey's ears dropped guiltily, with crumbles of chicken feed stuck to his black nose. "Time to feed the goats, boy."

Manz and Jen had four goats. They didn't hear us approach, so I called out their names as I tossed a leaf of alfalfa into their enclosure. "Rose! Blanche! Dorothy! Soph—" The name stuck in my throat as visions of a tanned, muscular man having sex with my fiancée in my bedroom flooded my head. A wave of nausea rose, and I steadied myself on the enclosure gate. I took a few breaths, swallowing hard in between, until the nausea subsided. Once the lava in my stomach cooled, it transformed into anger.

How could she do this? Just throw it all away? Just a few weeks past our five-year anniversary—five good years, or so I had believed. What had I missed? Where had it all gone wrong? Had I done something wrong? Was it me? Was I blind to all the signs and symptoms leading up to this?

And why the hell was she having sex with a guy? In our years together, she never mentioned being attracted to men. Sure, I knew there had been men in her past. But when she talked about sexy athletes or celebrities, it was always women on the list. So where did Romeo—as Manz so appropriately named him—come from? Who the hell was he? How and when did they meet? And why was he banging my fiancée? God, it hurt so much to even think about it.

My throat closed as the image of that red lace bra flashed before my eyes, and a hiccuping-sob escaped my throat. Hot, angry tears flowed down my face. Heavy drops created craters in the dust at my feet.

"I don't understand," I said aloud. The goats looked up at me in confusion. "Why would she do this?" It felt good to talk as they watched me with inquisitive eyes. "It had been good." I sniffled. "It had been so good until she asked for space…" Slowly pieces began falling into place. "Until she said she'd fallen out of love with me…" More tears fell. More pieces clicked. "She was already *not* in love with me by then…wasn't she? It was already too late." I covered my mouth with my hand as the goats continued to watch me. "Oh god, that's it." Dorothy baaed loudly at me. "That's when it started, isn't it? That's when she…" My words trailed off as realization struck like a thunderclap.

A hand started rubbing my back, startling me back to the present. "Damn, where'd you come from?" I quickly dashed tears away with the heels of my hands.

Ignoring my question, Manz said, "Fuck her, anyway," her voice still laden with sleep.

I sniffled hard as Blanche began nibbling the bottom cuff of my pants through the gate. I scratched the top of her head.

"They're good listeners, huh?" Manz said, watching Sophia and Rose playfully headbutting each other.

"Yeah. They drop some hard truths, though." I reached down and scratched Blanche's head again. "You gotta warn a girl next time," I said, gently pushing her away from my pant cuff.

We watched them in silence for a few minutes—young, mischievous goats doing young, mischievous goat things. The sun had risen, and diamonds of dew glinted on the grass. Bailey sniffed around the goat enclosure, sending puffs of dandelion seeds into the sunrise light.

"I'm done."

"With what?" she asked.

"With love. I'm done."

Manz grunted. "No, you're not."

"Yes, I am. I'm done. Just done with all of it. My heart is closed for business."

"You're off your goddamn rocker, Sam." She rolled her eyes at me. "Your heart's too big to call it quits."

I scoffed at her. "It's not worth it. It hurts too fucking much."

"So, what then? Go celibate? Enter a nunnery? Turn down the next cute girl who offers a smile or a wink? You're fucking full of it if you think you could stay away."

I stood quietly for a moment, wishing she were wrong.

"Nope," she continued. "The soft lips of a smiling woman, the feel of her warm skin against yours, that tingle of excitement when you know she's as hot for you as you are for her...It's a drug. It's an addiction we can never walk away from." She picked at a piece of flaking paint on the railing. "You'll heal." She tossed it over her shoulder. "You'll heal, and you'll love again. Simple as that."

"I hate your guts so much," I said, trying desperately not to cry again.

"Truth sucks, huh?" she said, nudging my shoulder with hers.

I didn't answer. I didn't need to.

"Come on," she said, turning to walk back toward the house. "Jen's probably done making breakfast, and I need some fucking coffee."

CHAPTER FIVE

Alyssa

"Here," I said, handing two bottles of wine to Amanda. "I couldn't decide, white or red, so I brought both."

"Ooh! Let's open both and decide which we like best."

I followed Amanda into the house. My mouth salivated with the smell of garlic and chicken.

"Hope you're hungry," Amanda said over her shoulder as I followed her through the living room to the kitchen. "Jen cooks for an army."

Jen stood at the stove, pushing sliced chicken off a cutting board into a skillet filled with pasta and vegetables. Amanda pulled eight wineglasses down from a cabinet and began opening both bottles.

Confused, I asked, "How many people are coming to dinner?"

"Just us four," she replied, filling the glasses. She emptied the bottles into the glasses, four with red and four with white. She turned and handed me one of each.

"Oh," I said, surprised. "You were serious about the taste test."

Before Amanda could reply, Jen interrupted, "Manz never jokes about booze."

I was confused again. "Manz?"

A tall woman walked into the kitchen from somewhere deeper in the house. "Manz is Amanda's nickname from our childhood. It just stuck."

"I like the white." Amanda—no, Manz—took a sip from her glass. She took a sip from the second glass and hummed with pleasure. "No, the red. Definitely the red."

The tall woman approached with her hand extended. "Sam. Nice to meet you."

Still holding two glasses of wine, I awkwardly turned to set them down on the counter behind me. I felt my face flush with heat. "Hi, I'm Alyssa," I said, shaking her hand.

Her skin was tanned, contrasting nicely with her light green eyes. She was a few inches taller than me and had sunglass tan lines at her temples, indicative of someone who works outdoors. Her body said she worked outdoors too—muscular but lean. Her dark hair was cut short, cropped close at the nape of her neck and almost long enough to keep tucked behind her ears on top. She wore an expensive-looking pair of dark jeans and a nicely pressed black button-up shirt rolled up to her elbows. She seemed confident without being arrogant. Her presence immediately demanded my entire attention.

She continued, "You'll have to forgive Manz's manners. I'd say she was born in a barn, but that's an insult to farm animals."

Manz, obviously ignoring her jab, took another sip of wine. "No, the white. Yes, I like the white best."

I chuckled at their easy banter and set my purse down at the end of the counter near my two glasses of wine. I settled myself onto a barstool, trying to lower my blood pressure with a calming sip of red wine.

Sam selected a glass of red wine and chose the barstool nearest to mine. *Man, she smells good too. Like clean pine trees, if that's even a thing.* I felt the heat creeping into my face again. *Why am I blushing?*

"So, Jen and Manz tell me Apricot is on your ranch now?" she asked. "How is she?"

"She's doing great. Settling in with my other two horses, putting on weight. She already looks better."

I could see the concern in her eyes. "She took Conway's death hard, huh?" she asked.

"Definitely. I know Jen and…" I hesitated, still getting used to Amanda's new nickname. "Manz did the best they could. But I think being here without Conway just broke her heart. She needed the distraction." I gestured vaguely, trying to find the right words. "A fresh start without the memories, you know?"

Sam nodded, her expression solemn and her eyes locked on mine. Her eyes had little flecks of gold and copper in the light green irises.

"But my gelding has provided plenty of distraction for her." I chuckled to myself. "Hickory is quite the character."

Sam nodded attentively without speaking, so I continued, "He's only two years old, so he's got the big body of an adult but the playful mayhem of a colt. He's my enormous puppy with hooves. His goofy energy has definitely put some life back into Apricot."

"I'm relieved," she added. "I was so worried when they told me yesterday." She took a slow sip of her red. *She has fantastic lips.* She stayed silent, looking at me to continue.

"I have another new addition to the ranch too—my new problem child, Maddox," I said as Sam continued her undivided attention on me. Could she be this fascinated by horses? Or was her attention due to…other motivations? Quit flattering yourself, I thought.

"I got her from the auction—she was destined for the slaughterhouse," I said, sipping my wine. Sam winced at the term. I continued, "And she was so scared and upset in that auction stable, I couldn't leave her behind. She was practically free, but that didn't matter—I would have paid more to get her out of there."

"I know some people buy at the auctions with good intentions, but some people are downright criminal in how they treat these horses." She shook her head in disdain.

"I agree," I said. "That's why I knew I couldn't leave her there." I took a sip from my wineglass. "Even if I can never ride her, or…" I chuckled darkly. "Or even put a hand on her at this point, at least she'll be safe and cared for."

"She won't let you pet her?"

"I can't even get near her, let alone pet or brush her. It took four of us to get her into the horse trailer at the auction. Which, I'm sure, did nothing to help her anxiety about humans."

"Wow," she added thoughtfully. "How is she getting along with Apricot and…Hickory, wasn't it?"

I nodded in confirmation. "Hickory is so easily distracted by everything, he doesn't even realize that she's actively ignoring him and often annoyed by him. But Apricot…" I took a small sip of wine. "That's a different story."

"Oh yeah?" she asked. "Good or bad?"

"Good, I think. At first Maddox was kind of a punk—some 'Get away from me' bites and kicks. But Apricot just stuck with it, kept following her, kept showing up…and eventually Maddox just started to tolerate her."

"Really?" Sam's voice was laced with excitement.

"Yes, so much so that I catch Maddox looking for her when I let them out of their stalls into the pasture in the morning. It's almost as though she's saying, 'I don't care anyway,' but her body language shows she very much cares."

"Body language is so important," she replied. Her voice had dropped, and her eyes were locked with mine.

Wait a minute. Is she…flirting with me? I felt the heat begin to creep up my neck and into my face again.

"Yes, it is," I said, holding her gaze.

CHAPTER SIX

Sam

Alyssa took a sip from her wine, still looking at me over the rim of her glass. Her hair was golden blond, with darker tones of copper and red. It was long and hung down her back in loose curls. Her eyes were startlingly blue—that crisp bright blue of a cloudless summer morning. Her look had an intensity to it, a familiar one that I hadn't received from a woman in several years.

Before my mind could travel down that path any farther, Jen announced dinner was ready. Alyssa and I stood simultaneously, coming nearly nose-to-nose as we stood.

We both laughed awkwardly, and her neck flushed scarlet. I gestured with an open palm to the dining room.

"After you," I said.

She carried her white-wine glass—the red glass stood empty on the counter—and began walking in front of me. She wore a deep purple pencil skirt with a lavender silk blouse, elegant with a hint of cleavage and lovely contouring of curves. Definitely not what I expected from the "rancher" Manz said she was inviting tonight. Her heels clicked on the tile floor, causing me to look down at her fantastic calves. She has better legs than Sophia, I thought. My stomach turned sour as I thought of that name, and the easy smile that had been on my face fell away.

At the transition from the tile of the kitchen to the hardwood of the dining room floor, the heel of her stiletto caught on wooden edging. She stumbled slightly, and my free hand instinctively caught her elbow to steady her.

"You okay?" I asked.

She regained her balance, and I moved my hand to her lower back.

"Yes, thank you," she said quietly.

"You didn't twist your ankle, did you?"

"No, I'm fine. Thanks."

I left my hand on her back as we took the last few steps to the table, ensuring she didn't slip again.

"So when can Sam come see Apricot?" Manz immediately launched in as we passed plates and bowls of food around the table. Two more bottles of uncorked wine appeared, and glasses were refilled. Pasta with grilled chicken and fall vegetables from the garden with a lemon, garlic, and white wine sauce. Garlic bread with feta cheese. Roasted brussels sprouts with herbed goat cheese and a balsamic reduction drizzle. A salad with fresh greens, sliced strawberries, Gorgonzola cheese, sliced almonds, and champagne vinaigrette. *Dear god. Decadent.*

Knowing Jen was an outrageously good chef, I heaped my plate with servings of everything and waited for Alyssa to reply.

Alyssa looked at me and shrugged. "Any time."

"You free tomorrow?" Manz asked.

"Sure. I'll be around."

Manz was the one talking to her, but Alyssa kept her eyes on me.

"What time?" Manz quickly asked.

"Babe, chill," Jen said.

"Whaaat?" Manz whined. "I'm fucking helping."

"Does ten a.m. work for you?" Alyssa was looking at me still.

Suddenly, it all made sense. This dinner. The gorgeous woman sitting next to me. The "rancher" who was not wearing the flannel and overalls I'd been expecting. My chat with Manz this morning. This was a setup, a blind date, and I was the one who had been blindsided.

I couldn't help it—my face fell. I shot a quick, angry look at Manz before replying.

"Ten a.m. is great."

Manz, completely oblivious to the mood shift, plowed onward. "Excellent," she said. "Sorry but Jen and I have plans—"

"We do?" asked Jen in confusion.

"...so we won't be able to join this time," Manz continued, undeterred. "But I'll be sure to give Sam directions."

I stabbed a bite of salad with my fork. I was struggling to conceal my frustration and took a deep breath. Thirty-six hours. Only thirty-six hours ago, my heart was broken when I caught Sophia cheating on me. Not even two full days, and Manz was already pushing me toward someone new. Unbelievable. The relationship that I'd poured my whole heart into for five years had ended in a flash. No warning. No explanation. And certainly no second chances. Not after that. Not after seeing everything I saw. How could I even contemplate meeting someone while my heart still bled from the wounds of another?

"Helloooo? Earth to Sam."

My head popped up, the sound of my name pulling me out of my thoughts. All three tablemates were staring at me.

"I'm sorry, what?"

"I said you might be able to give Alyssa some advice on her new horse while you're visiting Apricot tomorrow," Manz repeated.

Alyssa looked at me for a response, her face a mix of hope and concern. How long had I tuned out? What had I missed?

"Of course," I said half-heartedly. I took a deep drink from my wineglass and cleared my throat. "I'd be happy to."

"Did Sam tell you what she does for a living?" Jen asked Alyssa. Alyssa shook her head no, lifting her fork.

"I train animals. Usually for movie roles, but sometimes for high-profile clients or special consultation cases."

"Oh, wow. Impressive," Alyssa said, smiling at me. "What kinds of animals?"

"Horses and dogs, usually. But I've also worked with camels, llamas, parrots…" I took another bite. "And one time, a bear."

"A bear? Are you serious?" Alyssa's eyes got huge.

"Oh my god, tell that story. I fucking love it," Manz said, laughing.

Alyssa turned her attention back to me, smiling that bright smile.

"I was hired to train a client named Griz. That should have been my first clue. But the majority of my clients are horses, so I assumed that's what Griz was too."

Jen topped off my wineglass. With a quiet thank you to her, I took a sip and continued my story. "I traveled to Northern Canada to begin training Griz. Very limited information. It took three commercial flights, a private four-seater plane with those floats for landing in water, and an hour-long ATV ride to get to the client's location. Then…" I paused briefly for effect. "Then I met Griz's owner. His beard was gray and down to his waist. His clothes were as old as I am. Crazy old bat living out in the Canadian wilds with his horse. So this old-timer starts telling me about Griz—how he took him in after he was orphaned, how he raised him like his own child, spoiled him, trained him, even let him come in the house." Across the table, Manz was already giggling to herself.

"I thought raising a horse in the house and treating him like a human child was strange, but this old guy was clearly not dealing from a full deck, you know? So in a weird way, it made sense. I told myself, 'Train the horse and get back home.' So I asked him to take me to Griz. He pointed to a barn on his property and said Griz was probably in there. Then, he just walked away."

"Where'd he go?" Alyssa said, chuckling.

"Hell if I know," I said with a shrug. "Off to skin something or bottle the moonshine or some other mountain-man shit." I was momentarily distracted. *Alyssa really does have gorgeous eyes, doesn't she?*

"Anyway," I continued, trying to stay on track with my story. *Stupid wine.* "I figured there's no time like the present, so I walked down to the barn. Well, 'barn' is far too generous of a word. More like an old wooden hunting shack you'd find deserted somewhere in a horror movie. I opened the door, expecting stalls and lights, but it was pitch black. I couldn't see a thing. I could hear the horse moving, so I started talking to him. 'Hey Griz. Where you at, boy?' I groped the walls like an idiot, looking for a light switch, finding nothing. I finally thought to use the flashlight on my cell phone. I turned it on and all I could see was this enormous lump of brown fur. I figured it was an animal hide thrown over a table, so I started scanning the room with the flashlight for a horse.

"No horse in sight...but suddenly the hide on the table started to move. Suddenly I realized it wasn't a table—that huge lump of fur was alive. I couldn't believe my eyes when an eight-foot grizzly bear rose up onto his back feet in front of me. I was convinced I was dead. Gone. Goodbye, world. I was about to become a Sam-sized bear snack."

Alyssa was covering her mouth with her hand, following my story closely. I continued, "I suddenly remembered watching those nature shows years ago, but I couldn't remember what you're supposed to do when you encounter a bear. Are you supposed to act big and intimidating to scare it away? Or do you play dead, and it'll leave you alone? So I made the split-second decision—I dropped onto my knees into a ball and covered my head—"

"And kissed her ass goodbye!" Manz interrupted with laughter.

"Pretty much. So I curled up in a ball, covering my head. I felt him drop to all fours and pad toward me. I could smell him—like Fritos and wet dog fur. He kept walking forward until he was standing over me...literally, standing over the top of me. I could feel his body heat through my clothes. Then I could feel his hot breath on my face, and I could smell his breath. The bear's huge mouth was open. This is it, I thought. He's going to crush my head in those jaws like a ripe melon. And then…" I paused again for effect, holding Alyssa's gaze. "I felt a huge, hot tongue lick my face."

"No way," Alyssa said.

"Yup. From collarbone to hairline, the bear licked my face. Over and over and over, like a dog. Just licking my damned face! Do you have any idea how big a bear's tongue is?" I asked Alyssa. "So much slobber—like the Slimer scene from *Ghostbusters*."

Alyssa said, laughing, "I'd have peed my pants, I think!"

"I just about did!" I laughed with her. "So I was still lying on the floor of this shack, with an enormous bear standing over top of me, licking my face repeatedly, covered in bear slobber, when Old Man Time walked into the shack. He said, 'Well, shit, Griz…Buy her dinner first, at least!'"

CHAPTER SEVEN

Alyssa

The evening had drawn to a close, and it was time for me to head home. Mysteriously, our hosts had disappeared, leaving Sam to escort me to the door.

"I'll see you tomorrow?" I said, approaching the front door of the house.

Sam reached past me and opened the door for me. "Yes, ten a.m. You're safe to drive home?"

I nodded, touched by her concern. "It's been a few hours since I stopped drinking…despite Manz continuing to try to fill my glass."

Sam chuckled. "She can be rather bossy like that sometimes."

"Just sometimes?" I asked with a cheeky eyebrow raised.

She met my gaze and quickly looked at her shoes. "More like all the time. Believe me, you have *no* idea."

"You're a good friend," I said, putting my hand on her forearm. *What am I doing? This is so out of character for me.* Some magnetic force about her was drawing me to her. *Maybe that wine is hitting a little harder than I thought.* I let my hand fall.

"A patient friend. A very patient and understanding friend," I added. We shared a laugh.

"That's the truth," she said quietly. "She's a complete brat, but I love her."

I smiled but said nothing. It seemed their friendship, although very close, was purely platonic. They shared the teasing banter of sisters, built through their years together. I walked down the steps of the wraparound porch and again felt her hand supporting my elbow. A smile reached my lips at the sensation. Once I hit the level ground, the warmth of her hand disappeared.

"I'm excited to meet Hickory," she said.

I laughed quietly. "He's such a character. You'll love him. You can't help but love him." I unlocked my truck with the key fob but didn't immediately move to get in. I was content to stand here for a minute and look at those gorgeous eyes glittering in the porch light. My eyes strayed down to her lips, and I had to quickly look back up at her eyes before my thoughts became too distracted. *Man, it's been way too long since I felt any of this.*

"I'm excited to meet Maddox too," she continued.

I exhaled deeply. "That one's not quite so lovable. Not yet, anyway. I just can't seem to reach her." I scoffed. "Physically or psychologically."

"I have dealt with a few cases like this. Trauma and abuse can leave deep scars, but most of the time, they're not permanent. I just did some reading on the topic, actually. I'm curious to try a few things, if you're okay with that."

"I'm open to trying anything." My voice dropped and took on a husky tone. *Did I intend that to be dripping with innuendo? Because it certainly was.*

I looked at her from under my lashes, trying to gauge her response. Oh, it registered, all right. Her eyes got big as she returned my gaze. Now she was the one blushing. I allowed myself the tiniest smirk as I watched the red creep up her throat to her jawline.

She cleared her throat and reached past me again to open my truck door. Quite the gentleman. I smiled approvingly and gave her a quiet, "Thank you." I settled into the driver's seat and placed my purse on the passenger seat.

"Drive safely," she said, closing the door for me.

I gave her one last look and a smile before driving away. Backlit by the porch light, it was too dark to see if she smiled back.

I couldn't get a read on this woman. She seemed frustrated with Manz but also said she loved her. She was being so kind and gentle with me, but also slightly cold and awkward. She'd touched me several times tonight—but was it from a place of attraction, or just the normal chivalrous behavior she had with everyone? She'd also blushed when I pushed, but was it from attraction or embarrassment? I'd only just met her a few hours ago, but so far, I could tell she was funny and made me feel comfortable around her immediately. And those eyes...the way she looked at me. More than once tonight, her look made me think there might be something there. Something worth pursuing.

CHAPTER EIGHT

Sam

Once Alyssa's truck had turned safely onto the roadway, I entered the house, determined to confront Manz on the bullshit she pulled tonight. But when I reached their room, the door was closed with Bailey curled up against the outside. Faint moans could be heard from within. I growled quietly in frustration. My confrontation would have to wait until tomorrow. I called to Bailey to follow me and went to my room.

Fuck Manz's "No dogs on the furniture" rule. As unhappy as I was with her, I was certainly in no mood to obey. I patted the comforter at the foot of the bed, and Bailey eagerly jumped up. After a few moments of initial excitement and licks on my face, he spun three tight circles and lay down. After a quick face wash, teeth brushing, and change into PJs, I returned to the spare room to find Tuxedo curled up with Bailey. I climbed under the covers and tucked my feet under their warm bodies to sleep.

Early the next morning, I reflexively checked the screen of my phone and wished I hadn't. Three more multi-paragraph texts and one voice mail from Sophia. I deleted all of them without reading or listening to them. I just couldn't. And I certainly didn't trust myself to respond—not in this mood. I was still pissed off at Manz's meddling; I was not in a good place to deal with Sophia too. Besides, I figured, she had nothing to say that I wanted to hear. Even an apology would feel hollow, and it certainly wouldn't make anything better. I simply couldn't think of a single thing I wanted to hear her say.

Bailey and I left Tuxedo to groom his already perfect fur in a patch of sunshine while we went out to feed the chickens and goats. Something about the contented clucks of the hens as they scratched the ground felt like home. All of it, really—the quiet of the cool, fall morning; the sound of the goats beginning their day; the red-tailed hawk gliding overheard, hunting silently for breakfast; the golden rays of sunshine peeking over the eastern hillside. Perfection.

My calm and peace quickly disappeared as I heard footsteps behind me. I was relieved to see Jen join me at the goat fence instead of Manz.

"She told me I'd find you here." Jen's low voice rumbled from behind me.

I grunted in reply. I knew I shouldn't be rude to Jen—I was sure last night's setup was all Manz's doing—but she was still guilty by association.

Jen took a deep breath. "I tried to talk her out of it, I swear."

I rolled my eyes at her, saying nothing.

"I did," she said.

A long moment of silence ticked by.

"You're right. I should have tried harder. I told her you're not ready. It's too soon."

I continued standing in silence but took a deep, steadying breath. My eyes burned and welled with tears. I refused to let them fall.

"I'm sorry," she said, nudging her shoulder against mine. "It wasn't fair to ambush you like that."

Another moment of silence slowly ticked by.

"But…in Manz's defense…"

My head whipped around, and I glared at her in disbelief.

Jen put her hands up defensively. "Hear me out, okay?"

I returned to staring silently at the goats.

"She's like a cop in a B-rated movie: shoot first, ask questions later. She becomes so fixated on the end result, she doesn't always think through the plan to get there."

I didn't respond.

"Manz loves you. Like, *really* loves you. She wants so desperately for you to be happy and loved. But sometimes her methods are…questionable."

I scoffed indignantly.

"Plus, Alyssa is pretty awesome. Since her dad passed away, she's been running that ranch by herself. It's an amazing piece of property, but it's also a *big* property and a lot of work. She cares for her mom too."

My walls were dropping slowly, but I still wasn't ready to talk to her.

Jen continued, "She loves animals, like you. She has horses—your specialty." She began counting the traits off on her fingers. "She's kind. She's funny. She's easy to talk to. She's been single for a while, at least as far as we know. And she just happens to be attracted to women, which is rather convenient."

A mental picture of her laughing as I told my bear story last night flashed behind my eyes. I subconsciously pulled my bottom lip into my mouth and held it there with my teeth.

"And you could bounce a quarter off that delicious ass in that pencil skirt last night."

"Jennifer!" I yelled, slapping her shoulder.

"Hey!" She laughed, holding up her hands to ward off more hits. "So you *can* speak after all. I knew that would do it."

We chuckled together as we settled back into our spots on the fence, watching the goats again.

"She is hot though, huh?" she said.

I took another deep breath. "She's…very pretty."

"Very pretty?" Jen repeated. "No, love, sunsets are very pretty. Lamborghinis are very pretty. Wild mustangs running free through the desert," she said as she swept her hand across the horizon, "are very pretty."

I turned to look at her.

"Alyssa is not 'very pretty,'" Jen continued. "She is nuclear-meltdown-level hotness. She's fucking gorgeous."

She turned to look back at me, waiting for my response.

I sighed. "Fuck, she really is, isn't she?"

Jen laughed loudly. "Come on. Manz is cooking breakfast. We better get in there before she lights something on fire."

"Get it while it's hot," Manz said as we entered, scooping scrambled eggs, bacon, and fruit onto three plates.

My temper had cooled a bit after talking with Jen, but I was still unhappy with Manz. I took a plate from her and found a seat at the table, saying nothing. I didn't know what to say, and I didn't know how to start.

"So…excited to see Alyssa again today? Hmm?" She waggled her eyebrows suggestively at me. Leave it to Manz to bust the issue wide open like the goddamned Kool-Aid man.

"About that…" Jen said, shooting a cautionary look at Manz.

"Yeah," I growled. "About that."

"You're not upset with me, are you? Get over it, Sam. I did you a favor." She speared a piece of banana with her fork and pointed it at me. "Someday, you'll thank me." She popped the banana into her mouth.

"Thank you?" I scoffed incredulously. "I walked in on my girlfriend getting railed by a man in my bed only forty-eight hours ago. Less than that, actually! Not even two fucking days, and you're already setting me up with this woman."

"This sexy, intelligent, animal-loving woman who was *clearly* into you last night, I might add." Manz pointed her fork at me again to make her point.

Into me? Her words stunned me momentarily. Into *me*? Really? Maybe I hadn't imagined it.

"That makes it even worse!" I countered. "I'm not in a place to be…" I gestured around, looking for the right word. "Whatever it is she's looking for."

"Why not?" she asked innocently.

I looked to Jen. "Is she deaf, or just fucking clueless?" I looked back to Manz. "Two days ago, Manz. Two fucking days!"

"No time like the present," she replied cheerily in a singsong voice.

I sighed loudly in exasperation. "You are so damned infuriating."

"What are you waiting for? What are you holding on to? Are you hoping to reconcile with Sophia?" she asked.

"No," I answered quickly. "Absolutely not."

"Are you hoping she'll come groveling back, with promises of forever and fidelity?" She clasped her hands together and batted her eyelashes obnoxiously.

"No," I said again.

"And when she does—because I guaran-fuckin-tee she will—are you going to take her back like nothing happened?"

"No fucking way."

"So...is it safe to say that your relationship with Sophia is completely, utterly, and undeniably dead in the grave?"

"Yes," I growled. *Fuck, she's in attorney mode, and I'm in her crosshairs on the witness stand.* I knew I didn't stand a chance.

Manz planted her hands on either side of her breakfast plate and leaned forward across the table aggressively. Nearly nose-to-nose with me, she said, "Sure sounds like you're ready to move on to me. But what the fuck do I know? I've only known you your entire fucking life."

I continued staring at her, unblinking and without moving, until she withdrew back to her seat.

"Fuck you," I said flatly, my energy to fight depleted.

"Aww, I love you too, Sammy." She came around the table and hugged me.

"Asshole," I said and begrudgingly hugged her back.

CHAPTER NINE

Alyssa

In the early morning hours, I heard a tap-tap-tap on my bedroom window. I rolled over to see Sam's eager face peeking in, waving enthusiastically. I crossed the room and opened the window.

"What in the world are you doing out there?" I asked, helping her through the second-story window.

"I had to see you," she said, smiling broadly. "I couldn't wait until ten."

Once she was fully into the room, Sam stepped forward and hugged me. Pleasantly surprised, I hugged her back. But as her arms touched the skin of my back, I became suddenly aware that I was naked except for underwear.

"I'm sorry," I said awkwardly. "I don't wear pajamas."

"Don't apologize. These PJs fit you just fine." Sam began fingering the silky waistline of my thong underwear.

At least I'm wearing sexy ones, I thought.

She slid her hands down, cupping my naked ass with her hands. It lit a fuse in my brain, and my mouth involuntarily sought hers. Her lips were warm and pillowy soft. She wore minty ChapStick. She kissed me, closed-lipped at first, testing the waters for warmth. I gave her the warmth she sought when I parted my lips against hers, tracing her top lip with the tip of my tongue. She groaned into my mouth, meeting my tongue with hers. She bent slightly and lifted me from the ground. I wrapped my legs around her hips, her hands still holding my thong-clad ass. Her mouth locked on mine, our kisses building in intensity, and she walked me backward to the bed. Together, we collapsed onto my bed, her hips between my thighs.

I suddenly craved her skin—all of her skin—against mine. I stripped her shirt and bra away and dug my nails into her back as her hardened nipples touched mine. Still kissing passionately, she began sliding her hand down my stomach. My abs tensed in response, and she kissed me deeper. She slipped her hand inside my thong and dipped one finger into my warm, wet, hungry heat. My back arched at the intensity of that first touch, that first intense contact with my clit. I lifted my hips to invite her to more, to all of it, to anything and everything...

"Please..." I begged.

"Don't you...forget about me." Sam's voice was male. *What in the world?* "Don't, don't, don't, don't...don't you forget about me."

Realization swirled in, and the dream collapsed in a flash. Simple Minds was playing on my clock radio, and I reached over to turn it off.

My heart was racing, and my naked breasts were covered with sweat, my nipples hardened with arousal. I lay alone in the bed, awoken way too soon from an amazing dream. My clit was swollen and throbbing, aching for climax. I slipped two fingers between my legs—I was unbelievably wet. Immediately, Sam's intense green eyes appeared in my mind again as my fingers began to move. My body was already so ready, so hungry, it was not going to take much to finish. My mind traveled to Sam's lips and the feel of them against mine. And, as I kissed those lips and felt my fingers—her fingers—stroking my clit, the electricity coursing through my body intensified. My eyelids lulled shut as Sam kissed me, deeper and more passionately, as her fingertips gently but firmly brought me closer and closer to the edge. I continued kissing Sam in my mind, tracing her tongue and lips with mine, as my thighs quivered and my back began to arch. Unexpectedly, Sam's voice, guttural and flooded with need, filled my ears: "Come for me, Alyssa." And obediently, my body reacted as my back seized into an arch and wave after wave of climax raced through my veins.

What the fuck? I stared at the ceiling, my heart still raging against my rib cage. I swallowed hard, trying to tame my frenzied thoughts. I'd kissed girls before, but they were more the drunken college party kind of situations, not this. Okay, maybe a few fizzled first dates that never went any further. Nothing like this. And it certainly had never gone *that* far. If I was honest with myself, there had been attractions and flirting with women in the past, but it had never amounted to anything. Those few first dates—dinner or meetings over coffee—with women I'd met when I lived in The City or since I'd returned to town, had not progressed beyond that.

And, yes, there'd been dreams in the past, dreams of anonymous beautiful women with luscious curves and strong, knowledgeable hands. My fantasies and dreams about women were far more tantalizing than those I'd had about men, but I had always just figured it was the newness and exotic foreignness of it that aroused me so much. The only true relationships I'd had were with men. I had dated kind men and not-so-kind men, but none of them made me feel like this dream had—this *Am I having a heart attack?* kind of feeling. This *I'm being electrocuted with pleasure* feeling. This *Everything tingles from scalp to toes* feeling.

I had no issues with my attraction to women. In fact, I hoped to explore it more someday. I was blessed by the fact my parents didn't care either. But Sam's sudden appearance in my life—and my dream—had sent my mental train off the tracks. With the issues on the farm and Daddy's recent death, I wasn't sure I was in a place to dip my toe into that pond yet. I also wasn't sure I had the available emotional bandwidth to expose myself to this potential.

And yet… Again, if I was honest, Sam seemed kind and chivalrous. She was funny and—yes, I'd noticed—quite attractive. Her green eyes had caught my attention more than once last night. There was a spark of chemistry there—at least for me—that I clearly couldn't deny.

I hadn't been in a relationship for a few years—nothing beyond a first or second date anyway. *Am I ready? Am I able to open these doors that have been closed so long? And a woman, no less?*

My pulse had finally slowed a bit, and the sweat on my torso had cooled. *I don't need to decide anything today. Let's just be open and see where it all leads. What I need right now is a shower.*

* * *

What was I doing?

I stood in the kitchen, completely clueless, replaying the last few minutes in my head, trying to remember, without success. *Maybe if I walk back to my bedroom, it'll remind me.*

I walked back upstairs and into the master suite. On the nightstand, I saw my half-full water glass, which triggered my memory at last: Momma needed some water.

"Get your shit together, Alyssa," I quietly scolded myself and walked back downstairs to get the glass of water for her.

Momma's room was on the first floor. Since Daddy died, she didn't use the stairs anymore. For that matter, she didn't do much of anything anymore. Every day, she sat silently in a rocker facing the window. I helped feed her, encouraged her to bathe, tried to get her to join me to the farmers' market or the antique stores she used to love. Initially, it was, "Not today, honey," or "Maybe tomorrow." But those tomorrows never seemed to come, and now she wouldn't respond at all. Day after day, the shell of the woman I once admired so much sat wasting away in the back bedroom. It would be fair to say she died of a broken heart the day Daddy died, except her heart wouldn't listen and kept on beating anyway.

"Momma, you need anything before I head out to the stables?"

She sat staring out of the window, unresponsive.

"I'll put your water right here, okay? I'll be back in about thirty minutes. Call if you need me." I ensured that the water glass and landline phone were within reach before leaving the room.

On the walk to the barn, I checked the time: 8:45. Good. Enough time for morning chores before Sam arrived. The anxious flutter from last night returned to my stomach. I was curious to see how she acted when she wasn't around Jen and Manz.

Hickory heard me coming and nickered loudly from his stall. I entered the pasture to open the exterior stall doors for the horses.

"Hi, big boy," I said, throwing his stall door wide. He snorted, tossed his head, and nudged me in the chest with his huge head. He nearly knocked me off my feet, and I stumbled back a step to regain my balance.

"Hey, be gentle, Hickory!" I reprimanded him lovingly.

I continued walking to open the stall doors for Apricot and Maddox. Apricot came out immediately and began sniffing my pockets for food. Maddox did not emerge.

"No treats this morning, girl," I said as I ran my fingers through Apricot's mane to gently untangle it. "Where's Maddox, huh?" I kissed her inquisitive muzzle. "Where's your friend?"

Hickory approached, inserting his nose in between Apricot and me.

"You jealous, boy?" I said. "Fine, some kisses for you too." I gave his soft muzzle a few quick kisses.

Before leaving the pasture, I peeked into Maddox's stall. She was tucked into the farthest corner, butt to the corner and nostrils flared at me. Her eyes were wide as well, watching every move I made.

"Good morning, Maddox." Her ears flicked forward briefly before plastering back against her head again.

"Come on out and say hi, Maddox," I continued as I opened her stall door. She did not budge a muscle.

"Okay, girl," I said, feeling Hickory nibbling the back waistband of my pants. "I'll leave you be."

Hickory happily walked alongside me as I walked to the gate to leave. Apricot was still contentedly grazing on the freshly watered grass.

"Get back in there, Hick," I said, pushing his broad chest with both hands as he tried to follow me out of the pasture. He snorted at me but obediently took a step back. "I'll come visit you in a bit. A new friend is coming to see you today." His ears perked up in interest and an excited flutter settled in my belly.

As I latched the gate, Hickory suddenly burst into a case of the happy zoomies. He nickered loudly and began bucking wildly throughout the pasture. Apricot briefly lifted her head, realized it was just Hickory being Hickory, and went back to quietly grazing.

Once he'd gotten his burst of energy out of his system, Hickory trotted back to the gate. He extended his neck over the fence to me.

"Silly boy," I said, rubbing the base of his ears.

Before walking back to the house, I cast one last look to Maddox's stall. She was still in the stall but had advanced to the door opening. Only her head extended into the pasture, her ears pointed forward inquisitively. As we made eye contact, she pinned her ears back again and retreated into the stall. I sighed deeply and walked back to the house. Time to get cleaned up for Sam's visit.

I checked my watch: 9:55. I walked to the window and checked the driveway: no car. I walked to the bathroom and checked the mirror: exactly the same as the last time I checked five minutes ago. 9:56. *Oh my god, stop it. You're acting like a high school girl with a crush.*

I heard the distinct sound of footsteps on gravel and looked out of the window. Sam was walking up my driveway from the roadway. *Why is she walking? Why didn't she borrow one of Manz and Jen's cars?* One last peek in the mirror, I checked my teeth and lip gloss, and walked to the front door.

I walked down the porch stairs as she finished the last few yards of the driveway.

"Hey, good morning," I said, smiling.

"Hey, you," she said, returning my smile. "Great place you have here." She closed the distance between us and leaned in for a one-armed hug with a brief kiss to my cheek.

"Thank you." My heart rate leapt at her closeness. *Man, she smells fantastic.*

"How many acres?"

"Just shy of ten," I answered. "Although we really only use the front two." She followed my gaze toward the back of the property. "The back eight are undeveloped hills and oak forests."

"Beautiful," she said. I checked to see if she might sneak a peek at me when she said it, but her gaze remained fixed on the land.

"Come on in." I gestured to the front door. "Can I get you some coffee? Tea? Something to eat?"

"Coffee would be great."

She followed me into the house, looking around curiously. I went to the kitchen and retrieved two mugs.

"How do you take it?" I called to her.

"Black, please. Just a little sweetener is fine."

With two prepared cups, I rejoined her in the living room. She was looking at a framed picture of Daddy and his favorite Appaloosa, Whisper.

"Who's this handsome devil?" she asked, gesturing to the picture.

"That's my dad, Gerald. Jerry for short," I said, joining her side, looking at the picture.

"I was asking about the horse."

"Oh." I looked at her in embarrassment and quickly realized she was teasing me. "You brat." I playfully slapped her arm. "You totally got me."

Sam said, still laughing, "Sorry, I couldn't help it. You looked so serious." She continued, her tone becoming somber, "You really loved him, didn't you?"

My eyes began to sting. It took me a moment too long to reply. Through a tight throat, I said, "Yes. He was my everything."

"I'm so sorry," she said, placing a gentle hand on my arm. "I shouldn't have joked."

"No, nothing like that." I stood, looking at his gentle smile. "It's just…" I swallowed hard. "It's been hard since he died." I cleared my throat, and my voice regained some of its strength. "But, we're making it work, Momma and I. Little by little."

"Is your mom here?" She began to look around curiously. "I'd love to meet her."

I hesitated. "Yeah, um." My brain raced for the words. "It's just…There's something you should know first."

By her facial expression, I could tell she sensed my apprehension. "Boy, I've been in your home for five minutes and I've already stepped in it twice, huh?"

I gave her a half-hearted smile. "Come sit with me for a minute. Bring your coffee."

CHAPTER TEN

Sam

"My parents bought this ranch when they were first married before the North Bay was even on the map—back in the seventies when the property values were cheap and there were still huge parcels to buy." Alyssa paused to sip her coffee at one end of the couch, while I sat listening attentively at the other.

"He had a brilliant mind for numbers, and he could see the future value of land in this area. Over the years, my father invested and parceled out pieces of the hundred-acre property to cattle ranchers and vineyard growers that began flooding into the area. He kept the parcels around our house on the smaller side. He essentially created our little country neighborhood by parceling out small family-farm-sized plots.

"Mix in some smart investing, and Daddy and Momma retired comfortably, land paid for in full, and accumulated a nice little nest egg for themselves. They made some petty cash on the weekends boarding horses and selling produce and honey at the farmers' market, but that was more to have something to do than to earn money."

My eyebrows raised in surprise. "Wow. That's not easy to do in California these days."

She nodded in agreement. "Like I said, he had a fantastic brain for numbers." She took a long sip of her coffee. "Anyway, Daddy and Momma were high school sweethearts—classic love story, you know? So when the heart attack took him from us, it broke her. She just…never recovered."

She gazed off into the distance. I wanted to comfort her—to take her hand or hug her or something—but Manz's words that she was "into me" gave me pause. I didn't want to send the wrong message. Instead, I sat quietly and waited for her to continue.

She cleared her throat and continued with forced brightness. "So I live here with Momma now. Left the big-city life behind and became a horse rancher. I grew up here, so I obviously know how to care for the animals, how to run the ranch, and whatnot. That's the easy part, relatively speaking. But Momma…Momma is…Do you need more coffee?"

Her abrupt topic change caught me off guard. Without letting me answer, she took my still-half-full coffee cup from me and went to the kitchen. I rose and followed.

I heard a small sniffle from her as she refilled our mugs. The sound wrenched my heart.

"Alyssa," I said, placing a hand on her lower back. She turned, and her eyes were brimming with unshed tears.

"Maybe we should just go see Apricot. I've already wasted too much of your time with this nonsense." She took the mug handles and started walking back toward the front door.

"Alyssa," I said again, moving my hand to her forearm, stalling her movement. "Hey, stop for a minute."

I could see she was desperately trying to suppress her welling tears.

"I'm not in any rush," I continued. "And this isn't nonsense or wasting my time." I pulled out a kitchen table chair for her and directed her into it. Once she was seated, I sat beside her, pulling my coffee mug toward me. "It'll feel good for you to talk. Tell me about your mom."

"Ugh." She wiped her eyes carefully to not ruin her makeup. "This is so embarrassing," she said with a self-deprecating laugh.

I smiled and quietly disagreed. I encouraged her to continue.

She began turning her coffee mug slowly on the tabletop. "Momma's not doing well. She hasn't spoken a word since…" She trailed off, thinking. "I don't know. It's been weeks, maybe months." She took a sip of her coffee. Her hands were small, and her nails were clean and neatly trimmed. "Even when she used to speak before that, it was just one- or two-word responses." She resumed slowly turning the coffee mug. "She just sits and stares out the window, day after day. It's like…" Her voice trailed off, and her lips sealed.

"It's like what?" I prompted.

"It's stupid."

"It's not stupid," I said. "It's like what?" I had a suspicion what she'd say.

After a few moments of silence, she quietly said, "Sitting there, staring out the window every day, it's like she's waiting for Daddy to return."

Suspicion confirmed. I nodded to her.

"I hate seeing her like this, you know? The doctors say there's absolutely nothing wrong with her physically—it's all just her inability to cope with her grief. Her sadness has just eaten her alive. I think she wishes she were gone too…so she could be with him again."

I put my hand over hers.

She continued again, that tone of forced cheerfulness returning, "So, now you know. I didn't want you to meet this catatonic woman without some forewarning."

"I'd love to meet her, if that's okay with you," I said.

The room faced the west, and with the curtains thrown wide, Alyssa's mother's room was flooded with midmorning sunlight. A fresh vase of daisies sat on the table by the window. The twin bed was dressed in a quilt of bright, country fabrics. Next to the foot of the bed, facing the window, was a wooden rocking chair. In it sat a frail woman, hair graying at the temples but still retaining some of the golden color of Alyssa's beautiful, long hair. She sat utterly still, looking out of the window at the driveway.

"Momma," Alyssa said loudly as we approached her. "I'd like to introduce you to my friend, Sam."

Friend? Interesting.

"Sam, this is my mother, Marilee. Momma, this is Sam. Say hi to Sam, Momma."

Alyssa's mother did not move, aside from blinking and breathing. I quietly took a seat at the foot of the bed.

"It's a pleasure to meet you, ma'am." I reached over and gently squeezed her hand resting on the arm of the rocking chair. "This is a beautiful home you have. Thank you for letting me come visit." I sat in silence with her for a few moments, looking out the window with her, while Alyssa stood silently behind us.

"Alyssa told me you previously boarded horses. I'd love to do that someday. Have a nice, clean, little horse ranch, take in some boarders, maybe take in a few to saddle-break and train, or start a breeding program. But my real dream would be to do some sort of equine therapy program. You know?" I lapsed into silence again. Again, no response.

"I love horses. When my parents died, I was still really young." I heard Alyssa's body shift behind me. "My best friend's name is Manz—her parents were my godparents so they took me in after the accident. I was in a rough spot, you know? Grief and all that. Manz's family had horses. I'd go out and just talk to them. I'd talk to them for hours. Sometimes, I'd talk while I brushed them. Sometimes, it was when I'd untangle their manes and tails, or when I'd braid them. Sometimes, it'd be while I was cleaning hooves or stalls. It didn't matter what I was doing, I just kept talking to them. And each day, my grief got a little lighter and a little lighter." I snuck a look at Marilee—was that a tear pearled in the corner of her eye? "I'm convinced they saved me. So I'd love to build an equine therapy program where the horses can help other people too." I let another few more moments of silence slide by. "Thank you for listening, ma'am. It feels good to talk about my parents. It helps to keep them alive for me."

I reached over and gave her still hand another squeeze. She continued staring motionless out of the window.

"Well, I'll leave you to get some rest now. Maybe I could come back and talk to you again?" Marilee gave the faintest of head nods. "Great," I replied. "I'd like that."

CHAPTER ELEVEN

Alyssa

What in the world was that? This woman, that I don't even know, just elicited more of a response from my catatonic mother than I'd gotten from her in weeks! I was in utter disbelief.

Once in the living room, and out of Momma's hearing, I grabbed Sam's shoulder and pulled her to a stop.

"Thank you," I said quietly.

She smiled shyly and said, "Of course," in return.

"How did you do that?"

"Sometimes, you just have to sit in the silence," she replied. "Sit with the vulnerability."

I looked at her in complete confusion. With total sincerity, I said, "I have no idea what you're talking about."

Sam burst out in a short laugh. "Come on. Introduce me to your horses."

A loud nicker rang out from the pasture as we walked toward it.

"Oh, please tell me that's Hickory!" she said, smiling, her eyes glittering with excitement.

"It sure is. He can hear us coming."

Hick was prancing and pawing, tossing his head and turning in tight circles.

"He is a big puppy, isn't he?" she said.

Once we were close enough, he extended his neck as far as he could reach to sniff and nuzzle the newcomer.

"Hi, Hickory," she cooed, scratching his jawline. "Hi, handsome guy."

"And you recognize that pretty girl over there, I'm sure."

Beyond Hickory's large frame, Apricot was looking at us in curiosity from across the pasture. Behind her, paying close attention, Maddox also watched anxiously.

"It's good to see her out in the sunshine," I said. "Come here, Apricot! Come here, Maddox!" Hearing my voice, Maddox turned and quickly trotted back to her stall.

Sam's facial expression changed. She became pensive and serious. "Is Maddox a name you picked? Or is that the name she came with?"

"That's the name she already had."

"Have you thought about changing her name?" Sam was staring pensively at Maddox.

"Maddox's? No, why?" I asked.

"She reacted very negatively to it."

"She did? I had been thinking it was just my voice."

"No," she said. "I don't think so. She could hear us speaking and talking to Hickory, and she didn't react."

"Wow. Yeah," I said, thinking. *Not your most articulate moment, Alyssa.*

"It wasn't until you said her name that she turned and bolted back to the stall."

"So you think a name change might help?"

"It's worth a try." Her demeanor was very focused and determined. "Your job is to pick a name for her while I spend some time with these big ol' beasts," she said, playfully roughing Hickory's forelock.

"Okay," I agreed.

"May I?" she asked, reaching for the gate latch.

"Yes, please."

"After you," she said, opening the gate for me. As I moved past her, I felt the gentle pressure of her hand on the small of my back. *Chivalrous again. Nice.*

Once in the pasture, I gave Sam some space. I wanted to watch and learn as she interacted with my horses. And, equally important, I wanted to see their reactions to her. Okay, fine— she's just nice to look at in general, I thought.

Sam confidently walked up to Apricot, who began walking toward her as we entered the pasture.

"Hug?" Sam said as she approached, her arms extended wide. It wasn't a question, but it wasn't quite a command either. Her tone gave Apricot the choice to refuse. Apricot closed the distance. Sam wrapped her arms around Apricot's neck as Apricot tucked her chin over Sam's shoulder.

"You give the best hugs, Apricot." I could see Sam's eyes drift close as she melted into the hug. Before letting go, she rubbed her hands along Apricot's powerful neck. They both looked completely at peace. *I want to be hugged like that by Sam too.*

"Release." Apricot lifted her chin from Sam's shoulder blade and took a careful step back. *Holy crap, Apricot is trained to give hugs?* I had no idea.

I looked toward Maddox's stall. She was still inside but was peeking out at us. She made eye contact with me and took a timid step backward into the safety of the stall.

"Don't look at her," Sam cautioned quietly, running her hands along Apricot's ribs and haunches. *Her back is to me. How did she know?*

Sam continued running her hands over Apricot's coat, periodically checking her palms for the amount of shedding it released. Hickory approached Sam now as well, nibbling at the belt loop at the back of her jeans with his lips. Without turning, Sam continued her investigation of Apricot's coat and the musculature underneath it with one hand while stroking Hickory's soft muzzle behind her back with the other. Those hands—strong and gentle with such command. With barely perceptible movements, she prevented his nibbling and reinforced his nuzzles. As she moved to Apricot's other side to continue the health inspection, Hickory followed, his muzzle planted in her palm behind Sam's back. He had a trancelike quality to his movements, and Apricot stood in calm bliss, clearly enjoying the attention she was receiving.

And the entire time, Sam talked quietly to the horses, sometimes too quiet to be heard. "Your coat is growing back so nicely. Still a little patchy over here. That's okay, it'll be back. We've all had a bad haircut or two. We need a little more weight on these ribs though, girl. Maybe some more oats?" Apricot's ears perked. "You like oats, huh? Oats are delicious."

She began talking louder until she was at a normal speaking voice, her attention entirely on Apricot. Her hand remained behind her back, thumbing Hickory's muzzle in her palm, with him following her every step. I didn't think I'd ever seen him so calm. Sam continued circling Apricot, checking her eyes, her teeth, her legs, and her hooves, all the while Hickory stayed calmly in step with her.

I heard a hoof step to my right. I resisted the urge to look this time.

Without breaking tone or volume, Sam continued, "Apricot, your eyes look so good. Nice and clean. Alyssa, don't look to the stalls. And your mane is looking good too. Did Alyssa brush it for you? Almost tangle free. Someone has two hooves out of her stall. Oh, and you have a sticker in your mane. Here, let me get that out. Good boy, Hickory."

She began speaking to me, effortlessly weaving it into her chatter with the horses.

"Let's check out your tail, Apricot. She's watching us. Don't look. Don't speak. Oh, Apricot, your tail looks good too. Little bald spot there. Stay still, Alyssa. She's watching you."

How did she know? She hadn't spared a single glance toward Maddox. Not that I'd seen, anyway. I couldn't figure it out. How did she *know*?

"Okay, babies," she continued. "Alyssa and I are going to leave for a bit. But we'll be back." Her hands dropped slowly, and she turned to face me.

"Don't look," she said, slipping her hand into mine. "Stay looking at the gate and then we'll walk away without looking back. Okay?"

The shock of her fingers interlaced with mine had my heart doing backflips. We calmly walked out of the pasture, hand in hand. Still holding my hand, she latched the gate closed and walked me to the far side of the barn, out of the horses' line of sight. Only then did she let go of my hand.

"Excellent start. Did you see how far out of the stall she was?" Her green eyes glittered with excitement again. *My god, those eyes.*

"No," I said. "I didn't see anything. And to be honest, I can't figure out how you did either."

She smiled and dodged my inquiry. "Did you pick out a name for her?"

"How did you do that?" I asked, more direct this time.

"Something that doesn't start with M or have the X sound at the end. Something completely different," she said, ignoring my question and waiting for an answer.

"I'll answer if you answer."

She bit her bottom lip for a second, and her green eyes locked on mine. That lip bite made my blood pressure rise. The moment stretched into something tangible, and my blood pressure rose farther while she stood debating.

"Deal. I'll answer one question, but you have to answer mine first," she said at last, her eyes still fixed on mine.

"Whisper Two," I replied quickly. "Daddy's Appaloosa was Whisper, so...Yes, Whisper Two."

"Perfect," she said. "Now come and show me the rest of this ranch."

She turned to walk away, and I snagged one of her belt loops with a finger to stop her.

"Whoa, whoa, whoa, not so fast," I said. "We made a deal, and you didn't hold up your end of the bargain yet."

She spun, and we stood face-to-face, intensely close—close enough to smell her again. *Fuck, she smells good.*

"Bargain? What bargain?" she said innocently.

"How did you know that I'd looked at Maddox?" I asked again.

"Whisper."

"Why? Do you think the horses will hear us and catch on to your tricks?" I asked sarcastically, a feisty smile on my lips.

She chuckled. "Her name is Whisper Two now, not Maddox."

I rolled my eyes and playfully sighed. "Excuse me. How did you know that I'd looked at *Whisper*?"

"Because she quickly retreated back into the stall."

"Okay...but how did you know she'd retreated without looking at her? How did you know?"

"Oh, gosh, I'm so sorry," she said with mock regret. "But I've already answered your *one* question. You'll have to try again later."

"What? Are you serious?"

"Mm-hmm." She smirked. "Completely. You'll have to figure out some other way to get it out of me."

My mouth dropped opened in shock as I continued staring at her. With one gentle fingertip, she pushed my chin up, closing my mouth.

That smirking smile still on her face, she leaned closer to me, her breath sweet on my face. She cocked her head infinitesimally to the side, and her eyes flicked quickly between my eyes and my lips. *She is going to kiss me. Is this really happening?* Instead she said, with her voice low and velvety, "I'm confident you'll find a way."

My brain went blank. Empty. Wind whistling between my ears... *Is she flirting with me? Am I blushing? Dear god, I'm blushing again.*

"Come on," she said, taking my hand again and pulling me into a walk. "You gonna show me the rest of this ranch or what?"

CHAPTER TWELVE

Sam

It took all of my willpower to resist the urge to burst out laughing. The look on Alyssa's face was absolutely priceless. Or should I say "looks"? Confusion. Shock. Betrayal. Back to confusion. And then that blush...that delightful reddening creeping up her neck and face. It set butterflies free in my stomach.

But it took even more willpower to resist kissing those soft, pink lips. Had I missed an opportunity to kiss them? Or had I done the right thing to resist? It had to be the right thing, right? *I've only just met her.* But Jen and Manz were right—as much as I hated to admit it—we did connect on so many different levels. If I was honest with myself, the chemistry had sparked last night at dinner. And the spark hadn't fizzled out today. If anything, it burned brighter. So, what was holding me back?

"Here's the piggies," Alyssa said as we approached the first enclosure. At the sound of her voice, four pot-bellied pigs emerged from the shade of their little wooden house. Two were longhaired, with orangey-reds, blacks, and small patches of white. The other two were shorthaired—one mostly white with grays, and one black with a white diamond on its chest. We stood and leaned our elbows on the fence railing, shoulder to shoulder. The pigs came to the fencing, grunting and squeaking at us for attention.

"That one is Snoop Piggy Pig and that one is Mary J. Pork," she said, pointing to the longhaired redheads. "The white one is RUN P.I.G. and the black one is TuPork."

I chuckled at the names.

"I was big on nineties' rap at the time." She shrugged, slightly embarrassed.

"But where's Notorious P.I.G. and Ice Cubed Bacon?" I asked, shooting a playful look at Alyssa.

"Ooh, those are good. Crap, now I have to get two more pigs."

I nudged my shoulder into hers. We chuckled together for a few moments, watching the pigs, before she asked, "You wanna go in and meet them?"

"Can I?" I asked, my voice full of eagerness.

"Yeah, absolutely," she said, reaching for the gate latch. "But beware, they'll get muddy nose prints all over those expensive jeans."

Now it was my turn to blush, and I suspected she was enjoying it.

We entered the pen, and I squatted on my heels to get to their level. I extended a hand, palm up, for the pigs to sniff. After a few minutes of cautious curiosity, the piggies quickly decided I wasn't a threat. Almost immediately after I began to pet him, TuPork flopped on his side and lay perfectly still.

"Oh goodness!" I said in shock. "I've never spent time with pigs. Is he okay?"

Alyssa squatted next to me, the length of her lean thigh resting against mine. "He's a total slut for belly scratches." She began scratching him, and TuPork began making happy clicking noises in his throat.

"What in the world?" I said, listening to TuPork's strange sounds.

"He's a happy guy," she reassured me. "He's suckling from his momma in his mind, and that's his tongue sucking off the roof of his mouth. It's like…" She paused to think of an example. "It's like when cats make bread with their paws, like when they would knead milk from their mommas when they were kittens."

"Huh," I said. "How interesting."

"This is fun," she said, bumping her hip with mine. "It's the first time since I've met you that I know something you don't."

"Hardly," I said.

"Definitely," she said, looking at me.

Boy oh boy, her gaze was starting to have quite the effect on me.

"Okay then, Madam Pig Expert, educate me."

"Well, let's see. My two ginger babies are Kune Kune pigs. They generally have longer hair, and they usually have wattles," she said.

"Waddles, like a duck waddles?" I asked, confused.

"No, wattles with a T. It's these two tube-like things that hang down from their chin. Mary J., come here, baby, and show Sam your beautiful wattles." The smaller of the two ginger pigs approached, and Alyssa showed me Mary J.'s wattles.

"Oh, like goats have sometimes," I said.

"Exactly. They say the size of the wattle is indicative of testosterone level, so the bigger the wattle, the better the mate." She raised a cheeky eyebrow at me.

"I must be a terrible lover then, because my wattles are so small, they're nonexistent!" I laughed.

She mumbled something under her breath in a suggestive tone, but I couldn't hear what she said.

"Hmm? What'd you say?" I asked.

She pushed forward, ignoring my question. "The white one over there, RUN P.I.G., is a Juliana mini pig, and this guy"—she scratched TuPork's belly again—"is a Vietnamese Pot-belly."

"Man, I had no idea there were so many different kinds."

"Pigs are the fourth smartest nonhuman animal on the planet and have about thirty distinct vocalizations."

"Including suckling tongue clicks," I said, still scratching TuPork's belly.

"Lemme think. They don't sweat or have body odor, and their scent glands can smell sweet, like maple syrup. They're very clean, except when eating of course. Because...they're pigs." She flipped her long hair over her shoulder. "They keep separate areas for waste, eating, and sleeping." Jeez, only this girl could look sexy while talking about pig shit, I thought.

"Amazing," I said, trying to appear engrossed in petting and scratching TuPork's belly.

"And the males have corkscrew-shaped penises."

"Oh gross!" I yelled, the image popping unbidden into my mind's eye. I could feel my face scrunch up in disgust. "You don't have that, do you, TuPork? You're too handsome for that." He squeaked softly, clearly enjoying the attention.

"All right, time to put you to work."

I paused my scratching. "Work?"

"Yes, ma'am. This is a working farm," Alyssa said, adopting a Wild West accent. "And we ain't got no time to dilly-dally. Daylight's a-burnin'!"

I stood from petting TuPork. "And here I thought this was a social visit."

Alyssa tossed the handle of a rake to me. "No, ma'am. You gotta earn your keep if I'm gonna feed you lunch."

I raised an eyebrow at her again. "Oh, I'm staying for lunch, am I?"

"You have to," she said, closing the distance between us. "Because I still have to figure out your trick in the horse pen."

She closed the distance between us, and I froze as she got incredibly close without touching me. So close I could smell the sweet floral scent of her shampoo. *Is she using my own technique against me? Fuck. It's working.*

"And you said—and I quote—that you're confident I'll find a way to get it out of you." *She's shorter than me. I could look down her shirt if I weren't a gentleman.* I bit my bottom lip.

"And since I haven't done that yet," she continued as she leaned even closer, still not touching me, but close enough I feared she'd hear my racing heart. "You're not allowed to leave."

I swallowed hard. "Yes, ma'am."

Once the pig enclosure had been raked and the manure removed, I requested a brief ranch-tour-detour to go back to the horse pasture to do another quick session with the horses. I told Alyssa to stand a little closer this time—maybe ten feet away—and not look at Whisper Two. And certainly to not say "Maddox."

As before, Hickory was immediately front and center, demanding a hundred percent of the attention. I ignored him as I walked to Apricot. I didn't give Hickory attention until he'd calmed. Then I began talking to both horses, smoothing their coats, untangling manes and tails, and giving no attention to Whisper, who had retreated to her stall again. As I kept talking to, grooming, scratching, and loving on Hickory and Apricot, Whisper took one tentative step out of her stall. Then a second. I shot a look at Alyssa, who was staring at me, wide-eyed. Good. She'd heard those hoof steps too.

"That's a good, mellow boy, Hickory. I can give you lots of attention when you're calm like this." Without breaking tone or cadence, I started talking to Alyssa while I spoke to the horses. "Apricot, your hooves look good, but they'll need a trim soon. Alyssa, take three slow steps forward. Hickory, your nose is so soft. Perfect, Alyssa, stop there. Don't look. Don't move. Pretty horses. Beautiful babies."

Thank goodness Whisper hadn't retreated. I wanted one more step before we ended this mini-session.

"Can I braid your tail, Apricot? Oh, you're jealous, huh, Hickory? Okay, I can braid yours next. No nudging, Hick." I calmly pushed his nose down. "There—no tangles. Time for the braid. Should we do a regular braid or French braid? Regular is faster, and Hick is being so patient. Yes, you are."

I continued my inane chatter, listening carefully for Whisper's hooves to move. I finished Apricot's tail braid, untangled Hickory's, and began his braid when I heard it—two more steps forward. No, three. She must be fully out of the barn now. A quick peek—yes, she was fully out. That meant it was time to go.

"Okay, Hickory...Apricot...Whisper...we'll be back to visit you soon." I walked directly to Alyssa, interlaced my fingers into hers, and walked us out of the pasture to the blind side of the barn.

"Did you see that?" I whisper-yelled. "She was all the way out of the stall!"

"Again, no, I did *not* see it because I did *not* look—*like you told me not to*—and I still can't figure out how you're doing it. Your head didn't turn once."

"Trust me, then," I replied. "She had all four hooves out in the pasture with us."

Suddenly I realized, in my excitement, I'd forgotten to let go of her hand. Shyly—or maybe reluctantly—I let her fingers slip out of mine.

"So," I said. "I believe I was promised lunch."

CHAPTER THIRTEEN

Alyssa

"Make yourself comfortable," I said, setting a large glass of iced tea on the kitchen bar in front of Sam. "I need to check on Momma real quick."

Momma sat unmoved, still staring out of the window at the driveway. The glass of water I'd given to her earlier that morning had been drained halfway, the only sign she had moved at all.

"Momma, I'm going to prepare some lunch. Any requests?" I lightly squeezed her hand. Nothing. "How about a grilled cheese?" Again, nothing. "Does that sound good?" Still nothing.

I gave her a brief kiss on the temple and returned to the kitchen.

"Any dietary restrictions? Allergies? Vegan or vegetarian?" I asked Sam, who was now seated on a barstool.

"No, I'm not picky." Then, a mischievous smile crossed her lips. "Well, not about food anyway."

I chuckled and shook my head at her. "Grilled ham and cheese?"

"Sounds great," she said, tucking a short strand of hair behind her ear, making my own hairs on the back of my neck stand up.

Before long, lunch was ready. I quickly realized I had been so engrossed in making sure the sandwiches did not burn that I did not notice Sam had left the room. On the way to Momma's room with her lunch plate, I checked the hallway bathroom, expecting to find Sam there. She wasn't. I could hear a voice coming from farther down the hall.

I paused at Momma's door and absorbed the scene before me. Sam sat at the foot of Momma's bed again, holding Momma's hand. They both looked out of the window.

Sam was speaking. "...and then he says, 'Well, shit, Griz... Buy her dinner first, at least!'"

The corner of Momma's mouth twitched upward, and her shoulders subtly bounced up three times and stopped. *Is she laughing?*

"I know," Sam continued. "Pretty funny, huh? I mean, it was absolutely terrifying at the time, but I can laugh about it now."

Sam sat quietly for a moment. She leaned her ear to Momma's lips. "Can you repeat that?"

My eyes went enormous, and my heart raced.

"Oh yes, Griz and I became good friends after that. Old Man River and I...? Not so much. But that's a story for next time. Alyssa's here with your lunch."

How does she do that?

I stepped forward with Momma's plate as Sam returned Momma's hand to the arm of the rocker. I set the plate and a fresh glass of ice water on the table by her chair.

"I'll come check on you again before we go outside again. Love you, Momma." I placed a quick kiss on top of her head and left the room with Sam.

"What did she say to you?" I asked, setting the plates on the table and taking the seat next to her.

She shook her head slightly. "Nothing."

I looked at her, confused. "But you leaned forward and answered her question...She didn't ask a question?"

"No," she said. "But I figured that's the question I'd ask if she told me that story, so I answered it."

"But…why?" I asked, touched by her kindness to my mother but still completely confused.

"Well, I figured she might like to have a conversation, but…" She took a brief sip of iced tea. "But the words get stuck. This way, we could have that conversation without the pressure of actually speaking."

"How in the world does that make perfect sense and absolutely no sense at all…at the exact same time?" I asked.

"This sandwich is delicious. What kind of cheese did you use? Gouda?"

She is a master of topic changes, I thought. "Yes, smoked Gouda and sharp white cheddar."

"Ah, smoked Gouda. Yes." She took another bite, happily moaning in the back of her throat. "Absolutely delicious."

That moan…it sent vibrations straight to my stomach and— if I'm honest—a little farther south. I shifted my foot so that my calf touched hers.

"Thank you," I said quietly.

She tucked that same strand of short, dark hair behind her ear and caught me watching. Her green eyes sparkled mischievously, and she bit her lower lip again. *God, those lips.* The vibrations in my belly intensified.

"So, what's the plan for after lunch? More ranch tours, or should I be heading back to Jen and Manz's? I don't want to impose."

"No!" I said, too quickly. *Way to play it cool, Alyssa.* I cleared my throat to try again. "No, no need to leave, unless you want to."

"I don't want to," she said simply.

"Plus, you haven't seen the beehives or the chickens yet."

"Birds and the bees, huh?" That devilish sparkle was back in her eyes. "I can't possibly leave before you show me the birds and the bees."

And…the flush was back in my face.

CHAPTER FOURTEEN

Sam

"This time, we're going to be completely vulnerable to Whisper Two. We're going to show her we aren't a threat to her while simultaneously showing her we aren't afraid of her. We trust her not to hurt us. Follow my lead," I said, chuckling to myself. "Terrible horse pun fully intended."

Alyssa rolled her eyes. "Dad joke."

"Bad dad joke, definitely," I agreed. "In the pasture, do what I do. No eye contact. Don't speak, unless she comes close. And if she does, keep it to 'Hi, Whisper' or something along that line."

Alyssa agreed. I could sense she was nervous.

"Don't worry, she won't hurt us."

"Do you fucking read minds?" she asked.

"Maybe." I laced my fingers into hers again and began leading us toward the pasture gate. "Remember, horses are incredibly intuitive. They can read minds even better than I do." I gave her a cheeky smile. "So whatever you're thinking or feeling, she will too. So try your best to keep your thoughts and feelings calm and loving. I promise she'll respond positively to it."

I led us into the pasture, her small, soft hand in mine. Hickory came trotting up and nudged Alyssa's shoulder roughly.

"Hickory, we can't give you love until you're calm," I said.

He bolted into a bucking gallop around the pasture. Apricot barely budged, but Whisper Two retreated to her stall. Once his energy burst was completed, he calmly walked up to Alyssa and buried his nose into her empty palm.

"Good boy, Hicks," I said. "Now we give him some praise because he's being so good."

"That's my good boy, Hickory," Alyssa said with a low, quiet voice. She gave him some pets and scratches as we continued to the center of the pasture, thirty yards from Whisper's stall. Still holding Alyssa's hand, I led us to a nice, clean patch of sunny grass.

"Lie down with me," I said.

She looked at me with severe concern in her eyes but remained silent per my instructions.

"Do you trust me?" I asked, looking deep into her clear blue eyes.

She nodded solemnly, and we lay down in the warm grass, side by side.

This strange behavior clearly piqued the interest of the horses, and Hickory and Apricot approached to sniff us curiously. Hickory nibbled Alyssa's pant cuff as Apricot tickled my nose with the whiskers on her muzzle. And, as before, I continued chatting with the horses. Before long, I heard the first two tentative hoof steps emerging from Whisper's stall.

"No nibbling, Hickory. Alyssa, don't look, but someone's approaching. Apricot, I can see up your nose. Yes, I can."

After about ten minutes of my monotone chatter, Hickory and Apricot began to lose their interest in the strange humans lying in their pasture. Apricot stayed nearby but resumed happily grazing on the pasture grass.

I was elated when Hickory lay down with us. At first, he lay with his legs tucked but his head still raised. But before long, he lay down fully on his side, legs extended, head on the ground, in the perfect picture of relaxation and comfort.

Distracted momentarily by Hickory's napping extravagance, I did not hear Whisper's hoof steps until she was only a few feet away. Without moving my head, I looked over at Alyssa. She was staring at me, her eyes huge with excitement. Or fear? I hoped it wasn't fear.

"Whisper, come here, baby. Yeah, come closer, Whisper. You're safe here, sweet girl." I continued talking to Whisper, keeping my voice as warm and reassuring as I could. I gave Alyssa's hand a gentle squeeze. Another hoof step. And another. I could see her now. Whisper was less than five feet away.

"Yes, Whisper, come give me a kiss. Apricot gave me some kisses. I need a kiss from Whisper now. Maybe soon, Apricot can teach you how to give hugs too. Wouldn't that be nice? Come on. Give me another step."

Whisper stepped. Alyssa quietly gasped.

"Good girl. That's a very good girl. Give me another step."

Whisper stepped again. Her muzzle was so close, I could feel her breath as she cautiously sniffed my head.

"Gimme a kiss, girl."

Alyssa squeezed my hand tightly. *What does that mean?*

"One kiss, Whisper. You can do it."

With another step forward, Whisper's whiskers tickled my forehead, and I felt her nose brush over my hair.

"Thank you, baby," I cooed at her.

Whisper retreated a step and calmly walked away to graze with Apricot. Perfect. Mission accomplished. Time to go.

I slowly sat up, helped Alyssa to her feet, and we walked out of the pasture, hand in hand.

CHAPTER FIFTEEN

Alyssa

Once we were on the far side of the barn, I launched myself into Sam's arms. I hugged her neck and buried my nose in her hair. She smelled absolutely amazing—warm and comforting, like freshly cut wood waiting for a winter fire. I was hyperaware of the full length of my body pressed against hers, and I didn't want to let go. She wrapped her arms around me, hugging me back.

"I can't *believe* that just happened!" I said. "You're a fucking genius. I could kiss you right now!" The words were out of my mouth before I even realized I had thought them.

I reluctantly released my hug, my arms still loose around her tall shoulders.

"It worked," she said, excitement gleaming in her eyes.

"It worked," I repeated, smiling broadly.

"Your smile is gorgeous," she said quietly.

My belly did a backflip. I threw my arms around her neck again, fearing I'd kiss her if I looked into her eyes any longer. *Would it be so terrible if I did?*

"Thank you," I whispered quietly into her ear, leaning into her hug again.

Her hands slid slowly around my hips and waist until she was hugging me again in return. My eyes drifted closed, and a small hum of pleasure escaped unbidden. Her grip tightened ever so slightly.

With my arms still around her, I traced the tip of my nose from behind her ear, down her neck, to her shoulder. I placed one soft kiss on her neck, my heart beating like it might erupt right out of my chest. My arms still around her neck, I leaned back slightly, trying to evaluate her reaction. Sam's eyes were closed, and her lips were slightly parted. Her breathing was shallow and quick. *Is it possible? Is she feeling this too?*

As if on cue, her eyelids drifted open, locking her eyes on mine. With slow movement of her pink tongue, she pulled her bottom lip into her mouth and bit it again.

"You've got to stop biting your lip like that," I said as I ran the edge of my thumb against what remained exposed of her bottom lip, my voice low and husky with desire. "Or I'm going to do more than talk about kissing it."

I edged my lips closer and closer to hers, my eyes jumping between her lips and her eyes. Her gaze burned into mine. I hovered, mere millimeters from her lips, waiting for her to close the distance. She didn't move. She stood staring at me intensely, breathing quickly through parted lips.

Time to turn up the heat and force this amazing woman to make her decision. I slid my hand along her jaw until I cradled the back of her head, my nails raking gently through the short, dark hair at the back of her head.

Her eyes drifted closed again, and with delicious hunger that could be denied no longer, her soft lips finally met mine.

The kiss started slowly, her incredible lips exploring mine. But when she pulled my hips toward hers, fireworks exploded in my brain. I could not keep this kiss so sweet and innocent any longer. Visions of my dream that morning flooded my brain.

I slid my other hand up to cup her face and tentatively touched her bottom lip—that tortured and repeatedly bitten lip—with the tip of my tongue. A low, rumbling moan emanated from her throat, and the tip of her tongue touched mine.

My god, she tastes so sweet. My fingers weaved their own pattern through the hair at the back of her head. I deepened our kiss, and she joined me eagerly. My hands, my lips, my tongue each had minds of their own as I lost myself in her kisses, so much better than the dream.

With strong hands and confident movements, she guided my back against the barn wall. *Fuck, that's incredibly hot—my heart really might explode.* With her lips still locked on mine, her tongue teasing mine mercilessly, she pinned me to the barn wall with the pressure of her hips. Suddenly, it wasn't only my mouth that hungered for her kisses.

She broke the contact of our lips to kiss down my neck, across my collarbones, and back up to the tender skin behind my ear. Each kiss, each electrifying touch of her warm, wet tongue sent fresh waves of warm tingling low in my belly. My chin lifted involuntarily to give her access to whatever, wherever she wanted to kiss—everything was hers for the taking.

"I believe," she said, her lips tickling the skin on my neck as she spoke, "that I was promised a tour of your birds and bees."

I groaned, both because I was starting to catch onto her innuendo-laden sense of humor, but also because a tour meant a stop to our kissing. "Please…just kiss me a little longer." My voice sounded so foreign, thick with lust and desperation.

Obediently, her lips met mine again, and once again, electricity flooded my body. The juncture at the top of my thighs was throbbing, starving for her touch. Reading my thoughts yet again, Sam shifted and pressed her thigh there—right *there*—eliciting a small gasp of pleasure from my lips. Pressure where I craved pressure most—somehow it both satisfied the need yet only made the need worse. Sam grabbed my hips and pulled them even tighter against her thigh. I moaned with pleasure into her mouth. *Holy fuck, that feels good.* My hips subconsciously rocked forward, hungrily accepting the pressure of her body and craving more. So much more.

I kissed her deeply, stroking her tongue with mine and playfully sucking on her delicious lips. It took an incredible amount of willpower to keep my hips still, to keep my hands from removing her shirt, to allow the button and zipper of her jeans to remain closed. For now, at least, I compelled myself to be content with the divine exploration of her lips.

Before long, Sam's kisses slowed, and her lips reluctantly withdrew. I felt the loss of her warmth and pressure, and I subconsciously brought my fingertips to my lips. I rested my forehead against hers, trying to slow my breathing and the racing of my heart. *Has kissing always been like this? Is it always this intense? Or just with her?*

Sam still held my hips firmly against her thigh as she placed a gentle kiss on my forehead. Despite her calm demeanor, her quickened breathing betrayed her. Slowly—desperately slowly—she released her pull on my hips against her thigh. The easing of the pressure between my legs was nearly as delicious as when she had applied it, and I planted another lustful kiss on her lips.

"Fine, I'll show you around the rest of the farm," I said, sounding like a petulant child. "But I demand to be kissed like that again before today ends."

With a smirk, she said, "With pleasure."

CHAPTER SIXTEEN

Sam

I was pleasantly aroused as we walked hand in hand away from the barn. All the important places of my body were awake and humming. *Did that really just happen? Did this intensely hot woman just kiss me like that? And holy fucking shit, is she a good kisser…*

I could hear the hens clucking happily as we approached. A few ran up to Alyssa, begging for treats and pets.

"This is my friendliest girl, Nuggets." Alyssa lifted the hen for me to pet. "That one is Grilled," she continued, pointing out different hens. "This one is Drumstick. She's Tenderloin. That white one over there is Cutlets. There must be more resting or laying eggs in the coop because they're not all out here right now. That one is Extra Crispy, and that dark one is Rotisserie… obviously."

"Well, obviously." I laughed. "Looks like you have quite a variety here. I only recognize the Rhode Island Reds and the Leghorn."

"They lay different colored eggs too. That one lays bluish-green eggs." Alyssa pointed to another chicken. "And she lays pink speckled eggs. Those two," she said, pointing at hens farther away, "lay eggs that vary between terracotta and milk chocolate."

"Seriously? I've only ever seen the white and brown ones from the grocery store. Jen and Manz's lay brown ones, but definitely not milk-chocolate colored. Do they taste like chocolate too?" I said, playfully nudging her shoulder.

"Stay the night, and you can decide for yourself when I cook you omelets in the morning." She smirked and raised a devilish eyebrow at me.

How do I respond to that? I opted to deflect with humor. I gasped in mock horror and put a dainty hand over my heart. "I beg your pardon. What kind of a lady do you take me for? Even Griz had to buy me dinner first. And let me tell you, fitting a fully grown grizzly bear into a small Italian restaurant was no easy feat."

We shared a chuckle and returned to watching the hens happily scratching and pecking the ground.

"Do we have time to see the bees before we go back to do one last session with Whisper?" I asked.

"Sure," Alyssa said, turning away from the chicken coop. "Follow me."

She held out her hand to me, and I happily took it. We walked hand in hand toward an orchard.

"So, do you have clever names for all of the bees too?" I asked playfully as we stood a respectful distance from the five white beehive cubes.

"Well," she said, "considering there's about twenty thousand bees per hive, it's going to take a while for me to introduce you to all of them. But I'm game if you are."

"Wait," I said, doing some mental math. "You have a hundred thousand bees?"

"Mm-hmm." She nodded. "Give or take. Plus our five queens, of course."

"That's amazing. How much honey do they produce? Must be a lot with that many bees."

"I'd guess…" She looked at the hives with her head slightly cocked to the side. "Probably thirty pounds per year."

"Thirty *pounds?*" I asked, completely shocked. "That seems like a lot for these five little hives."

She looked at me, her expression deadpan. "No, thirty pounds per hive."

I did more mental math. "That's a hundred-fifty pounds of honey a year! I understand now why your parents sold it at the farmers' market. Otherwise, you'd be drowning in honey."

"Like Daddy said, 'Honey is money.' He planted this orchard to feed the bees, and then we'd sell the fruit at the market too."

"Amazing," I said, looking appreciatively at the trees. "What kinds of fruit?"

"Mostly apples, but there's cherries, plums, apricots, peaches…just about everything that he could get to stay alive in this climate. There's over a hundred trees—maybe closer to one twenty."

"Absolutely incredible. I wish I could have met him," I said, squeezing her hand. "He sounds like an amazing man."

"He was." Her gaze became distant. "He truly was."

"Okay, here's the plan," I said in a low and conspiratorial voice. "We're going in there hand in hand again—"

"If you insist," Alyssa interrupted with a mischievous smile.

"…and we're going to lie on the grass in the pasture again. But this time, I'm going to hide my empty hand behind my back, and yours will be out, palm up, by the top of your head, okay?"

"Okay," she said, turning serious.

"Don't be nervous," I added. "She won't hurt you. She's afraid of you, not the other way around. You need to project calm, loving, trusting energy to her. She'll feel it, trust me."

"I do trust you. It's Whisper I'm nervous about. I saw what happened at the auction when th—"

My turn to interrupt. "No, stop that right there. Not another word. We are being vulnerable and trusting of her, so that she can be those things with us in return. If this were a standoff, we're lowering our guns first. But if you hold that fear in your heart, she'll feel it, and she won't lower her gun. And she desperately wants to lower hers. I promise."

Alyssa took a deep breath and nodded. I leaned forward and kissed the furrowed lines between her eyebrows. Her face relaxed, and I began walking into the pasture. Apricot was grazing, and Hickory stood tall, watching our approach. By her stall door, but still in the pasture, stood Whisper. Her ears were alert and attentively facing us, and her tail whisked side to side anxiously.

"This time, you're going to do all the talking. Just remember, I'm here. And who cares what you say, as long as you keep saying the horses' names. Keep your voice low, monotone, and continuous. You've got this." I gave her hand a little squeeze as we lay down together on the grass. Discreetly, I watched Whisper, who still hadn't moved. A good sign—at least she didn't bolt like usual.

"Hi, Hickory," Alyssa began timidly. I could tell she was embarrassed to talk to the horses—whether it was because it was something she didn't normally do or, more likely, because there was someone else there to hear it.

"Thank you for being so gentle, sweet boy," she cooed. He approached and nuzzled her ear. "Your whiskers tickle. Where's Apricot? There she is. Hello, Apricot. Hello, sweet girl."

Alyssa continued her idle chatter, quickly becoming more comfortable with speaking to them aloud. Hickory and Apricot sniffed our heads and faces. Hickory nudged my side unsuccessfully to get to my hand hidden behind my back to give him pets and scratches. *Sorry, boy. This is Alyssa's turn to train you rascals, not mine.* Before long, he gave up and returned to Alyssa.

Apricot grew bored and wandered away to continue grazing. Hickory was not so easily distracted—he remained nearby, sniffing, nudging, and tickling us with his soft muzzle whiskers.

Eventually, Hickory bored of us too. *Perfect*, I thought. *Let Whisper see that there's nothing scary or dangerous going on with these weird humans lying on the grass together.* Hick began grazing his way toward Apricot.

"Keep talking to them even though they've wandered off, okay? Be sure to use Whisper's name too," I whispered into her ear. She nodded and continued to chatter.

I relaxed into the sweet sound of her voice, my thoughts wandering. I marveled at how comfortable I felt with this woman, lying in a field holding her hand, even though I had only known her for two days. Less than that, really, if you counted hours instead of boxes on the calendar. *And yet, why do I feel so at ease with her?* My mind wandered to that kiss—that glorious, pulse-quickening kiss—and the potential it promised. *She's a fantastic kisser—way better than Sophia.* The name rose in my mind without permission, instantly shattering the lovely daydream I'd been having of Alyssa's lips, her hands, her tongue against mine.

Sophia... I groaned internally. I'd managed to make it through most of the day without thinking of her. I couldn't decide which hurt more—that she cheated on me with a man or that she cheated on me wearing the heels and bra she knew were special to me. Both felt like a personal attack.

And all those texts, even though I'd only read one...all those deleted voice mails that probably said more of the same bullshit. Did she seriously think I was just going to forgive her and welcome her back with open arms? Welcome her back to our bed, his cologne still on her fingertips?

I had to resist the urge to physically move my head as I mentally shook those thoughts away. It brought me back to now—this pasture, this incredibly beautiful woman, her fingers interlaced with mine, her passionate kisses and, if I wasn't mistaken, our mutual chemistry.

It went without saying that this woman was way out of my league—an ordinary, humble mortal worshipping at the feet of a shimmering, beautiful goddess. I mean, I know I'm not ugly, but I'm not *pretty* either—not in the traditional sense of feminine beauty anyway. My work with animals had given me a lean but fit body. I had to maintain a reasonably high level of fitness to protect myself and keep up with the rigors of working with half-ton mammals with sledgehammers at the end of each long leg.

I was not blessed with a tiny waist or curvy hips. Sophia had always told me she loved my breasts and my abs, not that her opinion was worth a damn anymore.

But Alyssa...*Fuck*. It was laughable to even try to compete at her level—I was Little League while she was at the World Series. Long, loose, golden blond curls. Startlingly blue eyes. Lean, long lines with utterly delicious curves in all the right places. That hint of cleavage from the dinner at Jen and Manz's house—was that seriously only yesterday? Those lips. Those incredibly soft lips. My blood pressure was rising just remembering her lips against mine. If her passion and intensity while kissing was any indication... *Shit, I'm blushing again.*

My thoughts were interrupted by a hoof step shockingly close to my head. I must have been way down the mental rabbit hole to miss all the steps before it. Without moving my head, I snuck a peek. It was not Apricot's creamy orange foreleg. And it wasn't Hickory's chestnut coat either. It was a black leg, wearing a white "sock" at base just above the hoof.

Whisper. *Oh my god, Whisper's hoof is six inches from my forehead.*

"There you go. Good girl, Whisper. Good girl. I love you, sweet girl." Alyssa's voice continued talking, despite being thick with emotion. "Can I touch you, baby? Huh? Can I touch your nose, Whisper girl?"

I held my breath, waiting to see what would happen next.

"Oh!" Alyssa's voice had become much higher in tone, now threatening to dissolve into tears. "Oh, Whisper, your nose is so soft. It's nice to finally meet you, sweet baby."

After a few minutes, I summoned my courage to slowly turn my head to look at Alyssa and Whisper. Whisper's head lifted slightly in concern. She sniffed me, snorted, and returned to Alyssa's scratches and pets. Emboldened by Whisper's lack of fear, I slowly lifted my head, then my torso, and continued until I was sitting up. There was still no response from Whisper, so I gently tugged on Alyssa's hand, which I was still holding. She took the hint and slowly sat up also. Whisper took a half step back but soon closed the distance again. After extending a hand for Whisper to sniff, I joined Alyssa, petting Whisper and rubbing the base of her ears.

Hickory saw us sit up and came to investigate. His movement caused Apricot to cease her grazing. And before long, Alyssa and I were surrounded by three horses while we sat on the grass in the late afternoon sun.

Once all three horses were satiated with scratches, pets, and compliments, they began to drift away again to graze. Alyssa took the unprompted initiative to get to her feet while Whisper was only a few feet away. I feared Whisper would bolt. My heart swelled when Whisper not only held her ground, but instead closed the distance to be touched again by the now-standing Alyssa. Breakthrough.

Going behind the barn, out of sight of the horses, was no longer necessary since Whisper had progressed so far today. But Alyssa took my hand and pulled me there anyway.

"Since I was able to touch Whisper, it's time for you to pay up," Alyssa said once we exited the pasture. "You owe me." That flirty, mischievous sparkle in her blue eyes had returned.

"Oh, really?" I smiled as she pushed me backward against the wall of the barn. "Why do I owe you?"

"I faced my fears, exposed this *gorgeous* face to the hooves of an unpredictable horse…"

"It *is* a rather gorgeous face, I agree." I looped a finger through her belt loop and tugged her toward me.

"…and made friends at last with Whisper. So it's time for you to pay what you owe me." Her eyes became stormy with desire.

"And what is that, exactly?" I lifted her hand toward my face, the length of her delicious body pressed against mine. "Has anyone ever told you how soft your skin is?"

"Don't try to distract me. I demand an answer to my question."

"This skin riiiight"—I placed a soft kiss on the open palm of her hand—"here is particularly soft."

"Answer my question. How did you know when I'd moved this morning without turning your head?"

"This spot is nice too," I said, lifting her wrist to my lips.

"How did you know?" she persisted.

"And this spot," I continued, kissing the inside of her elbow. "And this spot." I pulled down the collar of her shirt to kiss her collarbone.

A small sound escaped her throat. "You're deliberately trying to distract me," she said, her voice losing all power and tenacity.

"Am I?" I asked coyly, placing small, light kisses up her throat. I could feel the intensity of her heartbeat against my lips.

"Yes…" she said, her voice barely audible, as I kissed her jawline. Her head tilted back and her eyes drifted shut.

"I guess you'll have to ask me later then," I said as I hovered my lips over hers, her breath warm and sweet.

"I will get it out of you," she said. "Someday."

"I'm sure you will," I said, deeply kissing her lips at last.

CHAPTER SEVENTEEN

Alyssa

I could kiss this woman for hours, I thought as we walked back to the house. The sun was setting, casting long shadows and hues of pink and peach across the ranch.

"Can you stay for dinner?" I asked, trying to sound nonchalant but probably failing miserably.

"I can't. I promised my parents I'd be home before the streetlights come on." She smirked.

I playfully nudged her shoulder. "You're ridiculous." *Ridiculously hot, that is.*

She chuckled. "Thanks, though, but I really did tell Jen and Manz I'd be back for dinner." She sighed. "Besides, Manz will want to probe me for all the juicy details about my day."

"She'd better not 'probe' you," I said, again trying to sound playful but failing.

"Oh god, no," she exclaimed. "With Manz? Eww!" Her torso shivered dramatically, and her shoulders rose to her ears. "That'd be like making out with my sister. Gross."

I laughed quietly. "So what are you going to tell her?"

She sucked in air sharply through her teeth. "That's a tough one. I have two choices—full disclosure or full denial. With Manz, there's no halfway. If she senses anything at all happened, she'll pester the living shit out of me until she has every naughty little detail."

"Naughty, huh?" I pulled her to a stop and kissed her hard on the lips. While still holding her close, I asked, "Can I see you tomorrow?" I couldn't help it. This time, my need was abundantly obvious in my voice.

"I'd love that," she said, tucking a wayward curl behind my ear.

"I'll drive you back to Manz and Jen's," I said reluctantly.

"Thank you, but no," she replied. "It's less than a mile, and it's a gorgeous evening." She placed a soft kiss on my lips. "Plus, I'm looking forward to the time to think. Lots to unpack from today."

"Only if you're sure?" I asked.

"I am," she replied confidently. "Besides, you need to check on your mom. Good night, gorgeous." She gave me a shy smile, a warm hug, and a long, tender kiss before starting her walk down the driveway.

"Hi, Momma," I said as I stroked her hair. "What can I make for your dinner tonight?"

No response.

"How about spaghetti? Or we have some fresh produce... maybe a salad?"

No response.

"There's some leftover meatloaf too, if you'd like that."

Wait...did she just nod? It was so faint, I was not even sure I'd actually seen it. Had she been communicating with me like this the entire time, and I'd missed it? Or did Sam's influence effect the change? I decided to take a play from Sam's book and run with it.

"Great! Meatloaf it is, then." I kissed the top of her head and took her empty water glass to the kitchen.

I returned shortly, carrying a tray with cutlery, two glasses of iced tea, and two plates of meatloaf with salad. After placing the tray with a dinner and a drink in Momma's lap, I sat at the foot of the bed where Sam had sat earlier in the day with my plate in my lap. Typically, I would guide Momma to the dining room, in the hopes the normalcy of it would bring her back to me. Dinner together as a family had always been important to Momma. But Sam's techniques today had resonated with me, so I decided to meet her in *her* comfort zone.

"What did you think of Sam today, Momma? Did you like her? Boy, I sure do." Imagining her question, like Sam had done, I continued, "What do I like? Well, honestly, I haven't seen anything I don't like. At least not yet, anyway. She's kind. She's *funny*. She's *fantastic* with our animals. She even shoveled pig manure today. And she finally got some progress with Whisper. Oh! I didn't tell you yet. Sam suggested we change Maddox's name. So I picked Whisper Two…you know, after Daddy's horse."

I let a little time pass. "I miss him too. Seeing Sam with the animals, working on our ranch…I don't know how to describe it. She has his same calm confidence. She's pretty incredible."

Knowing Momma, she would dive right into the personal stuff, so I reacted accordingly. "Momma! Oh my god, I can't talk about that." I playfully slapped her arm. My face flushed. "Fine, Ms. Nosey. Yes, we kissed."

Momma and Daddy had never cared what gender I dated as long as they treated me well. Even still, it'd been far too long since I'd dated *either* gender. Sam was the first person in ages to even appear on my radar, let alone been allowed to kiss me. And here I was, pursuing her. Out of character but long overdue, if I was honest with myself. I paused for her next imaginary question.

"I'm not sure who kissed whom. Mutual, I guess? But yes, I wanted to kiss her. I don't know—it just sorta happened."

Another imaginary question.

"Yes, she's going to come back over tomorrow. I'm not sure what we'll do but this is a ranch, and there's always things to be done."

Another pause.

"Oh, you're right, it is the farmers' market tomorrow. No, I didn't reserve a stall, but maybe we could go and get some fresh ingredients for a nice dinner. You'll have to let me know if you've got any requests. Or, maybe you could even join us, if you're feeling up to it."

I paused again.

"No, Momma! You wouldn't be a 'third wheel.' Sam would love it if you joined us. I certainly would too."

A pause.

"Well, you think about it, and you can give me your official decision in the morning, okay?" I reached over and placed my hand over hers.

"I love you, Momma. Make sure you eat and don't stay up too late. And call me if you need anything, okay?"

I gave her hand a squeeze. My heart jumped as she lightly squeezed my hand in return.

CHAPTER EIGHTEEN

Sam

I steeled my nerves to walk through the door and face Manz's inevitable interrogation. Deep breath. *Here we go.*

"Well, well, well, look what the cat dragged in," Manz said, pulling the cork from a bottle of wine. "Or should I say...what the pussy dragged in."

"You're filthy," I said, rolling my eyes at her. "Hey, Jen, what's for dinner? It smells fantastic."

"We're having chicken parm with garlic grilled asparagus," she replied.

"I'll set the table," I said.

Manz followed me as I carried the napkins and cutlery to the dining room.

"Soooo...?" she said suggestively. "Should I reserve the U-Haul for you two?"

"You're freaking ridiculous." I was stalling for time. To tell or not to tell? That was the question.

"It was a love connection, huh? You two will have beautiful babies."

Jen entered with two platters of steaming food, which temporarily distracted Manz's onslaught. Filling plates and wineglasses bought me a few moments reprieve to make the decision.

"Spill your guts, asshole," Manz said to me.

I took my time cutting my chicken and asparagus before answering.

"We had a very nice day. I met her animals and her mom. Apricot looks great and healthy. We made some great progress with her new horse that has some trauma in her past. She cooked me lunch, which was really delicious. And we talked for hours. An all-around fantastic day."

Manz let out an exasperated sigh.

Jen jumped in before Manz could speak. "Are you going to see her tomorrow?"

"Yes, she asked me to come again," I replied.

"Oh my god, just tell us the good stuff!" Manz belted out.

"Jen, this chicken parmigiana is outstanding," I said.

Another frustrated sigh from Manz.

"The secret is the chili flakes on the sauce," Jen said, spearing a bite of chicken on her fork. "Gives it a little extra pop."

"Please tell me. Please?" Manz's voice sounded so pitiful, I had to resist laughing.

"And is that parmesan on the asparagus?" I asked.

"Yes, I like to crisp the parmesan a little while grilling it. Gives the cheese a nutty flavor that I love," Jen continued.

"You're driving *me* nutty with this bullshit!" Manz yelled.

I took a long, appreciative sip of my red wine. "The tomato sauce pairs so nicely with the wine too."

"Seriously? You're a fucking wine connoisseur now?" Manz barked, glaring at me.

"I like a dry red like this pinot noir because it cuts some of the heaviness of the dish."

Manz groaned audibly.

"A zinfandel might be good too," I added.

"Oh, definitely. There's some gorgeous zins produced in this area," Jen said, stealing a glance at Manz.

In her true dramatic fashion, Manz pushed her still-full plate away, folded her arms on the table, and put her forehead down on her arms in defeat.

Jen and I looked at one another and burst into laughter.

"Success!" I said as I reached across the table for a fist bump from Jen.

"I hate you both." Manz's muffled voice came from inside her folded arms.

Still laughing, I walked around the table and hugged Manz from behind.

"We kissed," I said, finally giving her relief.

"Yeah?" Her voice was still muffled under her arms.

"Yeah," I confirmed. "We kissed but nothing else. She's a fantastic kisser."

"Yeah?" Manz asked again, lifting her head from her arms.

"Like...mind-blowing," I said. I mimed an explosion from the top of my head. I gave her a quick kiss to the top of her head and released my hug.

"See?" she said, gently slapping Jen's arm. "I told you they'd have chemistry."

"Chemistry? More like nuclear reaction!" *Yup, I'm definitely blushing now.*

In the morning, I woke to another phone call from Sophia. Again, I sent her to voice mail. I knew I had to rip this Band-Aid off eventually, but I certainly didn't want to hear her voice. I opened a text to her and simply wrote, *Please stop calling.* The predictable reply came a few minutes later, long and probably filled with I love yous and Come homes. I deleted it.

"Come on, Bailey-Boy," I said, waking him with a few ear pulls. "Come help me feed the animals." I threw on a pair of jeans and a San Francisco Giants T-shirt.

The hens clucked excitedly as we approached. I opened the coop doors and they flooded out, happily fluffing their feathers in the morning sun. I tossed out handfuls of feed and grain to the hungry girls. Nearby, the goats began bleating in jealousy, impatient for their turn at breakfast.

Manz approached with two cups of steaming coffee as Bailey and I finished feeding the goats. I gratefully took one of the mugs and took a deep drink.

"Mmm, thanks," I said. "Just what I needed."

Never one for subtlety, Manz launched directly into her train of thought. "Have you heard from Sophia at all?"

"Only five to seven times a day so far," I replied petulantly.

"Seriously? What do you say to her? I hope it includes the words 'Fuck' and 'Off,' in that order."

"I haven't talked to her at all. I've sent all of her calls to voice mail. But she's been texting too. Like, a lot. I've deleted them. I replied for the first time this morning—just said, 'Please stop calling.' I doubt it'll work, though, because she immediately sent me a text afterward."

"Oh, man, the nerve of that woman," she said. She began speaking in an Italian mafia voice, straight out of *The Godfather*. "You know, uh...Me and da boys, we could take care of this, uh, this little problem for you. A pair of concrete boots and"—she dusted her palms off against each other—"badda-bing, badda-boom, no more problem. Remember, Sammy Boy, family is everything. And they's nuttin' I won't do for family, kiddo. Capisce?"

I put my arm around her shoulder, hugging her into my side.

"I love you, bastard," she said, leaning into my hug and wrapping her arm around my waist.

"I love you too, shithead."

"But seriously though." She leaned slightly away from my hug to look into my face. "You need to get laid. Like, now."

"You are absolutely relentless," I said, looking at her incredulously. "Is sex all you ever think about?"

"No," she said. "I also think about booze." She continued after a moment's thought, "And food."

"Food, booze, and sex," I mused.

"And not necessarily in that order," Manz said with a mischievous eyebrow raised.

"No wonder Jen asked you to marry her." I laughed.

"Like Mom says..." she began.

I joined her in unison, "Do what you love, and do it as often as you can."

After a quick breakfast and a shower, I began my walk to Alyssa's house. As I turned into her driveway at ten on the dot, I could see Marilee sitting in her rocker in her room, staring out the window at the driveway. I gave her a big smile and a wave. She didn't respond, but I felt confident she had seen me.

Like yesterday, Alyssa didn't wait for me to knock—she opened the door and met me at the bottom of the porch stairs. Before she could close the distance, I produced a small bouquet of three small sunflowers from Manz's garden from behind my back.

"Oh my gosh, these are beautiful!" she said, her eyes sparkling with delight.

"Oh," I said, trying to sound awkward. "Those aren't for you. They're…for your mom."

She looked momentarily shocked and crestfallen before she could recover. "Oh, right. Well, I'm sure she will love them."

"*These* are for you," I said, revealing a second bouquet from behind my back—a dozen enormous gerbera daisies in bright pink, orange, yellow, deep red, and white, also from Manz's garden. A gorgeous smile exploded across her face.

"Thank you," she said quietly as she threw her arms around my neck.

I eagerly pulled her close, burying my nose in the floral scent of her hair.

Quietly, so very quietly, she whispered, "Can I kiss you? As thank-you for the flowers?"

The shy nervousness in her voice nearly broke my heart. Without answering, I met her lips with mine. Tender and soft, building into deep and warm, the kiss sent my heart into overdrive. The moment her tongue touched mine, a jolt of white-hot electricity shot through my body. *Why is she so nervous? Can't she tell I want to kiss her too? And how can this woman have that effect on me so soon? We've only just met.*

Then, the Devil on the other shoulder told the Angel to shut the fuck up and enjoy the kiss. So I did.

CHAPTER NINETEEN

Alyssa

"I'm torn," Sam said in response to my question, "between wanting to visit your mom and wanting to visit Whisper Two." We hadn't moved from the base of the porch stairs, with my arms around her neck and hers around my waist. She bit her bottom lip.

I couldn't resist that lip bite...I leaned in and kissed her again. *She's intoxicating. I absolutely lose my mind when her lips are against mine.* Thankfully, she eagerly kissed me back. She did that thing—that thing that stopped my brain dead in its tracks—where she pulled my hips in tight against hers. Such delicious torture, to be so close—all that glorious pressure and body heat—but still separated by infuriating layers of clothing. I involuntarily moaned softly into her mouth as we continued to kiss.

Keeping this kiss as relatively chaste as I could, while my imagination was light-years ahead envisioning the passionate entanglement of our bodies, was a feat of Herculean proportions. I desperately wanted to take her hand, pull her upstairs—out of hearing range of Momma's room—and surrender myself to her hands, her hips, her lips, and her tortuously soft tongue.

I lightly bit her lip in frustration, and I put my forehead against hers, my eyes closed. My heart was pounding hard against my ribs, my breathing quick and shallow. Sam slid her hand up to cradle my neck.

"Alyssa," she said but didn't continue. I heard her swallow.

I planted a quick kiss on her lips and returned my forehead to hers, my eyes closed.

"Alyssa," she said again. "I could kiss you all day."

"Don't say that," I said. "God, you can't say that because I'm impossibly close to taking you up on it."

"Come on," she said, dropping her hand from my neck to take my hand. "Let's go say hi to your Momma."

The remains of Momma's oatmeal with brown sugar sat on the table by her chair. She sat unmoving as we entered, still staring out of the window.

"Good morning, ma'am," Sam said. She took Momma's hand in hers, covering the top with her other hand. "I hope it's okay with you that I came back today to work with Alyssa and the horses a bit more. We're making great progress, and it's so exciting. Maybe soon, you can come out and meet the new and improved Whisper Two. Would you like that?"

Momma nodded faintly. I covered my mouth with my fingers, suppressing the urge to cry.

"Me too. But you'll have to be patient for me, okay? Because Alyssa and I have a little work left to do with her before she's ready for visitors."

Momma nodded again, and the lump in my throat grew.

"Well, unless there's anything you'd like to talk to me about, I should probably get over to the horses." Sam paused. No words or movement from Momma.

"Excellent! We'll come give you a full update on our progress in a bit. Okay, Marilee?"

Another faint nod from Momma. I took her used breakfast items away, and we left her room.

"She wants to talk. I can feel it," Sam said as we walked toward the pasture. "She's built this fortress of grief around herself and, now that the mortar has dried and the stones are set in place, she's trapped inside." She held my hand and rubbed her chin speculatively with the other. Her voice became distant and quiet. "When life closes a door, open a window. That just might do it." She was clearly speaking her thoughts aloud and not directing them to me.

"Care to share this little epiphany with me?" I said, gently squeezing her hand.

She bit her lip, still thinking. "Not quite yet."

As we approached the pasture, Hickory began galloping and bucking around the enclosure, nickering and whinnying the whole way. Apricot and Whisper watched his excited outburst for a moment before Apricot resumed cropping the tender ends of the green grass. Whisper, however, refocused her attention on us, her ears alert and pointed in our direction.

"You have any oats or other favorite treats in the barn?" Sam asked.

"Yes, oats and a mini fridge with carrots and apples," I replied.

"Perfect. Let's grab some before we say hi. Let's pique their interest a bit."

Once inside the barn, Sam looked around curiously. "Man, this place is great. I want a barn like this someday."

"I just realized, as much time as we've spent out here, you've never actually been inside the barn."

"No, but I have fond memories of the outside of that wall right there." Sam smiled and pointed to the location of our first kiss against the barn, and my face flushed hard.

Her smile grew more mischievous. "You're adorable when you blush."

I cleared my throat. "The farthest stall is vacant. Second to last is Whisper's. This one," I said, pointing to the closest stall to us, "is Hick's, and the middle one is Apricot's. She's a crotchety old lady, but both Hickory and Whisper want to be next to her. She's definitely the alpha of their little herd."

"And what about the five stalls on this side?" she said, gesturing to the stalls on the opposite side of the barn.

"Vacant for now, but maybe someday w—" I stuttered a little before continuing, "Maybe someday, I'll get them filled again."

Oh my god, I almost said "we." What the fuck is wrong with you, Alyssa? You're acting like a schoolgirl with a first crush. Get your shit together!

Sam didn't seem to notice my near miss. "And is this the tack room?" she asked, pointing to the enclosed room next to Hickory's stall.

"Yes, come see. That's where the treats are."

Shelves lined the back wall with the basics: equine first aid, hoof cleaning tools, brushes, and other equine maintenance tools. Horizontal posts affixed to the wall held five saddles—four Western and one English—and hooks held bridles, halters, and leads. The other wall had a thin table along the wall with a mini fridge humming under it.

Near the English saddle and smallest Western saddle, the wall was adorned with colorful ribbons, belt buckles, and photographs. Immediately, Sam gravitated to them, paying special attention to the photos with their curled edges and faded colors.

"I'm sorry…but are those braces?" she asked teasingly.

"Didn't we all have braces at twelve years old?" I replied.

"No way. I was born this gorgeous!" she responded with a teasing smile. She returned to the photos. "Gosh, you were adorable. So little." Pointing to one of the older photos, she asked, "How old are you here?"

"Um, eight, I think." I peeked over my shoulder as I snapped carrots into pieces.

"You were competing when you were that young?"

"No, I was *winning* when I was that young." I smirked. "My favorites were Western saddle barrel racing in the gymkhana events and English show jumping. But I did them all."

"I see that," she said, looking at the wall filled with ribbons and belt buckles.

I began chopping an apple into slices. I was surprised to feel her arms slip around my waist, her thumb rubbing low on my belly.

"I'm going to cut myself with you distracting me like that," I said.

She began nibbling the ridge of my ear, sending shivers down my spine. "I didn't know you're such a talented and decorated horsewoman," she said quietly into my ear.

"I'm serious. Let me finish," I said, laughing. I tried to concentrate as her hands migrated over my stomach, my hips, my thighs, and teased at the button of my jeans. She ran her fingers along the fly of my jeans and back up. My hand-eye coordination was quickly becoming compromised as I made the final slice and set down the knife. I placed my palms on the table and tried to keep my knees from going weak.

Sam began kissing my shoulders, my neck, and my ears. Her breasts were pressed against my back, and her hips were tight against my ass. My eyes drifted shut as one hand slid under my shirt. Her strong hands were so soft against my skin, which tingled everywhere she touched. Her hand softly stroked my stomach, my abs, and the insanely sensitive skin on my sides.

Her other hand slid across the top of my jeans, one finger dipping just inside the waistline of the denim. The touch of her fingertip on that sensitive skin was maddening. She followed my waistline to my side. She slid her hand down over my denim-covered hip while her other hand still mercilessly touched the bare skin of my stomach. Her fingers found the ridge of underwear elastic that encircled my thigh and began tracing its path over my jeans down, down, down in the crease of my thigh to that hungry, throbbing place between my thighs.

But halfway there, her hand retreated back up to my hip, and I groaned in frustration. Her other hand continued its sensual exploration of my abs and ribs as her fingers began trekking down the crease of my thigh again. My head fell back against her shoulder with pleasure at her touch. Her hand went to the midway point and just past before reversing to my hipbone again. Delicious torture.

With her other hand still softly stroking my stomach, her fingers traced the crease of my thigh yet again. Each millimeter—each glorious millimeter—built my anticipation higher and higher. When she finally reached the apex of my thighs, my arousal was nearly unbearable.

Sam began tracing her nail against the denim seam between my legs, causing vibrations between my legs. I inhaled sharply at the sensation, and my jaw dropped open. My clit began to throb, aching terribly for her contact. She continued that slow teasing of the seam between my legs. Her other hand drifted up to cup one breast over my bra. My knees grew weak, and I had to hold her neck over my shoulder to support myself. She continued stroking between my legs, the vibrations of her nail on the denim bringing me closer to the brink. Her warm hand softly squeezed my breast, and my nipple pebbled small and tight at her touch. She lightly pinched my nipple through the satin of my bra, causing warm, slick arousal between my legs. It took conscious effort to keep my hips still. *I can't stand much more of this...*

"Sam," I moaned.

She didn't reply. She just continued stroking the denim between my legs while gently rolling my erect nipple between her thumb and forefinger.

"Sam, please," I said again.

She kissed my throat.

"I don't want the first time you make me come to be fully clothed in my tack room."

She kissed my neck again and slowly returned her hands to my hips. I leaned against her for a few more moments until I trusted my knees enough to move. I turned in her arms to face her, wrapping my arms around her neck.

"I ache for you," I said into her ear, my voice strained and foreign.

"We're going to get nothing done today at this rate," she said, her breathing elevated in my ear. She tucked one of my blond curls away from my face and gently stroked my cheek with her thumb.

"Tempting, though, isn't it?" I asked playfully.

"Incredibly."

CHAPTER TWENTY

Sam

Armed with carrot segments and apple slices, Alyssa and I walked out of the barn to the pasture gate. Hickory had, at last, worn himself out and stood watching us approach, with Apricot and Whisper.

We entered the pasture, and my heart dropped when Whisper took a step backward toward her stall. But, when her progress stopped and she retreated no farther, my hope began to bloom again.

Alyssa followed my lead as we took three or four slow steps into the pasture and stopped. Hickory quickly approached and began nuzzling our hands, smelling the treats and trying to locate them.

"Not yet, Hick," Alyssa said.

Apricot soon followed and, like Hickory, began nosing around to find the treats. Her calm, methodical approach quickly located the bag of carrots and apples Alyssa held.

"Let's give one to each," I said. "Give lots of praise and use their names."

Alyssa gave each a carrot segment, which they chomped loudly. "Good boy, Hickory. Very gentle. Thank you. Did you like that carrot, Apricot? Yeah? Delicious, huh, sweet girl?"

While Alyssa's attention was focused on Apricot and Hickory, I snuck a peek at Whisper. She stood in the same place, her eyes and ears trained on us.

"Feed them another carrot each. Keep your voice sweet but loud, okay?" I instructed.

Alyssa complied, and the horses happily ate their snacks. I took a carrot segment and set it on the ground about five feet behind Apricot. Whisper did not move, but her eyes watched everything I did. I returned to Alyssa's side and waited hopefully.

"Give them one more carrot segment each, and then let's be quiet and watch," I told Alyssa.

She continued talking to and petting the horses until both had finished eating their carrots. Then, as requested, she fell silent.

I was hoping my instincts were correct—that Whisper's fear of us would be overrun by her desire to outrank Hickory in the herd's hierarchy.

As expected, once Hickory realized no more pets or treats were coming, he began to move around Apricot to eat the carrot on the ground. And, as I hoped, Whisper saw his intention, moved forward, and picked up the carrot before Hickory could. Slowly, I took a carrot and placed it in Alyssa's hand. With a gentle pull, I signaled that she should offer it to Whisper.

Without my direction, Alyssa began talking to Whisper in a low, quiet, soothing voice. Alyssa took one step toward Whisper, her open palm extended with the carrot, and stopped. She's learning fast, I thought. *Let Whisper close the distance. Let her make the decision to approach. Come on, Whisper! You can do it.* I mentally willed Whisper's hooves to move.

Nothing. It was a staredown akin to the O.K. Corral, minus the tumbleweeds and gunslingers. Alyssa stood motionless, carrot extended, and Whisper stood motionless, watching Alyssa.

And who should come to the rescue? None other than that carrot-loving, gallant steed Hickory! Hick spotted the carrot, advanced one step closer to retrieve it, and Whisper again closed the distance to take the carrot from Alyssa's palm.

"Good girl, Whisper," she said, tentatively smoothing her forelock of mane. "That's a good girl. Want another one?" Alyssa palmed another carrot to Whisper's muzzle, who happily accepted. Hickory approached too, sniffing for a treat.

"Here's an apple for my Hicks. How about you, Apricot? Huh? Come get your favorite—apples! Come here, girl." Soon, all three horses were happily munching carrots and apples while I stood back watching, trying desperately not to cry.

Alyssa was absolutely buzzing with excitement when we exited the pasture.

"She came to me!" Alyssa jumped into my arms, and I spun us both in a hug.

"I'm so proud of you," I said. "You did it."

"Me?" she said, shocked. "I didn't do anything. I just did what you told me to. You are the genius behind this miracle, not me."

"No way," I retorted. "I showed you the starting line today, but the rest of it was all you."

"Let me repay you," she said. "The farmers' market is today. Let's go choose some great local ingredients, and I'll cook dinner for you."

"Yeah?" I asked. She nodded enthusiastically. "All right, that sounds great. Think your mom would want to join us?"

Alyssa shrugged. "Let's go ask," she said as she led me back to the ranch house.

We inferred from Marilee's lack of response that she'd prefer to stay in her rocker. We left a fresh glass of water and a sandwich for her and made our way to the farmers' market. I rode passenger in Alyssa's F-250 truck, holding hands on the center console. .

The booths were decorated with dried stalks of corn and leaves the colors of fall. A Lynyrd Skynyrd cover band was playing "Gimme Three Steps," and the entire market area had an autumn festival atmosphere. Somewhere nearby, I smelled the mouthwatering aroma of barbecue and heard the sound of kettle corn being stirred in a huge copper cauldron.

Alyssa did not reach for my hand in our first public outing together. I wasn't expecting her to. I understood her desire for privacy in a small town—after all, these were her people, not mine—but missed the warm comfort of her small hand in mine.

"Well, I don't believe it. Is that you, Alyssa?" A woman in her sixties approached, smiling ear to ear.

"Hello, Ms. Rhonda," she said warmly, kissing the woman lightly on the cheek. "This is Ms. Rhonda, one of my horse instructors as a kid, and this is my friend Sam."

Friend. Accurate, but also somehow insufficient.

"Pleasure to meet you, ma'am," I said, shaking her hand.

"Now, you both make sure to drop by the booth, okay? James will be upset if he missed seeing you."

After parting ways, Alyssa said quietly, "James will always be Mr. Westbrook to me, my high school biology teacher. He and Ms. Rhonda run one of the floral booths around here. You should see his gardens and greenhouses—they're breathtaking."

We wandered through the booths, sampling candied almonds and miniature spoons of wildflower honey. Alyssa bought a pair of lavender-colored chenille socks for her mom. I bought a sign for Jen and Manz—okay, mostly Manz—that read, "Kinda Country, Kinda Hood."

My competitive side flared when I saw the homemade salsa booth had free samples.

"You like spicy food?" I asked.

"The spicier, the better," she said.

I nodded toward the salsa booth, adorned with a range of salsas from mild to "We warned you" hot.

"Care to make a little wager?" I asked.

"What...who can handle the hottest salsa? You'll lose but I'm in."

"What's the wager?" I knew I could handle the heat.

"How much have you got to lose?" she asked with a cocky smile.

The salsa seller, a young Hispanic guy wearing an apron emblazoned with the words "The Salsa Man," overheard our conversation and said, "Ooh, I like the sound of this!" He began setting up two rows of little disposable plastic bowls with a basket of tortilla chips in the middle.

"Twenty bucks," I said, throwing out a starting bid.

"Aww, c'mon. Let's make this interesting. Up it to fifty bucks," the Salsa Man said.

"Okay, I'll do fifty dollars," I said.

"One hundred dollars!" Alyssa said loudly, pulling in a crowd of spectators. She extended her hand, which I shook enthusiastically.

"Now *that's* what I'm talking about," Salsa Man said. "Folks, we're in for a treat! These two lovely ladies are going to battle for the hottest salsa title, and the wager is one hundred dollars."

Still holding my handshake, Alyssa leaned in close and whispered confidentially, "A hundred bucks if you win. But if I win, you have to stay the night with me tonight."

I swallowed hard and felt my face go crimson. "Deal." I released her handshake, and our spectators cheered us on.

Salsa Man began pouring the first salsa. "Okay, folks, first up is one of our mild salsas, Mango Citrus Pepper Chutney."

We each took a bite.

"Sweet, a little sour, with a nice mild heat," the Salsa Man added. No problem for either of us.

"Next is one of our medium salsas—think Pico de Gallo but a little more heat. This one's called Tio Pepe's Salsa."

Again, no problem for either of us.

"Our third salsa is also a medium salsa—The Green Pig— charred tomatillos slow-simmered with shredded chile verde pork to give it that great roasted pork undertone."

"Easy-breezy and freaking delicious," I said, taking a second bite.

The Salsa Man was fully embodying the salesman role at that point. "Okay, folks, time to step into the hot zone!" He poured salsa into our little bowls, followed by some oohs from the crowd. "This is called Sangre de la Madre. It's made with chiles de arbol, tomatillos, and a heaping dose of garlic."

I took a bite. "Finally, something with some heat."

"Heat?" Alyssa looked around theatrically. "Where?"

"Well, let's give the lovely lady what she wants, huh?" The Salsa Man encouraged the growing crowd to clap us on. "Into the Extra Hot category we go!" He poured salsa into our bowls, and the spice and vinegar immediately hit my nose. "This one is our Hab You Seen My Tastebuds? It's mangoes, pineapple, and habaneros with the seeds, ribs, and pith included." The crowd reacted with wows and oohs.

Wow, that shit's hot. "Delicious," I said, bluffing as hard as I could. No readable reaction from Alyssa whatsoever.

"Folks, these ladies are brave to say the least. This next salsa—My Scotch Bonnet's on Fire—is too hot for me to eat. And I'm a born and raised authentic Mexican!"

I took a bite. *Jesus, Mary and Joseph. My brains are boiling.* I discreetly wiped sweat from my upper lip. The heat kept building and building. I ate a chip without salsa, hoping to flush the oils out of my mouth. For the record, it didn't work. I stole a peek at Alyssa—not even a single bead of sweat to be seen anywhere on her beautiful face.

"Folks, I can't believe they've made it this far! Let's give these gals a big round of applause." The crowd eagerly complied.

Wait...is it over? Did we tie?

"Only two salsas left to test," the Salsa Man continued.

Fuck.

"Here we have The Flaming Ghost," he said, pouring a serving into our bowls, "made with the infamous ghost pepper." My eyes burned from the fumes. I swallowed hard.

"You ready?" Alyssa asked. She lifted the little bowl and poured the entire contents onto a chip.

I nodded hesitantly, and she popped the chip with its heaping contents into her mouth. Not to be outdone, I did the same...and regretted my bravado immediately. My brow started running rivers of sweat that I didn't stand a chance of concealing. I sniffled as my nose began to run. I looked at Alyssa, who stood cool as a winter breeze.

"I don't believe this, folks! They've made it to the final round—the Carolina Reaper. The Reaper is up to two hundred times hotter than the jalapeño. One of the hottest peppers in the world, so hot that these ladies have to sign a waiver to taste... The Devil's Asshole," he said theatrically. He placed waivers and pens in front of us. Alyssa signed without hesitation. I signed... but definitely not eagerly.

The Salsa Man donned goggles and latex gloves to pour the salsa. *Are you serious? You need protective equipment, and I'm supposed to eat that? Whose brilliant idea was this?*

Alyssa made her chip selection and dipped it generously into the salsa. My mouth still burned painfully from the ghost pepper salsa, and this hellfire awaited its turn? *Oh hell no.*

"Bottoms up," she said, and with a quick chew and swallow, the Carolina Reaper salsa was gone. I studied her face—not even a flinch. Not even a flicker of pain or distress.

I picked a chip, dipped it into the salsa, and stood staring at it. My nose and eyes watered at the smell. I willed myself to take the bite but my arm simply refused. I set down the chip and, with downcast eyes, I extended my hand in defeat.

"Ladies and gentlemen, we have a winner!" the Salsa Man yelled to the crowd, who began clapping enthusiastically. Alyssa shook my outstretched hand, and I raised it over our heads in celebration of her victory.

"To the victor go the spoils—a free Salsa Man apron for...?" He leaned in to hear Alyssa's name. "For Alyssa!" The crowd cheered again. Some drifted away as others stepped up to make purchases. He handed the apron to Alyssa, and I put a five-dollar tip into his jar. Alyssa unfolded the apron to read the slogan: *The Salsa Man makes me hot!* with flames and chile pepper decorations.

"That was impressive," I said as we walked away.

"Did you throw that to me?" she asked.

"What?"

"Did you throw it to me," she said, her voice dropping to a whisper, "so you can stay the night with me?" Alyssa's voice was tinged with hope. "Because I fully intend to hold you to the bargain."

"I'll never tell," I said coyly. "But I do need a milkshake immediately."

Milkshake in hand and fiery tongue quenched, we continued wandering the farmers' market.

"You know what I just realized?" she asked. "We've bought nothing for dinner tonight so far."

"No, no, no," I said playfully. "That's not it at all. We're just fully surveying the options before we commit to a menu."

"Ah, yes, of course," she said, smiling. *Man, her smile is infectious.* Butterflies danced in my belly.

"Aww, fuck," she mumbled and dropped her chin.

The butterflies disappeared as I looked at her in concern.

"Please play along. I'll owe you," she said, sliding her small, soft hand into mine as she lifted her chin again. She squared her shoulders with a defiant air about her. I looked up to see a tall, rather handsome, athletically built man walking confidently toward us.

"I thought that was you," he said, smiling and placing a chaste yet overly familiar kiss on Alyssa's cheek. Discomfort radiated from her in waves.

"Hello, Tom," she replied, her tone devoid of all its usual warmth.

"Hi there," he said confidently as he extended his hand to me. "Thomas Kentfield, Tom for short. Nice to meet you." His teeth were impossibly straight and white. He looked like a hunky Hallmark movie beau and smelled like old family money.

I briefly released Alyssa's hand to shake his. "Samantha Monroe, Sam for short." I imitated him, intentionally leaving off the pleasantries. He noticed and the wattage of his smile dropped by a few volts. Alyssa quietly chuckled as he held my gaze just a little too long. He clearly wasn't used to being challenged.

"Alyssa, I want you to meet Cecile, my girlfriend. Ceece, come here." It was a command, not a request. What a douche, I thought.

A bottle-dyed blonde approached. It took me a moment to figure out who she reminded me of before it hit me—a cheap, knock-off version of Alyssa's natural beauty and grace. The one that got away, I thought, looking at Alyssa. Cecile hung herself on Tom's arm and stared up at him adoringly.

"Ceece, this is Alyssa…the one I told you about." His smile became tainted like the sinister sneer of the villain wolf in fairy tales.

"Tom, this is Sam…my girlfriend."

I didn't react, not externally at least. *Girlfriend?* Fireworks exploded in my brain. *Please play along. I'll owe you*, she had said. This mattered to her. All of this mattered. *So let's turn up the volume.*

Tom's smile finally fell as he looked between Alyssa and me, and back again.

"Baby," I cooed, my voice velvety and sweet. "You said yes, remember? I'm your fiancée now, not girlfriend." I pulled her left hand—notably missing an engagement ring—behind my back and kissed her passionately on the mouth. She kissed me right back, her free hand caressing my cheek. Tom's face darkened further while Ceece stood staring, a clueless and confused smile still on her face.

Alyssa withdrew from the kiss, her body still pressed against mine, and touched the tip of her nose to mine. "I love you, baby."

I kissed her again. "I love you too." It was acting, I knew, but my stomach backflipped anyway.

"Well," Tom said a little too loudly. "It seems you're happy. I'm glad to see it." His tone of his voice did not convey the sentiment of his words.

Still looking solely at me, Alyssa said, "Likewise."

"We should get together and have dinner!" Ceece said brightly, utterly clueless to the intense emotions boiling beneath the surface tension.

"Shut up, Cecile," Tom said quietly.

"Aww, please, Tom? Can we?" She sounded like a child begging for a treat. "We haven't been out to dinner in ages. It'd be fun."

"I said." Tom's voice was now a growl. "Shut up. We won't be having dinner with *them* any time soon."

"Have a great day," Alyssa said brightly, waving cheerfully.

"You too," Ceece said equally cheerfully but completely oblivious to Alyssa's thick layer of sarcasm. Tom took her hand and roughly pulled her away.

Once their backs had melted into the crowds of the farmers' market, Alyssa threw herself into my arms. She wrapped her arms around my ribs and buried her face against my chest. Shorter than me, her petite frame fit so perfectly into the contours of my body. I hugged her neck and gratefully smelled the floral scent of her hair.

"Thank you," she said, her voice muffled against my chest. "Thank you, thank you, thank you."

"That guy's an asshole."

"You have no idea." She groaned.

Inferring he was an ex, I asked, "What did you ever see in that prick?"

"Chalk it up to the idiocy of youth." She snuggled deeper into my hug.

"There you are!" Ms. Rhonda approached quickly, and Alyssa untangled herself from our hug. Ms. Rhonda gently took Alyssa's forearm. "He won't say as much, but James is just dying to say hi to you."

We followed Ms. Rhonda to a booth a few spots down. The pop-up tent and table overflowed with bouquets of colorful flowers. The aromas wafting from the booth were intense and intoxicating. A few lazy honeybees bobbed and landed on the flowers, happily ignoring the passersby.

"Good afternoon, Mr. Westbrook," Alyssa said. Her voice became small and shy, with an almost childlike quality to it. It gave me a small glimpse of this powerful, determined woman in her younger, tender years.

"Good afternoon to you, Alyssa. How's my star pupil these days?" His voice was deep with a warm, fatherly tone.

I shot an eyebrow at Alyssa. "Star pupil, huh?"

"Oh yes, Alyssa was an extremely bright student. Not just in my class either. Honor Roll and everything," Mr. Westbrook bragged.

Alyssa blushed and hurried to change the topic. "Mr. Westbrook, this is my friend Sam. Sam, this is Mr. Westbrook, my biology teacher."

Demoted to friend again.

"Her advanced placement biology teacher, she means. And her AP chemistry teacher and her AP physics teacher," he continued, shaking my hand.

"Wow," I said. "Horse ribbons and academic scholar."

Alyssa was squirming uncomfortably. "Your flowers are beautiful, as always, Mr. Westbrook."

"Aww, thank you," he said, looking around the booth. "And please, call me James. I'm not your teacher anymore. How's your momma doing?"

"Um, about the same. Healthy but disconnected," Alyssa said but didn't elaborate further.

"Well, it's no wonder. Your dad sure did love her."

"Yes, sir, he did," she said. Her mood became somber.

"I'm sorry, kiddo. I didn't mean to pull a rain cloud over you." He came around the table and gave her a tight, one-armed dad hug. "You kids should come on out to the farm and pick some flowers for your momma. And you let us know if you ever need something. Rhonda and I are just a call away."

"Thank you, Mr. Westbrook," she said shyly, still quiet and childlike in her demeanor.

"It's James," he said again.

"Thank you, sir, but I don't think I can."

After getting a quick lunch of chicken teriyaki skewers and corn on the cob from a food vendor, we found a picnic bench in the shade to eat. Nearby, the band played a decent rendition of "Sweet Home Alabama" while a warm breeze rustled the dry leaves overhead. We discussed dinner menu options and settled on chicken and steak fajitas.

"With *mild* salsa for me," I said. "Maybe medium, tops."

"Too much heat for you for one day?" she asked, sliding her hand up my thigh under the picnic table. My heart did a stutter-step and sent electrified tingles southward.

"Definitely hot, that's for sure," I said, looking at her and letting innuendo drip from my voice.

She leaned in conspiratorially and whispered, "I'd have gone three more rounds to claim my prize." Her hand inched a little farther up my thigh.

"And I should have thrown it two rounds sooner," I said, sending her a playful wink.

We returned to the Salsa Man and bought a jar of the Green Pig salsa for our fajitas. From other booths, we collected some fresh tortillas, Mexican cotija cheese, and bright, crisp bell peppers and onions, and began our walk back to Alyssa's truck.

Once seated in the truck, she immediately reached for my hand. My heart leapt—I'd missed that simple contact with her while navigating the farmers' market. She drove out of the parking lot and proceeded about a mile before she pulled into an empty and secluded bank parking lot.

Confused, I asked, "What are we doing here?"

She unbuckled her seat belt and leaned over the center console with a twinkle in her eyes. "It's been *hours* since I've kissed you."

"We kissed in front of Tom, remember?" I teased.

"Mm-hmm. I remember," she said, sliding that mischievous hand up my thigh again. "But I want to kiss you without a homophobe watching."

"Well, I should warn you..."

"Yes?" She leaned closer to my lips.

"I should warn you," I repeated, hovering my lips millimeters from hers, "that I had the Devil's Asshole on these lips today, and kissing me might be really, really hot."

"I beg to differ." When I looked at her quizzically, she continued, "I had the Devil's Asshole on *my* lips today. You surrendered. So, technically..." Alyssa lightly bit my lip. "Kissing *me* will be really, really hot."

My heart was racing, and the arousal was building quickly. Her touch was pure electricity, jolting directly to that greedy place between my legs. I was not accustomed to someone having this level of power over me. I was usually the pursuer, and this incredibly sexy woman was pursuing me. It was new and exciting.

"You're definitely a Carolina Reaper then," I said. "Scorching hot and just might kill me if I can't kiss you soon."

She licked my upper lip with the warm tip of her tongue, and the time for talking was done. I met her tongue with mine, and those now familiar tingles flooded my body. The kiss started shallow, tongues and lips exploring teasingly. But soon, my fingers were entwined in the hair at the back of her head, and she moaned softly into my mouth. It might have been five minutes or five hours—I had no idea. I lost myself entirely in the sensual enjoyment of her mouth against mine.

With a final frustrated bite to my lip, she pulled away to drive again. She looked into my eyes, her passion and lust clearly on display there.

"You're lucky there's a center console in the way," she said devilishly.

CHAPTER TWENTY-ONE

Alyssa

Back at the ranch house, I excused myself to check on Momma. I looked in her room, then stood in confusion and replayed the morning in my mind. Yes, before we left, Sam and I had left a glass of water and a PB and J with chips on Momma's table for her. I was sure we had. Positive, in fact.

So, where was the plate? And why did her water glass have iced tea in it? Obviously, I knew Momma moved around when I left the house—she used the restroom, changed her clothes, got into and out of bed. But this? This was very different. She had never gotten food or drink before.

"Hey, Momma," I said, sitting at the foot of her bed.

No response—she sat completely still, staring at the driveway.

"You got some iced tea, huh? That's excellent. Can I get anything else for you?"

No response.

"Okay, if you change your mind, you let me know, okay? Dinner will be ready soon. Love you." A quick kiss on the temple, and I left for the kitchen.

To my surprise again, I found Sam slicing vegetables at the counter, completely at home in my kitchen, with a clean dishtowel draped over her shoulder.

"Excuse me, but I'm supposed to be cooking you dinner, not the other way around." I planted a quick kiss on her lips.

Sam chuckled at me but continued slicing onions into strips. In a skillet behind her, seasoned flank steak and chicken breasts sizzled. The aromas immediately made my mouth water.

I glanced at the drying rack and noticed Momma's lunch plate clean and dry.

"Did you wash this?" I asked Sam, pointing to the plate.

Sam briefly paused her task to look over her shoulder. "No, why?" She pushed onion scraps into the trash.

"Huh," I said, thinking it through. "Momma must have." I turned my attention back to the plate. "She's never done that before."

"Really?" Sam wiped her hands on the dishtowel slung over her shoulder.

I shook my head. "She poured herself a glass of iced tea too."

Sam's eyebrows rose. "That's promising."

"Hope so."

"I have a strange request," I said to Sam as we filled three plates with rice, beans, and fajitas. "Not particularly romantic, I know, but would it be okay if we ate dinner in Momma's room?"

"Great idea," she said, picking up two plates.

In her room, I set a plate with cutlery on Momma's lap. I sat next to Sam at the foot of Momma's bed. Instead of handing me one plate, she handed both to me.

"Hold this for a sec," she said. "I want to try something."

Holding her dinner plate, I watched as Sam opened the window in front of Momma. Her earlier commentary to herself returned to my mind: *When life closes a door, open a window. That just might do it.* The warm fall breeze filled the room, lightly fluttering the curtains that flanked the window. The loamy smell of damp earth and rotting leaves from the planter below the window drifted into the room. I could also smell the sweet, dry grasses and pungent tang of the oaks. I could smell the smoke of a neighbor's burn pile and the manure of the cows and horses on the farms surrounding us. It smelled like autumn. It smelled like home.

I watched in shock as Momma's eyes lulled shut and her head drifted back against the headrest of the rocker. And, amazingly, she smiled.

The events that followed are blurred and delightfully messy in my mind—a watercolor memory left behind to spread and blend in a spring rain. I barely felt Sam's thumb as she wiped the tear, which trailed down my cheek. Come to think of it, I hadn't felt the tear at all. I don't recall kneeling at Momma's feet, my face in her lap, or moving her dinner plate out of the way. I don't remember bunching the fabric of her flowing skirt in my fists or the moment that the racking sobs began.

I do, however, with crystal clarity, remember crying out, with a voice foreign and strained, that I missed him too, and I couldn't stand to lose them both. I remember begging her to come back to me. I remember screaming she was selfish for withdrawing from me and becoming subdued as I acknowledged that I, too, was selfish for being unable to embrace her grief in the way she needed to experience it. I told her of my fear that she would, quite literally, die of a broken heart and leave me behind to mourn them both. I remember telling her of my overflowing love for her and my heartfelt wish for her to find her path out of this darkness.

All of this, I watched from a distance, a spectator outside of myself, watching like a captivated moviegoer before the big screen. I remember being confused that somehow time had both slowed and sped up simultaneously. I remember the steaming tears of rage and grief that soaked her lap and the hoarse dryness of my throat as I cried months of unshed tears. The walls, the bed, Sam, that dreaded rocker—all of it disappeared into nothingness, leaving only Momma and me, fighting our way to the surface of this tragedy together.

And, like the snap of a finger, the room whipped back into reality as a hand—a frail, soft, motherly hand—smoothed my hair. Words whispered, on a voice dry and cracked from months of disuse: "I love you, baby."

Miraculously, the months of burden, fear, and anxiety I had been carrying lifted away. My mother's voice, a sound I had feared I'd never hear again, was real and alive. It was there in the room with me, physically tangible in its gravity and purpose as a manifestation of her survival, her triumph over grief.

"I love you, Momma," I said, my voice still strained with emotion. "I've missed you so much." A fresh wave of tears began to flow as she continued petting my head resting in her lap.

"I'm sorry. I'm so sorry, baby," she said, her voice finally breaking with the weight of tears withheld.

I lifted my head and moved to hug her, her frame so thin from months of stillness, a mere shell of the bold and vivacious woman she had been. And yet, her return hug was fierce and strong, conjuring memories of comfort after scraped knees and lost toys. I poured every drop of energy I had into that hug, trying to fill her empty reserves with everything I had left to give. Yet somehow, this impossibly fragile woman still managed to strengthen me instead.

With Momma resting peacefully at last, Sam and I left her room and returned to the kitchen. Once there, I fully intended to clean the dinner dishes and package leftovers, but suddenly the weight of it all made my knees weak. I stood at the kitchen counter, bracing myself there, and allowed my chin to drop to my chest.

"Come here," Sam's gentle voice said behind me.

I turned and wrapped my arms around her waist, resting my temple over her heart as I had after seeing Tom at the farmers' market. She wrapped her strong arms around my shoulders and kissed my forehead. And my tears began to flow again.

"I am so incredibly proud of you," she murmured into my hair.

"Me?" I said incredulously, my tears staining her shirt.

"Yes, you." I could hear the smile in her voice. "Running this place by yourself, taking care of your Momma, rehabilitating heartbroken Apricot, rescuing Whisper from the slaughterhouse—"

"From the auction house, you mean," I interrupted.

"Same thing, and you know it," she said. "My point is you've been carrying all of this alone for so long. Too long." She kissed my hair again. "And I respect the hell out of you for it."

I dried my eyes, trying not to smear mascara everywhere. "You're the strong one. I'm here crying like a baby because my mommy said, 'I love you.' You probably think I'm nuts and can't wait to get away from this madhouse," I said, jokingly.

"Hardly," she said, tucking my hair away from my eyes.

"Okay then, be vulnerable," I challenged.

She scoffed at me.

"I'm serious," I said. "I need to see this tender little underbelly." I poked her stomach. *Holy shit, her abs are rock hard!* "When's the last time you ugly cried? Like, really let the faucets run?"

"Two days ago," Sam replied without hesitation.

"What?" I leaned away to look into her face. I did some quick mental calendaring. "The day I came for dinner? The day we met?"

"Mm-hmm," she said simply.

I took her hand and pulled her to the couch. "I need to hear this. Sit. I'll be right back."

I quickly uncorked a bottle of cabernet and brought it with two wineglasses to the couch. I filled the glasses and handed her one. I sat beside her, allowing my thigh to rest full length against hers.

"Make me feel better about my ugly cry and tell me about yours," I said.

"I'm gonna need this," Sam said, taking a deep drink from her glass. "Where to start?" Another sip. "I came to stay with Jen and Manz for this week after I caught my girlfriend cheating on me."

I nearly spit my wine across the room. "Girlfriend?" I sputtered. Her tone was so monotone and matter-of-fact, but the contents of her words were earth-shattering.

She nodded. "Fiancée, actually." She looked down into her wineglass, slowly spinning the stem between her fingers. Mad? Sad? Guilty? Her expression was hard to read.

"Oh god, I had no idea," I said.

"Of course you didn't. Why would you?"

"I'm sorry I kissed you," I said quietly. "I mean, I'm *not* sorry I kissed you...but I'm sorry I kissed you while you're engaged." I was shamelessly fishing for their current relationship status, couched in an apology, but I didn't care—I needed to know. "I hope you believe me I wouldn't have interfered in your relationship if I'd known."

"First of all, I kissed you, not the other way around," she said with a mischievous smirk. "Second, we are not currently, nor will we ever be ever, ever again, in a relationship. That ship has sailed." She took another sip. "No, that ship has sunk. Hacked apart with an ax, burnt to a crisp, and sunk to the bottom of the Pacific."

I sat for a moment, processing the revelation and trying not to smile at Sam's single status that had so nearly slipped between my fingers. "What's her name?" I asked at last.

"Sophia."

"How long were you together?"

"Just past five years."

"Ouch. Long time."

"Yeah, it was a shock to say the least."

"So...you caught her? I'm scared to ask..." I said, adding wine to her glass.

"Oh yes, I caught her, all right. I caught her getting hot and heavy with a man in our bed."

I gasped. Yes, I literally gasped. "A man? She was bi?"

"Not that I knew of."

"Shit," I said. "That's awful."

"Yes. Hence the ugly crying."

"Understandable," I said. "I'm so sorry. That must have been terrible." After a moment's thought, I added, "On second thought, I should send her a thank-you card." I took a sly sip from my wine, eyebrow raised.

Sam chuckled, and I was relieved she wasn't upset with my joke.

"I mean," I continued, feeling brave. "If you think about it, she did us both a favor."

"Yeah, how's that?"

"If she hadn't been a complete fucking idiot by cheating on you, you wouldn't have come to stay with Jen and Manz…"

"Mm-hmm?"

"…and you wouldn't be single right now," I continued.

"Yeah?" she said again.

"…and I wouldn't be allowed to do this," I said, sliding my hand up her thigh.

"I see."

"…and I certainly wouldn't be able to do this." I slid my hand under her shirt. Her abs tensed at my touch.

"Mm-hmm."

"…and I definitely couldn't do this." I threw my leg over hers, straddling her lap.

Sam placed her hands on my hips and swallowed hard. "Anything else?"

"I can think of a few other things."

"Yeah? Like what?"

"Well, this, for one thing." I leaned down to kiss her throat. "And this," I whispered, kissing her cheek.

Her grip on my hips tightened.

"And this," I said as I licked her top lip and rocked my hips forward.

Sam's lips parted with the touch of my tongue, and her breath quickened.

"Or this." I rocked my hips back, arching my back and pressing my breasts against hers.

Sam said nothing, her hands warm on my hips.

"Or maybe…" I rocked my hips forward again. "This." *Jesus, that feels good.* I was supposed to be torturing her, not myself.

Sam's eyes widened at the increased contact and pressure. She pulled my hips in tight against hers and looked deep into my eyes. I cupped her face with both hands and slowly moved my mouth to hers.

"I definitely couldn't do this," I murmured as I softly kissed her delicious lips. My eyes involuntarily lulled shut. She kissed me back, matching the tender, sweet pace I'd set. It was torture, this slow, exploratory kissing.

Sam's hands moved from my hips to my ass and, in a flash, my dream flooded back. Those hands, those strong, confident hands carrying me to my bed in my dream made my desire for her overflow. I touched my tongue to her top lip again, aching for more. But when her tongue touched mine, I couldn't keep it sweet and innocent anymore. I wanted hot and passionate, and I wanted it now.

I kissed her deep and stroked her tongue with mine. Arousal flooded my system, making my skin tingle and my nipples harden. I rocked my hips forward again—an involuntary but not unwelcome movement—which caused Sam to moan into my mouth.

Unexpectedly, Sam grabbed the back of my thighs and stood, lifting me into the air, with her lips still locked on mine. *Fuck, she's strong.* Without saying anything, she carried me to the staircase. I expected her to set me down to climb the stairs myself, but she didn't. With no perceived effort, she continued carrying me up the staircase.

At the top of the stairs, I gestured to my left to my bedroom door. Somehow, she knew without looking or breaking our kiss. Inside my master bedroom, she closed the door and pressed my back against it, my legs still wrapped around her waist. She pressed her hips into mine for the first time, and I heard her groan softly in satisfaction.

I began removing my shirt, briefly breaking our kiss to pull it over my head. Sam followed my lead, and I helped to remove her shirt. The sight of the swell of her breasts peeking from the top of her sports bra was too much to resist. I released the grip of my legs and lowered my feet to the floor.

I had to see them. I needed to see more of her, all of her, everything. I bit her lower lip and sucked gently as I reached to remove her bra. I fumbled for a moment but, when the elastic released from under her breasts, the anticipation became almost too much to bear. Before I could strip it away, Sam reached behind me and, with only one practiced hand, she quickly unclasped my bra.

I released my hold on her lip and raised my eyebrows at her. "Show-off."

She chuckled. "The skills of a misspent youth."

Before kissing her again, I pulled her bra away and let it slide down her arms. I had no idea where it went or if it ever landed—my eyes were glued to her amazing breasts. Fuller and larger than I expected, I couldn't resist bending to kiss each as I took them one by one in my hands.

So feminine, so innately female, and utterly intoxicating, my mind reeled and my heart raged. This was all new territory, new experiences. Of course, I'd seen breasts of other women in movies or the gym locker room. But like this, attached to an incredible woman who wanted me—*me*—and I wanted intensely in return, was entirely new. How had it taken me all these years to find myself here for the first time?

"You're gorgeous," I murmured, momentarily stunned. I stood staring, taking in all of her beauty—her strong, toned shoulders, her muscular arms, her surprisingly voluptuous breasts, and dear god, those abs. Pretty sure I could grate cheese with those abs. "You've been hiding this under those clothes all this time? If I'd known, I would have kissed you the night we met."

"You should talk. You're absolutely stunning." In my worship of Sam, I hadn't noticed that my own bra had fallen away. Sam's lips were parted, and her look was pure hunger. She bent and buried her face in my breasts, inhaling my skin and kissing my breastbone. I cradled the back of her head as she gently held my breasts to her face and kissed them affectionately.

"Fucking stunning," she said as she stood again to kiss me. I threw my arms around her neck, kissing her intensely as her breasts and stomach pressed against mine. I felt my nipples harden again at the sensation, sending a similar tightening sensation between my legs.

"Absolutely fucking stunning," she said again as she walked me backward to the bed.

The backs of my thighs hit the mattress. I expected us both to collapse backward onto the bed, as we had in my dream. But instead, she dropped to her knees before me. She looked up at me as she slid her hand up my flat belly to my breast. She cupped it gently as she began to kiss along the waistline of my jeans. Reminiscent of her teasing me there in the barn, my heart rate increased. My nipple pebbled at her touch as she rolled it lightly between thumb and forefinger. She kissed my belly as she unbuttoned my jeans. She lowered my zipper slowly, kissing each newly revealed inch of skin. I ran my fingers through her short hair, trying to keep my knees from buckling. When my zipper hit its base, she folded down the corners to reveal the black satin waistline of my thong.

"Oh, Alyssa," she whispered but didn't continue.

I hooked my thumbs into the back of my jeans and began slowly lowering them down over my hips. Sam's eyes grew huge as she watched with her lips parted. I concentrated on her incredibly green eyes as I continued slowly lowering my jeans inch by inch over my ass.

Still on her knees before me, Sam slid her hands around my hips to my ass. Her hands were warm but dry and sent electricity zinging through my nerves. I lowered my jeans to my thighs, and Sam lowered them the rest of the way, helping me liberate one foot at a time from the denim. I stood before her, naked except for my thong. The lust and hunger in her light green eyes as she devoured every inch she could see lent me confidence.

"Alyssa, you're so beautiful."

"Thank you," I murmured as I looked down into her eyes and ran my fingers through her hair.

She hooked one finger into the waistline of my thong and pulled down slightly. She kissed the skin exposed there just above my shaved hairline, and my eyes lulled shut. She pulled it down a little farther and kissed again. My neck went weak and my head drifted back as my breathing became labored. One more pull, one more kiss, and I nearly lost control.

I couldn't wait. I pulled the thong down over my hip as I cradled the back of her head, with her mouth on my stomach. My thong slipped down, down, down until it came free and dropped to my feet.

CHAPTER TWENTY-TWO

Sam

I admit—I'd made love to my fair share of women: beautiful women, fit women, confident women, sexy women. But this? This absolutely fucking gorgeous woman, standing naked before me and looking at me like I was a feast and she was starving, was a wholly new experience. Half of me wanted to pounce like a tiger and ravish every incredible inch of her like a greedy carnivore, while the other half wanted to slowly melt her on my tongue like a piece of decadent chocolate, savoring every moment and sensation. The latter had to prevail, but it would take all of my willpower to keep the tiger at bay.

I knelt before her, cradling the impossibly soft skin of her ass in my hands as I surveyed the delicious landscape of her body before me. Above, her breasts were firm and high with her nipples impossibly tight. Her stomach was flat and soft, with a small belly-button ring in her navel. Below, she was shaved except a nicely trimmed blond landing strip down the middle, drawing my eyes to the split between her legs. I leaned forward and kissed the manicured hair, letting my tongue devilishly explore. I kissed a little lower, still well above the area that was beckoning me home. Alyssa's hand tangled in my hair, held lightly in her fist. I kissed her mound again, this time my tongue barely reaching the beginning of that tender spot I sought. Alyssa moaned and her fist, full of my hair, tightened. Without withdrawing my lips, I reached my hand up over her belly and gently pushed her backward onto the bed. She complied and lay down, throwing her arms up above her head in a posture of utter surrender and trust.

It was too delicious to resist. I had to kiss all of this new horizontal skin before continuing. I kissed the crease of her thigh—that same crease I'd played with so mercilessly earlier in the day. I kissed and nibbled her hipbone, causing her to squirm. I kissed my way up her ribs to her breasts. I took one small, hard nipple into my mouth, sucking lightly and stroking with my tongue as my hand gently held the other. I slid my denim-clad thigh between her legs, pressing it in just the right place. Her eyes were closed, and she moaned, high and frustrated. Good. I wanted her frustration.

I kissed northward again, over her collarbone, her throat, her jaw, to her lips. She dove into the kiss, hungry and passionate. She ran her hands down my bare back until she hit the waistline of my jeans and froze.

"Oh no," she said, withdrawing from our kiss. "Oh no, no, no, this is unacceptable. These have to go. Now." It was not a request.

I knelt on the bed, straddling one thigh as she lay on the bed watching me. Her face was framed in those gorgeous golden curls, and her bright blue eyes sparkled with lust. I unbuttoned my button-fly jeans with three slow pulls. Her eyes strayed over my body from eyes to knees. I lay over top of her, holding myself up in a one-armed push-up position as I negotiated the removal of my pants.

"No, no, no, these too," she said, snapping the elastic waistband of my boy shorts. I removed them also, still holding myself aloft, as she ran her hands over my arms and shoulders appreciatively.

"These are…" She bit her lip. "Nice."

I lowered myself slowly, savoring each new millimeter of my naked skin touching hers. I pressed my thigh between her legs as I kissed her lips and felt the vibration of her moan on my tongue. I rocked my hips to press harder, and Alyssa eagerly spread her thighs to allow it. While I caressed her breast, thumbing her nipple into a firm peak, I continued to rock my hips, rubbing my thigh between her legs and enjoying the warmth and wetness of her arousal there. I savored the sweet taste of her mouth as I continued kissing her, continued grinding my thigh against her sex, continued touching her erect nipple with my thumb. Soon, her breathing changed, became deeper and husky with lust. I slid my hand away from her breast, across her stomach to that deliciously cropped landing strip.

Alyssa's breathing hitched, and her back arched slightly. I took the invitation to slide my fingers farther. She was warm, wet, and inviting. She squirmed slightly as I teased with gentle touches, random caresses of her clit and the opening to her depths. I ached to taste her, but I wouldn't allow myself that pleasure yet. There was still more torturing to be done.

I kissed her mouth, bit her lips, and kissed her throat and the sensitive ridge of her ear, all the while touching and caressing between her legs. I kept it random, enough to stimulate and torture but no repetition to build toward climax. Not yet. Not quite yet.

I moved so that I was fully between her legs, touching and sliding through the slick heat below and kissing and nibbling above. I kissed my way down her neck to her breasts while I slid two fingers slowly, slowly, so slowly into her. Her gasp of pleasure told me what I needed to hear. And her slippery arousal told me I'd tortured this poor woman long enough.

I stroked my fingers inside of her slowly, deeply, with conscious rhythm as I kissed my way down to that landing strip again. I dipped the tip of my tongue into that delicious split, and her fingers entangled themselves into my hair. She gently pulled my face closer, deeper, not letting me retreat as I stroked her pulsing clit with my tongue.

"Fuck, you taste so good," I said.

"Sam, please...don't stop." Her voice was high and strained as her hips moved in time with my stroking fingers.

Her clit was swollen against my tongue as I began drawing slow ovals around it, stroking up and down its hardened length with the tip of my tongue. I listened carefully to the sound of her breathing, the motion of her hips, the ferocity of her fingers in my hair to guide me. As her breaths became pants, I moved my tongue and fingers a little faster. And as her pants became gasps, I moved a little harder, a little deeper.

"Oh fuck, Sam, don't stop. Please don't stop." She gasped, her voice strained with passion. I moved my fingers and tongue in unison, driving her ecstasy higher.

Her free hand gripped the fitted sheet tight in her fist. She whimpered under my continued stroking, sliding in and out of her wet heat. Her breasts heaved as her breathing became ragged. *Shit, I might orgasm too, just watching this.* I had to focus to keep my pressure and rhythm steady.

I reached my free hand up to gently tweak her nipple as I slowly began stroking her throbbing clit faster with my tongue. Faster...faster...a little more pressure...and I felt the first clench of her impending orgasm around my sliding fingers. I pushed deeper, giving reciprocal pressure on her clit. She clenched again, and her abs tightened. Her knuckles went white on the fitted sheet, and she started grinding her hips against my tongue, her fist of my hair holding me in place. *Don't worry, beautiful, I'm not going anywhere.*

"Oh fuck, oh fuck, Sam, I'm going to—"

Her abs tightened hard, lifting her head from her pillow as wave after wave of orgasm seized around my fingers. I rode the waves with her, enjoying each pulse of pleasure, savoring the sweet taste of her orgasm on my tongue.

Her abs released at last, and her head fell back on the pillow. I slowed the pace, but not the pressure, riding the slick of her orgasm, shallow and teasing again. I licked her clit slowly, and patiently waited for her body to reset. As I continued playing and teasing, realization seemed to dawn on her that I was guiding her toward another orgasm.

"Oh my god, what are you doing to me?" She began to pant again. *Oh yes, I knew there was more than one hiding in there.*

CHAPTER TWENTY-THREE

Alyssa

Holy fucking shit, is this woman trying to kill me? My limbs were limp and heavy, my head was swimming, and my heart beat like it might erupt out of my chest. And yet, she was still going, driving, pushing, steering my body toward ecstasy again. Was that even possible? I'd always been a one-and-done kind of gal. But my body—specifically, my clit—didn't get that message and was obediently following where she was leading.

Sam was torturing my already highly sensitized body with this slow, sensual teasing. And unbelievably, that feeling—yes, *that* feeling—was beginning to grow again low in my belly. It was building and quickly gaining momentum. It made my toes curl.

"Sam." I grabbed her hair again, holding it like a life preserver, fearing I'd be lost forever if I let go. My chest felt tight, like there was no longer enough air. I could feel a warm sheen of sweat beading on my forehead and across my breasts.

I looked down to see this gorgeous woman—this incredibly sexy woman—with her face buried between my legs. Instantly, the spark low in my belly blazed into an inferno of desire.

Sam must have sensed the change because her slow, teasing touch became focused and intense. I could feel every ridge of her fingers, every swirl of her tongue, as she guided me closer to the brink. My back arched and my breasts lifted toward the ceiling. I took my nipple in my fingers and twisted hard, aching to ground myself in this moment as my mind was floating away. The electric tingle began dropping lower and lower, a direct line from my nipple to my clit.

"Oh my god, baby," I whispered. *Baby? Did I just say baby? Oh, fuck it, who cares?* "Yes, please. I'm going to come again. Oh god, Sam, please don't stop!"

At the last moment, she took my clit into her mouth and sucked hard, stroking her tongue along its length, a delicious blend of pleasure and almost painful fervor. I moaned audibly— or maybe it was a scream—as my ab muscles seized hard. For the second time tonight, the intensity lifted my head from the pillow involuntarily as I cradled her head between my thighs. My grip on the sheet and her hair tightened as wave after wave of orgasm flooded my body. I drove my clit deeper into her mouth, and she met me eagerly, continuing the spasms around her thrusting fingers. Electricity coursed through me, and every square inch of my skin tingled.

Finally, my abs released, and I collapsed back onto the pillow. My throat was hoarse. *Was I screaming?* A sweet, gentle tear trailed down my cheek to my ear. My breathing was still shallow and quick as Sam climbed up my body to rest beside me. She tenderly kissed my cheek as I lay languid and stuporous. I was wholly at her mercy; my muscles had disappeared entirely, and I lacked any form of coherent thought.

Sam leisurely ran her hand over my hips, my belly, my breasts, my throat—a silent and sensual worship as my mind slowly returned to my body from the unknown. I managed to roll my head toward her, reaching for her lips to kiss. Her mouth tasted of my arousal, like the double orgasm she'd just delivered to me with her talented tongue. It was sensual and sexy, knowing my pleasure was tangible there on her gorgeous lips.

"What the fuck did you just do to me?" My voice sounded thick and slurred, drunk on endorphins.

Sam smiled a cocky half-smile.

"I've never..." My voice trailed off. How did I intend to finish this sentence? My muddled brain wasn't functioning yet. *I've never orgasmed twice before*, or *I've never had sex with a woman before*. Both were true, but I honestly didn't know which I'd intended to say.

Sam swept my hair away from my eyes and tenderly kissed me. "Never what, Alyssa?"

The sweet roll of my name off that talented tongue almost brought another tear to my eye.

"I've never orgasmed twice before," I slurred, opting for the easy response. "And I've certainly never orgasmed like *that* before."

Sam propped herself up on her elbow and looked down into my eyes. "Really?"

I silently shook my head, looking into her green eyes.

"Wow." She seemed honestly surprised. "I'm so sorry for that. There is nothing sexier in this world than making a beautiful woman orgasm." She ran her hand tenderly over my stomach and breasts, causing my skin to sizzle with residual electricity. "To see you experience that level of pleasure, and to know I could be so trusted and so blessed to be chosen to give you that pleasure? Well," she said, running her fingers over my hipbone. "I guess I'm greedy."

"Greedy?" I scoffed. "How in the world would that make you greedy?" My powers of speech were slowly returning.

"I'm greedy," she said, pausing to kiss my collarbone. "Because I don't want you to stop at just one."

"Marry me," I said suddenly, causing her to chuckle. "Marry me tomorrow."

"Now you're really a lesbian stereotype," she said, still chuckling.

That word: lesbian. It stopped me in my tracks. Was I? Did that shoe fit? This was certainly the best sex of my life—so intense I doubted I could walk yet, in fact. I certainly had never considered myself a lesbian before now, but I wasn't one for labels and boxes either. I'd love who I loved, and be attracted to whomever caught my eye. It just happened to be that I was infinitely more attracted Sam than to any of the men I'd ever dated. More than anyone I'd ever met, male or female, for that matter.

"Did I say something wrong?" she asked quietly, using her thumb to smooth the furrows in my brow that must have gathered there.

"No, it's just..." My voice trailed off again.

"What, baby?" *Baby. I liked the sound of it from her lips.*

"It's just...I don't know."

Sam didn't say anything. She just lay next to me, her beautiful, naked body pressed against mine.

I took a deep breath. "That's not true. I do know."

I suddenly became incredibly shy. I rolled toward her and curled into her arms to hide my face. She wrapped her arm around me, and I rested my forehead against her chest. *Maybe I can just hide here forever.*

"Don't hide from me," she said softly, reading my mind and tucking my hair away from my face again. "You can tell me anything, sweetheart." *Sweetheart. Jeez, this woman is quickly winning my heart.*

I took a deep breath and dove in, my voice muffled against her chest. "I want that—what you said—to give you that pleasure too. But I..." I swallowed hard, my throat suddenly dry. "But I...I don't know how."

"Don't know how? What do you mean?" Her voice was still quiet and patient.

"I've never..." I tried to swallow again. "I've kissed a few women, and even had a decent make-out session or two, but I've never..." My throat went dry again and the words disappeared.

"You've never made love with a woman?" she finished for me.

I nodded my head, still hiding my face in her chest like a coward. "And you are so, so, *so* good at that. I don't want to disappoint you."

I was confused by the shaking of her body for a moment until I realized she was laughing.

"Are you laughing at me?" I asked, playfully indignant.

"Sweetheart, you could never disappoint me."

That word again. I emerged slightly from my hiding place under her chin.

"I'm serious. I almost orgasmed with you just now, and you weren't even touching me."

I scoffed incredulously but said nothing.

"Listen, okay?" She tilted my chin up the rest of the way to look in my eyes. "There're only three rules, got it?"

I nodded.

"First rule: No faked orgasms."

My eyes got huge. I couldn't imagine needing to fake it after what she just did to me.

"I'm serious. Neither of us learn anything that way. I want to please you and faking anything gets us nowhere. Agreed?"

"Agreed."

"Which leads us to the second rule: Tell me what you want. What you need. You won't hurt my feelings. My entire goal is to give you pleasure. So if you need harder, faster, deeper, slower, or something else entirely, I want to know. You want to try something different? I'm game. Your pleasure is my pleasure. Agreed?"

"Agreed."

"And Rule Three—and this one is one you already learned the hard way, it seems. We're not done until we're both fully satisfied. If that's two orgasms or ten, I'm all in to make that happen."

"I didn't even know more than one was even possible before tonight," I said, the shock still clear in my voice. "I thought it was just something they said in Hollywood or porn."

"Oh yes, it's possible. It's very, very possible. Oh, and one last bonus rule that should go without saying: We won't do anything you're not ready to do. No pressure. No rush."

I nodded again.

"So do you agree to these terms?"

"Yes. I agree." I took a deep breath and exhaled slowly. It felt good to tell her. It had felt like a secret I was carrying, and now that it was disclosed, my heart felt lighter.

Sam lay on her back, one arm around me and the other under her head. I lay snuggled against her, resting my head on her shoulder. Her full breasts were displayed before me, begging me to touch.

"So…" I said, testing my arm muscles to playfully stroke her breast. "About these rules…I think it's only fair to give them a trial run." I raised an eyebrow at her. "You know, just to be sure I fully understand them."

"Mm-hmm," she said, nodding sternly.

"I'm particularly interested in Rule Two," I said. "Specifically as it pertains to you."

"How so?"

"Well," I said, trailing my fingertip around her nipple and watching it pucker and harden. "I am just wondering what you like. I mean," I said, reaching to tease her other nipple into a hardened peak as well. "Rule Three says we're not done until we're *both* done…and you're not done yet."

"True," she said simply.

Feeling empowered, I went for the direct approach. "What do you like?"

Sam looked at the ceiling and raised her eyebrows. "What would you like to try?" she asked, artfully dodging my question.

"What you just did to me was pretty fucking fantastic. That's definitely an option on the menu."

She smirked but said nothing.

"Would you mind if I just…?" I let the question hang as I moved to straddle her hips.

Sam's eyes got huge as she put her hands on my thighs, her thumb sneaking into the crease of my thigh.

"Nuh-uh," I said, peeling her thumb away and placing it back on my hip. "It's my turn now."

Sam smirked again but complied.

I slowly rocked my hips, grinding her pubic bone against my still vibrating clit. My intention was to arouse her by straddling her and figure out how I'd make love to her in a minute. But her closely groomed triangle of dark hair was sending a delightfully arousing sensation through my body. It felt so good, I didn't want to stop. I bent over her, placing my palms by her ears, and continued grinding against her. Just a little longer, I told myself. She began lifting her hips slightly, just enough to add depth and pressure to my already aroused clit. Her eyes became intense, glinting with desire. Her grip tightened, following the movement of my rocking hips. I let my eyes lull shut as I savored the sensations—her warm hands on my skin, her body rocking in time with mine, my hardened nipples tracing the skin of her breasts, and the curtain of my hair forming a halo around her head.

Shit, I'm supposed to be pleasuring her, not myself. But it felt so good, so incredible, that I didn't want to stop. I'd have never guessed a third orgasm could be lurking within me, and yet there it was, standing up and demanding to be noticed.

"I'm supposed to be pleasuring you," I said, my voice husky and panting. "Not the other way around."

"Alyssa…" she said, her voice equally strained with passion. "You *are* pleasuring me."

Fuck it, I thought. *I'll take care of her needs in a minute. I'm too close now.*

My breathing became ragged, and sweat broke out across my shoulders. Sam began breathing through her mouth as my movements became more focused and deliberate. That tingling tension began low in my belly, and I knew my climax was coming.

"Fuck," I said, the word not much more than a breath.

"What do you need?" she asked, her voice barely a whisper.

I couldn't answer—I simply grabbed her hand from my hip and placed it on my breast. I sat vertical again, grinding my clit hard against her now, holding her hand against my breast as she pinched my nipple.

"Come for me, Alyssa."

I moved faster, my head swimming, my nerves firing electrical sparks in every direction.

"Yes, baby. I want to feel you come."

Her words threw me over the edge as my orgasm crashed in, grinding myself hard against her pubic bone. Each movement, each pulse, each wave of ecstasy rocked my body. My mind went blank as sounds I had never made before emitted from my throat. I dug my nails into her shoulder as my body clenched and spasmed. Sam moaned along with me, carried along by the magnitude of my ecstasy. I felt the slick wet heat of my orgasm between my legs, feeling both embarrassed and impressed at the incredible effects this woman was having on my body and mind.

I gently eased myself down to lie against her chest, my hips still straddling hers. I tried to slow my breath, bringing my blood pressure down from the fantastic heights I'd just reached. Like before, she stroked my bare back with her hands.

"You are so beautiful, Alyssa," she murmured in my ear. "I could worship you like this forever."

Forever. My heart skipped.

I breathed deeply as I kissed her neck and collarbone. Although my mind was still off wandering the galaxy somewhere, my body was hungry for more. I groggily kissed the valley between her breasts, the hot swell of one, then the other. I kissed her nipple and marveled as it hardened again against my tongue.

"Relax a minute," she said, trying to slow my pace. "We're not in a rush. Recover for a minute."

But I didn't want to recover. I didn't want to rest. I had to have the taste of her on my tongue immediately. I couldn't wait. I had to have her writhing in pleasure at my touch while I was still reeling from the pleasure of hers. I needed to share this high with her before it ebbed away.

I kissed and stroked her nipple with my tongue as I slid my hand down between her legs. She let out a small, deep moan as I tentatively played with the outside of her sex. I touched and explored. I teased and tried to find my courage to go further.

I took a deep breath and pressed lightly, plunging at last into the warm, slippery heat of her arousal. She didn't stop me or resist—in fact, if the expression on her face was any indication, she was enjoying it. Like, a lot. So far, so good.

Now, let's be clear. I've touched myself, both alone and with some of my male partners. I am obviously familiar with the female anatomy and its, um…reactions to sensual stimuli— the whole "home court advantage" thing. But let me tell you, feeling that same arousal on another woman, knowing I *caused* that arousal, was utterly mind-blowing. Insanely intimate. Deliciously sensual. Fantastically satisfying. And, in some strange way, it activated my predatory instincts. Somewhere before me, lying dormant in this insanely sexy woman's body, was an orgasm, and it was my sole mission to find and capture it. Mission accepted.

I began to suck her nipple, firmly pressing it between my tongue and the roof of my mouth, as I slid my finger deeper and deeper into her. Her soft moan turned into groans of pleasure as I began sliding in and out, in and out. Still working her nipple with my tongue, I slid out of her and up, touching her clit with fingers wet with her arousal for the first time. I watched with satisfaction as her mouth opened with a gasp of pleasure.

I played with her clit, swirling my slick fingers around and around. I could feel her tension rising, her muscles tightening, and her breathing spinning out of control. I kissed my way up to her throat, her jaw, and finally her sensual lips. Our kisses were deep and passionate as I rubbed rhythmic laps around her clit like she had done to me. I stroked her tongue with mine, mimicking the pace and pattern of my fingers between her legs. I pressed my fingers harder and slowed my pace, eliciting a sharp cry of pleasure from her into our kiss.

"I'm sorry, Sam…I can't wait anymore. I have to taste you." I pulled away from our kiss and ran the warm tip of my tongue down her neck, over her full breast and nipple, and over the tense ridges of her ab muscles. I moved my body down, and she seductively spread her knees for me. I kissed her thighs as I continued stroking her clit with slick fingers. I kissed closer and closer. That first touch of my tongue to her clit, that first warm, inviting, sensual taste of her, and suddenly, the final missing puzzle piece of my sexuality clicked into place. Every question was answered, every doubt was erased, and every fear was subdued.

This is heaven, I thought as I enveloped her clit with my lips and sank my fingers deep inside of her. The musky scent and the sweet taste of her on my tongue was, quite possibly, the sexiest thing I'd ever experienced. I couldn't resist my own moan of pure ecstasy as I felt her rapid heartbeat from inside. My tongue, lips, and fingers worked in unison as I found a pace that seemed to be driving her insane. She tossed her head on the pillow, her short, dark hair shielding her eyes. One palm lay flat against her stomach, the other flung over her head, holding the headboard of my bed.

Why the fuck did it take me so many years to get here? Why in the world haven't I tried this sooner? Nothing I had ever experienced before could even compare to this divine thrill of pleasing and being pleased by another woman. It was exquisite.

I tried to keep my rhythm slow and teasing, but my own excitement took over as I watched her writhe in pleasure. My speed and pressure increased as instinct took over, reading the cues of her body to know what she needed. I felt the first clench of her sex around my fingers and the corresponding increase in warm, slick arousal. It was delicious and erotic. It was sweet and absolutely addictive. I knew exactly what it meant, and I wanted all of it.

Her body clenched again, and I knew I couldn't hold off any longer—the wait was torturing me. Still sliding in and out of her, still mercilessly stroking her hardened clit with my tongue, I slid my free hand around her thigh and pulled her hips closer. It deepened my kiss on her clit and the thrust of my fingers inside her. I felt her body climb to the edge, awaiting the final push from me into the oblivion of ecstasy. I sucked her clit, stroking slow and firm, as I withdrew my fingers from within her. I played with her entrance, letting her truly feel each and every penetration of my fingers. I continued pushing and withdrawing, pushing and withdrawing. With one final, hard press of my tongue against her clit, her body tensed and her voice hit a new octave. Her back arched impossibly, pressing her clit even harder against my mouth and plunging my fingers deep inside of her. Pulse after pulse after pulse, her orgasm continued, eliciting guttural moans from Sam's throat. I didn't ever want it to end. I rode the waves with her, trying desperately to concentrate as my own arousal threatened to overwhelm me.

As the clenching around my fingers began to slow, I slowed my pace to match. I withdrew my fingers and licked her as deep as I could. Her answering groan let me know she'd noticed the difference. Surprisingly, her hips began to move against my tongue, which was buried as deep inside of her as I could reach. I slid two fingers up to play with her clit as I continued searching her opening with my tongue.

The rocking of her hips gained tempo, and I increased my pace to match. Those incredible abs constricted as she lifted her head from the pillow to watch me through eyes half closed. She cradled the back of my head, pulling gently, and I licked even deeper within her. I began stroking her clit with my fingers more intensely, building her climax to the breaking point.

"Alyssa, don't stop. It feels so good."

I dug the nails of my free hand into the skin of her ass, pulling myself as deep as I could. I stroked my fingers furiously against her clit, trying desperately to keep my rhythm consistent.

"Oh, fuck, it's coming. Don't stop. Please, don't stop!"

I did as she instructed.

"Yes. Yes. Right there. I'm going to come." Suddenly, with another back-breaking arch, she groaned with animalistic intensity and ground her hips against my mouth in time with my fingers. I kept the pace even though my forearm muscle burned, until her hips slowed, her back relaxed, and she collapsed into a sweaty mess of limbs on the pillow.

I could feel my own wet arousal coating the tops of my thighs as I rested my temple against her relaxed leg. I stared adoringly at her glistening and swollen sex, the ridiculous ridges of her toned abs, the full swell of her breasts heaving as she breathed, and her gorgeous face, tossed to one side and utterly spent. I kissed her thigh affectionately but she didn't stir. She lay completely inanimate and vulnerable before me. In that moment, she was the most beautiful thing I'd ever seen.

I could fall in love with her, I thought. I marveled at how my life had changed in the last few days. I had been a habitually single, country recluse with two busted horses, a ranch I could barely manage, and a nonverbal, grieving mother. Now I had a healthy herd, a mother on the road to recovery, and an insatiable lust for the woman in my bed.

I crawled up to nestle myself against her, and she stirred enough to drape her arm around me. Her eyes stayed closed as she tenderly kissed my forehead.

"I can't move. You broke me," she mumbled, her voice a low, sleepy rumble.

I chuckled quietly. Okay, maybe a little cocky smile snuck in there too.

"Alyssa, you're a liar."

I scoffed indignantly and tickled her ribs.

"Hey! Watch it." She laughed, pushing my hand away.

"I am *not* a liar. What did I lie about?"

"There is no way in the world that was your first time with a woman. I don't believe you for a hot second."

"Well," I said saucily. "What can I say? I'm a fast learner, I guess." *Okay, I've now gone from a "little" cocky to flat-out arrogant.* "Besides," I continued. "I had a pretty fucking awesome teacher." I planted a kiss on her still sleepy lips and nestled my head into her shoulder again.

CHAPTER TWENTY-FOUR

Sam

I woke in a dark and unfamiliar room, completely confused where I was. As my tired eyes cleared, I recognized Alyssa's bedroom. The beautiful curves of her naked body glowed in the moonlight from the window. I lay on my back with her head resting on my stomach, her arm possessively holding me around my waist. I carefully tucked her wayward blond curls away from her face. Her face was serene and angelic with flawless skin and incredibly long eyelashes. *How have I never noticed her eyelashes before?*

The memories of our evening together flashed back through my mind—the sweet scent of her hair, the silky softness of her skin, the delicious, feminine curves of her hips, her tight ass, her small, perky breasts, and her equally small waist. Memories of the sounds she made sent tingles of arousal low in my belly.

When she had said she'd never made love to a woman before, I was honestly surprised. She seemed so confident and assertive with her advances toward me that I had simply assumed there had been others before me. I mean, she seduced *me*, which was definitely a fun role reversal from my usual plotline. At the time, I'd simply figured this wasn't her first rodeo. And then, her kisses, her touches, her expert handling of my needs... *My god, how could this possibly be her first time?* It was like she had tapped into my mind, read my desires and wants, and executed them perfectly. She was a prodigy who had picked up my violin body for the first time and made it sing like a virtuoso.

The other thing I couldn't understand: Why was she single? Smart, funny, kind, sexy as hell with dangerously seductive curves that need warning signs, successful, beautiful, an animal lover... The list went on and on. *Why hasn't some hot, single horsewoman scooped her up yet?* I could hear Manz's voice in my head: "Hey dumbass, *you* are the hot, single horsewoman destined to sweep her off her feet." Probably followed by a slap upside my head. I mean, this is Manz we're talking about here.

Manz. Oh my god. I never told Jen and her that I wouldn't be coming back to their house tonight. My absence would be the only confirmation Manz needed to know we had "bumped uglies," as she so eloquently put it. Oops. I laughed silently and had to stop myself—it was making Alyssa's sleeping head bounce on my stomach—which, of course, made me laugh even harder. Holding back my giggles made it even worse, and soon, Alyssa's head was bobbing uncontrollably.

"What the..." Alyssa's groggy voice came from my belly.

"I'm sorry," I said, my voice high and strained with the effort of desperately trying to stop my laughter. "I'm so sorry. Go back to sleep, beautiful."

She lifted her head to look at me, her expression confused. "Are you laughing?" She moved up to rest her head on my shoulder. "What could you be laughing at..." She lifted her head to check her clock radio. "...at 3:29 a.m.?"

I wiped a tear from the corner of my eye. "It's nothing, I swear. It's so stupid. I just started laughing and couldn't stop, and your head started bouncing, which of course made me laugh even harder. It's dumb." I took a deep breath, trying to stave off my giggle attack. "I really didn't mean to wake you."

She snuggled against me. "Mexican food was a risky dinner choice for a sleepover. I figured I farted in my sleep or something."

With that, I completely fucking lost it. All the suppressed laughter came erupting out of me, tears streaming from my eyes and my already sore abs screaming in pain. Alyssa laughed with me, pulled into my contagious ridiculousness. I couldn't breathe. My laughter no longer had meaningful sound, just that crazy wheezing noise that occurs when laughter takes over.

Once I could finally breathe again and the tears had stopped flowing from my eyes, I kissed the top of Alyssa's head.

"You just might be my dream girl," I said.

"So…" she said, her voice beginning to drift off to sleep again, "Does that make me your girlfriend?"

I thought for a moment and couldn't come up with a single reason why not. "I guess it does."

"Mmm," she said, snuggling deeper into my embrace.

CHAPTER TWENTY-FIVE

Alyssa

I woke to my bedroom flooded with midmorning light. I turned to my clock radio—9:12 a.m. *Oh. My. God. How the fuck did I sleep so late?* I turned to wake Sam, but she was gone.

My mind replayed scenes from last night: the moment Sam had spread her knees for me, the exquisite arch of her back, grinding myself to orgasm on her, those deliciously full breasts in my hands and mouth, and being able to make her orgasm, not once, but twice. I blushed as I remembered our final conversation before I fell asleep. *Did I really ask to be her girlfriend? And had she really said yes? And where the hell is she now?*

Through the closed bathroom door, I could hear the shower running. Perfect. I slipped out of bed, still completely naked, and quietly opened the bathroom door. A quick peek behind the curtain revealed that her back was to me, and she was rinsing her hair and face. I snuck into the shower unnoticed and snaked my arms around her bare waist. I pressed my naked breasts against her warm, muscular back.

"Marilee! You can't be in here. Your daughter will catch us," she said. She immediately started laughing and turned in my arms to face me.

"Ugh! You are such a bastard!" I laughed, tickling her sides, still slick with soap.

"Hey, quit it," she said, wiggling in my arms, trying to escape my tickles.

I stopped tickling her and settled my body against hers. Slippery, hot, wet, and completely naked. My entire mood underwent a polar shift as my libido woke again. I slid my hands down to cup her naked ass in my hands and pulled her hips toward mine.

Sam's eyes got huge. "You're insatiable."

"And you're incredibly sexy," I replied.

I turned her around again and pulled her ass to my stomach. She complied and braced her hands on the shower wall.

"Remember Rule Two?" I said, rubbing my hands across the slick, soft skin of her lower stomach, upper thighs, and groin.

"Uh-huh."

"The part where you said you're game to try anything?" I slid my hand up to hold her breast while my other hand began rubbing lightly between her legs. *They've got to be D cups. Too big for Cs.*

"Mm-hmm," she said, spreading her feet a little. *God, that's so fucking hot.*

"Well," I continued. "A few years ago, I dreamt about this." I slipped my fingers along her opening. She was already slick with arousal for me.

"And I never saw what she looked like because she was behind me the whole time..." I began teasing her with two fingers, pushing and withdrawing without penetrating her depths. Her chin dropped to her chest as she continued bracing her palms against the shower wall, the hot water streaming down her toned back.

"But she started doing this," I said as I toyed with her entrance, sliding forward to stroke her clit, back to her entrance, and forward again, repeating my pattern.

"Yes." Sam's voice was breathy.

"And she started doing this," I said as I continued a little faster and a little harder. I sank my teeth into the muscle of her shoulder.

Sam didn't speak—she groaned.

"And as I started to orgasm," I said, stroking her clit exclusively in long, consistent movements.

"Oh fuck, yes," she said, getting close to climax.

"She asked me a question," I said, still stroking, my own arousal rising with hers.

"It's coming," she whispered. "Please keep going."

"She asked me..." I said, then cruelly withdrew my hand entirely. "How did you know when I moved in the horse pasture without turning your head?"

She froze. "What?" Her voice was strained with passion and frustration. "What are you talking about?"

I slid my hand up her stomach and spun her nipple between my thumb and forefinger with each word. "How. Did. You. Know?"

"Oh, come on, Alyssa, I'm so fucking close," she said, whimpering in agony.

"Answer the question first," I said, biting her shoulder again.

"Like this," she said without moving, her palms still on the shower wall and her chin still on her chest.

I was confused—just like in the pasture, she hadn't moved. "Like how?"

"I looked under my armpit at your feet...at the horses' hooves," she said quickly. "Now please...I'm begging you... finish what you started?"

I slid my fingers down her stomach and between her legs again, smiling with triumph.

"Yes, ma'am."

"I can't believe I slept that long," I said, pulling jeans up over a clean thong. "I never sleep in like that. I've gotta get out and feed the animals and make Momma some breakfast too. Wanna come?"

"Already done," she said.

I looked at her in confusion as I pulled my shirt on. "Already done? What do you mean?"

"Well, almost all done. Momma's got her oatmeal and coffee out on the porch. And the horses are fed and watered. I didn't know how to feed the pigs or the bees, but the chickens are done too."

I stood frozen in shock. She called her "Momma"? And made her breakfast? Wait, Momma's out of her room and on the porch drinking coffee? She fed the horses and chickens? My heart warmed at her thoughtfulness and help.

"When did you have time to do all of that?"

"Hours ago." She shrugged. "I'm an early riser." She stood in jeans and a sports bra with her hands on her hips. Drops from the shower still clung to her shoulders and ab muscles. "And you looked like you could use the sleep." She tucked my hair behind my ear. "You looked completely worn out, in fact." She gave me a devilish wink.

"I…" I sat hard on the bed and didn't know how to finish the sentence.

"You…need coffee? Coming right up." She put yesterday's shirt on and kissed my cheek. She left the room, tousling her wet hair in her fingers.

When she returned a few minutes later, a mug in each hand, I still hadn't moved.

"Lots of milk, no sugar, right?" she asked, handing one of the mugs to me.

I stared at it incomprehensibly. "You know how I take my coffee?"

"Mm-hmm," she said, taking a long sip from her mug. "I pay attention."

"You know how I take my coffee," I repeated. "I can't believe you know how I take my coffee."

She sat next to me on the bed. "Yes, I do."

"Sam?" I said, my voice small and nervous.

"Yes?" She looked at me with concern.

"Can I ask you something?" I stared at the mug in my hand in my lap, picking idly at my cuticles.

"Anything," she said, then paused. "Wait…this isn't like the question in the shower, is it?"

I chuckled quietly. "No, I promise."

"Okay, then what's your question?"

"Sam…did you mean what you said last night?"

She reached over and placed her hand over mine, preventing me from abusing my cuticles any more.

I continued, "Did you mean it when you said…about me being your girlfriend?"

Sam looked out the window at a blue jay perched in the oak outside and took a sip from her mug. "Yes, I meant it. I want you to be my girlfriend."

My heart swelled and butterflies danced in my stomach.

"Really?" I asked, my voice very small.

"Yes." She paused for another sip of coffee. "I mean, as much as it pains me to let Manz be right, we do make a great match. And you're quote 'fucking gorgeous,' unquote."

I scoffed. "She said that?"

"More than once. Obnoxious little turd that she is."

"So…" I continued with my train of thought. "I'm new to this, so forgive me, but…" My voice trailed off again. *Why am I so fucking nervous? Spit it out, nitwit.*

Sam looked at me in concern. "What's on your mind, gorgeous? You can ask me anything."

The soft sincerity in her eyes bolstered my courage. "I'm new at this women-loving-women stuff, and I don't know the rules or whatever…"

"We already went over the rules last night, remember?" she said with a cocky smirk.

I blushed slightly. "Maybe 'rules' is the wrong word. More like…vocabulary, I guess."

She nodded for me to continue.

"Does 'girlfriend' mean 'monogamous'?" I couldn't look at her. *God, please don't say no. It'll crush me.* I just stared at the back of her hand still covering mine.

"Do you *want* 'girlfriend' to mean 'monogamous'?" she asked.   .

Yes, I want you all to myself. Yes, I think I might be falling in love with you. Yes, I know this is all super fast, but I can't help how I feel. Yes, I don't want your ex, Sophia, to swoop back in and steal you from me. Yes, because I don't ever want you to leave. Yes, because absolutely all of this feels so fucking right.

Of course, I said none of that. I just sat there, still staring at our clasped hands, willing myself to speak.

"Hey," she said sweetly. When I didn't look up, she turned my chin gently toward her face to look into my eyes. Those eyes. Those sparkling green eyes I could lose my soul in forever.

"Hey, talk to me," she repeated. "Do you want us to be monogamous?"

I nodded shyly.

She didn't reply. Instead, she brought her lips to mine and softly—so heartbreakingly softly—pressed her lips to mine. I kissed her back, entwining my lips with hers. Her warm hand caressed the back of my neck. I love kissing you, Samantha Monroe, I thought.

She withdrew from the kiss and rested her forehead against mine. With her eyes closed, she whispered, "Me too."

CHAPTER TWENTY-SIX

Sam

"So, what's Jen cooking us for dinner?" I asked into my cell phone, trying to sound as nonchalant as possible.

"Us?" Manz asked, her tone thick with innuendo.

"Yup. I'm bringing Alyssa home for dinner." It was the first time we'd spoken since I failed to let her know I wouldn't be coming home last night. I tried not to sound like a teenager caught making out on the porch after curfew.

"Gosh, well, I'll have to see if we're free," she said, feigning disinterest. "We have a very busy social calendar these days."

"Sure, sure, sure," I said, not believing a word she said. "C'mon, you can spend the whole night plying us with booze and trying to elicit scandalous details from us…" I let my voice trail off teasingly.

After a moment's silence, Manz yelled loudly into the phone, "Jennifer! You're cooking tonight. Maybe that pork loin I love. We have guests coming. Sam and her wife-to-be are bringing dessert!" Returning to her normal speaking voice, she said, "Be here at six, and don't be late, you good-for-nothing hussy." Without saying goodbye, Manz hung up.

"Oh my god, she is such a brat," I said, staring at the darkened screen of my phone. I turned to look at Alyssa. She was leaning toward the mirror, applying lip gloss to her parted lips. *How the fuck am I supposed to form coherent thoughts while she's doing that?*

"You're sure you want to do this?" I asked. "Manz is a force to be reckoned with…and you're fresh meat."

"I think I can handle it," she said, finishing her lip gloss and doing that sexy thing where girls rub their lips together afterward. *As if I needed any more of my attention drawn to her sumptuous mouth.* She double-checked herself in the mirror and turned to face me.

"Besides, if we stay here…" She closed the distance, placed her hand on my breastbone, and tipped her face up to mine. "I'll just spend the whole night ravishing you like a wild animal, and I'm sure you wouldn't want that."

My heart skipped. "I'm calling to cancel right now." I unlocked my phone, but she covered it with her hand.

Laughing, she said, "No, we have to go. We can't be sexual hermits, and I need to share you with Manz. You need to stay there tonight." She stifled my protest with a finger to my lips. "Have some quality time with your friends, gossip with Manz about your overwhelming feelings for me, and return to me in the morning. I mean, you did come here to see *them*, not me."

"It's not my fault Manz introduced me to better company," I said, sliding my hands to the nape of her neck. "Better, sexier company." I kissed her lips. She tasted like strawberry. She returned my kiss and lightly stroked my tongue with hers. My knees went a little weak. *Is kissing her always this fantastic?*

"You stole my lip gloss," she said into our kiss. "Now I have to do it all over again."

"Darn it," I said, smiling.

It turned out Alyssa's mom was a massive daytime TV fan. Or maybe it was just the months without it that made it so alluring. Either way, she was perfectly happy to sit with the remote and a glass of iced tea to laugh at sitcom reruns while Alyssa and I contemplated tonight's dessert.

I clapped my hands together and rubbed my palms. "Okay, let's see. Dessert…Whatcha got?" I asked.

"What have I got? I figured we would head to the store on the way and buy something to bring." She opened the cabinet door, staring blankly. "I don't bake."

"Well, not so fast," I said, looking over her shoulder into the cabinet. "I assume you have honey?"

She nodded. "We've always got plenty of that."

"Okay," I said, rubbing my chin while I thought. "What fruits are ripe in your orchard right now?"

"Apples and pears are in season for sure," she said. "I think there's walnuts ready too."

"Hmm. I can definitely work with that. Do you have the basics for a crust—flour, shortening, butter, stuff like that?"

"We should. Momma baked a lot for Daddy. He had a vicious sweet tooth. Her baking gene must have skipped a generation, so I'll have to be your sous chef."

I tossed a clean hand towel over my shoulder and got to work.

The afternoon sunshine glinted off Alyssa's golden hair, and I marveled at how beautiful she was when she smiled. I tried to think of ridiculous things to say, enjoying the soft melody of her laugh. We walked slowly, hand in hand, back to the house, laden with freshly picked apples, pears, lemons, walnuts, and eggs.

I pulled the crust dough I'd made earlier from the fridge and removed the plastic wrap. I set Alyssa to work rolling it out while I peeled, cored, and sliced apples and pears. I simmered them slowly in red wine, honey, cinnamon, cloves, and nutmeg. Soon, the house smelled warm with spices and mulled autumn fruit.

Working together hip to hip, Alyssa and I spiraled the fruit vertically in the crust, resembling the petals of a rose. We drizzled it with sauce made with the reduced mulling liquid, honey, lemon juice, and a tiny bit of cornstarch to thicken it, topped with candied walnuts and small hearts cut from extra crust, and suddenly, we had something resembling a dessert. We stood back and surveyed our labor.

"I can't wait to see it all browned and gorgeous once we bake it," I said, rubbing the small of Alyssa's back.

"I can't believe we just made this from stuff I already had here at the ranch," she marveled. "You made the house smell so good."

"We did." I leaned in for a quick kiss. "You ready to face the firing squad?"

"Manz?" she asked, one eyebrow raised.

I nodded.

"No time like the present, I suppose. Let me go freshen up, and we'll head over there." She playfully grabbed my ass and headed for the staircase.

I joined Marilee in the living room with two glasses of iced tea, one of which she gratefully took. She reduced the TV volume and turned to face me.

"Would you like to come to dinner with us tonight? My friend Manz is a wild card, but Jen is a phenomenal chef. Good food and some laughs. I'd love if you'd join us."

She patted my hand. "Very sweet of you to think of me, but I'm happy here."

"Can I make some dinner for you before we go?"

"No, my dear. There's plenty for me here." After a moment's silence, she continued, "I don't know that I'm quite ready for the outside world yet."

"When you're ready," I added.

"Thank you." She squeezed my hand again and returned her attention to *The Office*.

After a few moments, she turned it down again. She locked eyes with me, her expression serious.

"Don't hurt her, okay?" Her abrupt topic change took me by surprise. "She's already been through so much. Part of that's my fault, I know…" She lapsed into silence. When she spoke again, her voice was choked with emotion. "But I just want her to be happy."

"You ready?" Alyssa's voice startled us from the staircase.

I squeezed Marilee's hand and stood to carry the two bottles of wine and our apple-pear pie-slash-tart invention to the car. I was stopped in my tracks when I saw Alyssa. She was wearing a curve-hugging, dark gray skirt that stopped just above her knees, accentuating her tiny waist. Her sleeveless, silky, dusty-blue blouse had a distractingly low neckline. Her stiletto heels, also dusty blue but with a subtle leopard print and a pointed toe, clicked authoritatively on the hardwood floors. And her legs—my god, those legs. I stood unabashedly staring, devouring every inch with my eyes.

"Are you ready?" she repeated, laying a hand softly on my forearm.

Her touch switched my brain out of neutral at last. "You look incredible." I was, quite literally, salivating at the sight of her.

"Thank you, baby." She handed the dessert to me and picked up the two bottles of wine.

"God, you smell good too. And I'm over here wearing yesterday's clothes still," I said with a chuckle.

She kissed me quickly, and then seemed to change her mind and returned for a slightly longer kiss. She finally broke away and turned her attention to Marilee.

"I'll be home later, Momma. Do you need anything before I go?"

"No, sweetheart. Have fun."

I guided Alyssa's elbow over the doorjamb and down the porch stairs. She dangled the keys in front of me with one lifted eyebrow.

"You trust me to drive your truck?" I asked.

"It's less than a mile on empty country roads. I'll take the chance."

I took the keys and opened the passenger door of her truck for her.

"So chivalrous," she said, giving me another kiss.

On the porch of their farmhouse, Jen took the dessert from me and lightly kissed Alyssa's cheek.

"You look fucking hot. Thanks for coming, Ms. Eye Candy," Jen said to Alyssa.

"Quit getting handsy," I joked.

"You're jealous, huh?" She slapped my ass. "Fine, you can have some too. Gimme some sugar." She puckered up and leaned toward me with her eyes squeezed shut. Laughing, I palmed her face, and she planted a loud raspberry on my palm.

"Forgive my wife," Manz said, exiting the front door. "Our chef has been sampling the wine since you called."

"What do you expect? I had to soak the golden raisins for the pork loin. I couldn't let it go to waste."

"Likely story," Manz and I said in unison. I gave her a hug as we laughed together.

"Well, I'm way too sober for my wife to be hitting on anyone that looks *that* gorgeous," Manz said, flapping a hand at Alyssa. "So get your skinny asses in the house and pour us some wine." She hooked her arm through Alyssa's and walked her into the house. "After all," she said as an aside to Alyssa but loud enough for Jen and me to hear. "What good is it having our butch lovers around if we can't have them do our bidding?"

Alyssa blushed hard but joined in good-naturedly. "Yes, I'll take red, and make it quick."

As we walked into the house, I threw my arm around Jen's shoulders. "So what's for dinner, drunken chef? I heard something about pork loin?"

"Yes, we're having a pork loin embedded with white-wine-rehydrated golden raisins and rolled with herbed goat cheese then roasted to perfection. We'll also have a Caesar salad and roasted sweet potatoes." She lifted the dessert she held to eye level. "And whatever this delicious-looking creation is."

"Um, we're not sure either," I replied with a chuckle. "Somewhere between an apple tart and a pear pie, if that even exists, with some honey-lemon drizzle and candied walnuts."

"We?" she teased.

"Definitely we," I said, smiling.

"I'm so happy for you, Sam." She gave my waist a squeeze.

CHAPTER TWENTY-SEVEN

Alyssa

"Just then, Dad yells, 'Wait! You have to put it in gear first!' And the Bug starts rolling backward down the hill, picking up speed, with Sam looking terrified in the driver's seat."

Manz, Jen, and I laughed as Sam covered her face. "I thought the pork loin was the only thing getting *roasted* at this dinner," she said, blushing.

Manz continued, "So instead of hitting the brakes, Sam yanked the wheel hard to the side."

"Did she wreck the Bug?" I asked.

"She didn't just wreck it," she replied, taking a sip of her wine. "She high-centered it on Mom's planter box."

"No!"

"Yes!" Manz said excitedly. "We had to call the neighbor's sons over to help us lift the fucking Bug out of the planter box. And she spent the next two days replanting Mom's petunias."

"Using my allowance money," Sam said, pouting playfully.

"Maybe I shouldn't have let you drive us here," I said with a smirk, running my hand over her thigh.

"I never replaced that back fender either," Sam added.

"Dad hung it on the wall in the garage over his workbench like some sort of dented memory of Sam's first car accident," Manz said.

"Is that why there's a bumper on the wall in their garage?" Jen asked. "I've always wondered."

Manz and Sam nodded as I took a bite of dessert. The apple-pear-lemon-honey-walnut-pie-tart thing was surprisingly delicious. A scoop of vanilla ice cream from Jen and Manz's freezer completed it perfectly.

"So, tell me about how this began," I said.

"This what?" Sam asked, confused.

"This," I said, pointing to the three of them with my fork. "How did this Terrific Trio come into being? Y'all have obviously known each other forever."

"We have," Sam agreed. "As you know, after my parents died, Manz's parents took me in so we could stay together. Our parents were best friends, and they were my godparents. I will truly never be able to repay them for saving me from foster care or some distant relative I've never met. Plus, it meant we could all finish school together. Manz's parents live just north of here, so we all grew up around here. Even back then, everyone knew that Jen and Manz were destined for each other. That is, everyone *but* Jen and Manz."

"Jennifer was in denial about the true extent of my awesomeness," Manz said flippantly.

"No, I was overwhelmed by the fact that you never stop talking," Jen replied.

"Agreed," Sam added.

"So we ignored each other for years," Manz continued, ignoring Sam and Jen's verbal jabs. "Until I finally just said, 'You're gay. I'm gay. We're both single. We should, like, hook up sometime or something.'"

"And then it hit me like a Mack truck that, deep down, I'd had feelings for Manz for years," Jen said, taking Manz's hand.

"And I thought she was great in bed and would cook for me, so I said yes when she asked me to put a ring on it," Manz added.

Jen rolled her eyes, and I laughed.

"And you two?" I asked, pointing a forkful of pie and ice cream at Manz and Sam.

"She was a loner, and I took pity on her sorry ass and said, 'Fiiiine, you can hang out with me on the monkey bars. Just don't embarrass me, okay?'" Manz said.

"Ignore her," Sam instructed. "We met in kindergarten."

"Mrs. Alexander's class. She looked like a turtle." Manz scrunched her neck and chin as far down into the collar of her shirt as she could. I chuckled.

"She shared her pickle with me," Sam said.

"I did no such thing, you vulgar lesbian!" Manz donned a look of mock horror. "The scandalous things you say about me."

"Just keep ignoring her," Sam continued. "No, she literally shared a pickle from her lunch with me, and we were inseparable ever since."

"Bonded over a pickle," I mused whimsically. "A phallically shaped vegetable soaked in salt and vinegar. Seems pretty perfect, ironically enough."

"Wanna hear how I found out Manz is gay?" Sam asked.

Unperturbed, Manz waved her away. "No one cares. Seriously, Attention Whore, stop trying so hard. You're embarrassing yourself."

I turned toward Sam, marveling at how her beautiful green eyes sparkled when she smiled. I knew I was dangerously close to falling completely in love with this woman.

"It was prom night, and Jen and Manz were still deep in denial about their inevitable future together. A bunch of us rented a limo together, and Manz went with some nitwit jock named...What was it? Robbie? Johnny?"

"Ronnie," Jen said helpfully.

"Ronnie! Yes, thank you, Jen," Sam continued. "Ronnie the running back."

"One too many hits to the head for that one." Manz tapped her temple with one fingertip. "He really was dumb as a box of rocks."

"We danced, we talked, Manz spiked the punch bowl...your standard prom experience for the most part." Sam continued with the story. "Then Ronnie came up to me and said he couldn't find Manz anywhere. I checked the bathroom, outside the gym, anywhere I could think to look. No Manz anywhere. I sat on the bleachers to scan the dance floor again and think of other places to look.

"In the quiet lull between songs, I heard the telltale, 'Uh! Uh! Uh!' of someone having sex." Sam did an unsettlingly good impersonation of a porn soundtrack. "Our bedroom walls were thin growing up, and I thought I recognized Manz's exclamations of pleasure."

I snuck a look at Manz, who shrugged and said, "What can I say? I had a voracious sexual appetite from a young age."

Sam continued, "Curiosity killed the cat, so I went to the end of the gym bleachers. I was hoping to bust her in the act. I couldn't see anything in the dark of the gym, so I had to sneak closer. I carefully crawled through all the crossbeams under the bleachers, dodging empty chip bags and discarded bubble gum. Once I was close enough, I waited for the strobe lights to circle around again so I could see who it was. They were still going at it and hadn't even noticed me. By then, I was pretty sure it was Manz, but I was just dying to know who she was having sex with under the bleachers. Especially since her date, Ronnie the running back, was out on the gym floor looking for her."

"You're such a fucking perv, standing there, watching me get eaten out. Alyssa, you've been warned. She's a total sexual deviant," Manz said.

Sam went on. "And I was right. It was Manz all right, with some long-haired dude tongue-deep between her legs. Except, the guy had…boobs? I was so confused. The strobe light circled around again, and I realized it wasn't a guy at all, it was Raquel Ingalls…the girl who picked her nose and smelled strongly of beef and onions."

"Oh no, that's not attractive." I laughed and looked to Manz.

Manz shrugged again. "In the dark, head is head. And I like getting head…a lot. Get it where you can, I always say. But I did have a strange craving for pot roast afterward."

I shook my head, laughing.

"Needless to say, Ronnie didn't take me to any more dances after that." Manz feigned remorse, palms up. "Whoopsie."

"Ronnie wasn't the last man whose heart Manz broke," Jen added.

"And Raquel wasn't the first to paddle my pink canoe." Manz smirked, and then turned to Jen. "Thank goodness you're good in bed, babe. Weeding out the duds is tough work, but somebody's gotta do it." She finished, sighing at the sheer exhaustion of her sacrifice.

"I warned you, she's ridiculous." Sam looked to me. "If you need me to tie and gag her, just say the word."

"Careful," Jen warned. "She'd enjoy that."

"Thank you for another delicious dinner, Jen," I said, air-kissing her cheek goodbye.

"Thanks for coming, but you gotta go now," Manz interrupted. "I have cross-examination techniques to use on my bestie to get every nitty, gritty, sweaty detail out of her."

"Are you *sure* I can't stay with you tonight?" Sam's eyes were huge and pleading.

Jen jumped in. "And deprive Manz the opportunity to torture you for the night instead of me? Not on your life!"

"Fine." Sam pouted adorably. "Can I at least walk her to the truck without supervision?"

Manz pointed her first two fingers at her own eyes and then at Sam. "I've got my eye on you, so no funny business. Escape attempts will be dealt the most severe punishment allowed by law."

Once the door closed behind them, Sam took me into her arms. "I'm going to miss you tonight."

"Me too," I whispered, melting into her embrace and turning my face up to hers.

"Can I see you tomorrow?"

"You'd better," I said. "And bring your toothbrush."

"Dental hygiene is very important." She nodded seriously.

I ran my fingernails through the short hair on the back of her head. She moaned softly and closed her eyes.

"That feels good," she said.

"Yeah?" I pressed myself a little closer to her.

"Mmm, that feels good too."

"What?" I said innocently. "You mean this?" I pushed her backward against the driver's door of my truck. "Or do you mean this?" I pressed my hips suggestively against hers, my breasts just below hers due to our height difference. Our bodies interlock so perfectly, I thought.

"All of it," she said, looking down at me.

"How about this?" I slid my hand over her shirt to cup her full breast in my small hand.

Her eyes closed again, and a small smile crept across her lips.

"Or maybe this?" I slid my thumb over her nipple, feeling it tighten and rise under my touch.

"What else you got?" she asked, playfully challenging me. *Oh, don't challenge me. I promise I'll win.*

"Let's see," I said, sliding my hand under her shirt, up her insanely tight abs, to her bra. Her breath stuttered as I slid my hand under her sports bra to lightly pinch that hardened nipple. Her skin was warm and incredibly soft.

"I see," she said, draping her arms loosely over my shoulders, her eyes still closed.

"I want something like..." I slid my hand out of her bra, down the ridges of her abs, and between her legs. I used my nail to scratch along the denim of the seam between her legs, teasing her the way she'd teased me in the tack room of the barn.

"Oh, that's not fair," she murmured.

"Not fair?" I smirked. "I'll show you 'not fair.'"

I slid my hand into her jeans and began stroking between her legs, over the fabric of her boy shorts. She made a sound that didn't sound human—something deep and guttural. I easily found her clit, swollen and hard to my touch.

"Alyssa," she groaned.

"Yes, baby?" I said, continuing to tease her clit through the fabric.

"Please let me come home with you."

"No, ma'am."

"Why not?" She was definitely whining now.

"Because," I said, stroking faster. "I want you to think about me all night. I want you to imagine my tongue on you as you touch yourself until you fall asleep. I want you to dream about tasting me, licking me, making me come on your face." I continued stroking her clit through the fabric, feeling the cotton begin to dampen with her arousal.

"Oh god."

"I want you to wake up sweaty from a night full of wet dreams about me. And then, I want you to come over and reenact every..." I stroked slower and harder, emphasizing each word. "Single. Scene. With. Me." I studied her face, her eyes closed and mouth open in an expression of desire and frustration. I slid my hand out of her jeans, feeling the moisture of her arousal that had escaped through the fabric on my fingertips. Her eyes fluttered open and I met her gaze, hazy and unfocused, lusty. On impulse, and without breaking eye contact, I sucked the taste of her from my fingers. It was tantalizing and delicious, and I immediately wanted more.

"You're cruel."

She kissed me deep, her fingers threaded through the hair at the back of my head. I kissed her back, hungry and passionate. Electricity jolted to my clit as she slipped her tongue past my teeth. I playfully bit it, flicking the captured portion with the tip of my own tongue. She kissed me again and I released her tongue, allowing myself to completely unravel against her lips. I submitted as she gently bit my lip, nibbled my neck, and tugged my earlobe with her teeth—she'd earned a little bit of revenge.

I pulled her phone from her pocket and noticed she had seven unread text message notifications and four unheard voice mails, all from someone named Sophia. *Isn't that the name of her ex who cheated on her? Why is she calling and texting so much?* I felt a pang of possessive jealousy, which I quickly tried to suppress. Instead, I returned to my task and entered my cell phone number into her address book.

"Text me if you need inspiration."

With one last kiss, I got into the truck and drove away.

CHAPTER TWENTY-EIGHT

Sam

I walked back up the stairs to Jen and Manz's house, my knees weak with arousal and sexual frustration. I took a deep breath to calm my racing heart, wiped the sweat from my brow, and steadied myself on the doorknob before entering the house. *Fuck, I need a drink. This woman knows all my buttons to push.*

I found Jen and Manz on the couch, Manz's feet in Jen's lap, and Jen massaging them lovingly.

"I expected the walk of shame from you, but I thought for sure Alyssa would make you work harder for it," Manz teased.

"I changed my clothes before dinner," I said defensively, popping the collar of my button-up.

Manz and Jen laughed quietly.

"So, spill your guts, you filthy whore," Manz said, handing me a very full glass of red wine.

I drank a long sip and flopped onto the love seat. "I'm in deep shit, y'all," I said, rubbing my face with my hand.

"Why? You two looked mighty cozy at dinner. What's wrong?" Jen asked.

"That's the problem. She is utterly fantastic. Beautiful. Smart. Kind. Funny. An Energizer Bunny in bed. Strong but tender. She's completely amazing."

"So?" Jen looked confused. "What's the problem?"

"The problem is…my life is in Denver. Her life is here. I'm here visiting and—"

"And you're welcome to stay as long as you like," Jen interrupted.

"I did *not* authorize that," Manz joked.

"And I have a home and career to return to. I can't just pick up and move back to California, and she certainly can't relocate to Denver. It's doomed to fail before it even begins," I continued, running my fingers through my hair.

"Bullshit," Manz said.

"Bullshit? What's bullshit?" I countered.

"Everything out of your mouth is complete and total bullshit."

"How do you figure that?" I asked, trying not to lose my patience.

She mimicked me in a whiny voice. "'My home and career are back in Denver. My whole wooooooorld is back there.' You're joking, right?"

"No, actually, I'm not. Everything I said is entirely factually accurate."

"No, it's not. You're full of shit." She took a sip of her wine and took her feet out of Jen's massaging hands. She planted her feet on the floor, put her elbows on her knees, and began counting off on her fingers. "First of all…"

"Ooh, girl, you're fucked now," Jen said, eyebrows raised at me.

Manz shot her wife a cocky grin of appreciation before turning solemnly back to me. "I hate to remind you, but your relationship with Sophia is over. Dead. Done. Nothing to return to."

My stomach dropped at the sound of her name. I clenched my jaw and stayed quiet.

"Second," she continued, ticking off her second finger. "The house you shared with Sophia is no longer your home. You'll have to sell it because neither of you can afford to buy the other out. And even if you could, I doubt you'd want to keep living in that house where you walked in on her cheating on you."

I grunted, begrudgingly agreeing with her.

"Third, with Sophia out of the picture, all of your people are back in California. Sorry, babe, but you've got no social circle in Denver, and you're an orphan with no extended family. Your 'parents' are my parents, and Jen and I are your only 'siblings.' And all four of us are here in the North Bay."

"God, you're annoying," I said, feeling like a petulant child. "Fifth—"

"Fourth, babe. You're on 'Fourth,'" Jen said.

Manz shot a look at Jen, who raised her hands in surrender.

"Fourth, do you or do you not travel for work?"

"I do." *God, I hate when she lawyers me.*

"Do the clients you train *ever* travel to you?"

"No."

"So it's safe to say that a hundred percent of your work is done at the client's home, on set in Hollywood, or on location for a film somewhere, correct?"

"Correct." Manz wasn't fazed by the growl in my voice.

"Is it also correct that you could not only do your job from basically anywhere in the US, but in fact relocating to California would actually be *closer* to your primary work location in Los Angeles?"

"Yes." I'd never seen her in action at work, but she must be absolutely vicious in the courtroom.

"Fifth," Manz continued, shooting another look at Jen, who nodded approvingly. "Well, I'm not sure I actually had a fifth argument, to be honest. I was on a roll, and wine is delicious." She took a sip from her glass.

"And your point is?" I asked, secretly impressed with her rationale but unable to let her have the win just yet.

"My point, hon." Her tone softened, and she joined me on the love seat. "Is that there's nothing and no one waiting for you in Denver."

Ouch. That's gonna leave a mark. I must have physically winced, because she took my hand and gave it a squeeze.

"Tough love sucks, and I'm sorry to lay the hard truths on you, but I'm just *sooooo* fucking good at it."

I couldn't help but chuckle.

"Go to Denver. Pack your shit. Sell the house. Kick Sophia in the ovaries. Stay with us until you find your own place," she said, squeezing my hand again. "Or better yet, until Alyssa rents you a U-Haul. We'd be neighbors!"

I rolled my eyes at her.

"Don't roll your eyes at me, bitch. I've seen how she looks at you. You're an ice-cold glass of water, and she's dying of thirst." After a moment, she said, "And to be honest, you look at her the same way. It's adorable and gross as fuck, all at the same time."

I let out a loud sigh and flopped dramatically against the back of the couch. I stared at their vaulted ceiling. "But this is all so new. I'm going to move back here in the hopes of spending my forever with a girl I've only known a few days? That's crazy."

"'Spending my forever?' What the fuck kind of poetic crap is that? Did I stumble into the script of a Hallmark movie all of a sudden? You're not moving back here for her. You're moving back here for *you*, because this is where your support network is. This is where your social circle is. Where your family is. Where your true home is. Where your career is. Plus, my fabulous ass is here, which is always a bonus."

"It is a fabulous ass too, babe," interjected Jen.

"Thank you, wife." Turning her attention back to me, Manz said in a loud stage whisper, "I pay her in orgasms to say that shit." She briefly laughed at her own joke and then grew serious again.

"And, if it works out with Alyssa and you ride off into the sunset or 'spend your forever' or whatever bullshit it was you said, all the better. Icing on the cake. Cherry on top. Cheesy movie montages and little baby Sams and Alyssas running around everywhere."

She put her hand on my knee as I continued staring at the ceiling. "And if it doesn't, I'll be here to pick up the pieces and superglue your sorry ass back together again."

"And then play matchmaker with the cute dyke who works the paint counter at Ace Hardware," Jen added, lifting her feet as Manz playfully kicked at her.

"Shut up, Snookiebear. Besides, I was right, wasn't I? They're banging like bunnies, Sam's moving back to NorCal, and it's all because of me."

"Does the Prosecution rest?" I asked, donning my best judge's voice.

"Fuck yeah, I do," she said smugly.

I changed into flannel PJ pants and a threadbare Eagles concert tee and climbed into bed. Tuxedo the cat and Bailey the dog must have found better accommodations for the evening because the bed was empty. I settled in and picked up my phone to text Alyssa. *Should I start out sweet and sentimental? Or dive into flirty and dirty?* I unlocked my phone and saw several missed texts and voice mails from Sophia. *Ugh.* I deleted all of them. *Great. If that's not a mood killer, I don't know what is.*

I opened a text box to Alyssa but suddenly couldn't think of anything to say. The cursor blinked and blinked and blinked at me. Actually, no, that's not true. It wasn't that I had nothing to say to her—quite the opposite. I had *so many* things to say, all crowded in my brain and demanding airtime. *I can't stop thinking about you. I want to spend every moment with you. I want to fall asleep with your head on my chest and wake you in the morning with gentle kisses. I want to watch your naked ass flex and fall as you walk to the bathroom in the morning. I can't wait to hear what you'll say next, and I want to know absolutely everything about you. I want to know the story of every scar and worship every freckle. I want to kiss each curve and worship you until you scream with ecstasy. I want your nails in my skin, and my skin slick and sweaty against yours. I want all of it. I want to saturate myself with you and drown in the bright blue of your eyes. I want to hear your laugh and meditate on the sound of your voice. I want to hear about your dreams and make each and every one come true.*

But how could I say that? How could I type the immense volume of my thoughts and feelings into this tiny text box? That cursor continued blinking, mocking my silence and timidity. It was calling me a coward, and I knew it was entirely right. I took the easy choice.

Sam: I miss you.

Immediately, the three dots appeared, indicating she was typing a response.

Alyssa: I miss you too! How did your chat with Jen and Manz go?

Sam: I'd hate Manz if I didn't love her so much. She's such a brat. (Winking face emoji)

Alyssa: It's clear how much she loves you.

Sam: You looked beautiful tonight. Took my breath away.

Alyssa: Thank you

Sam: What are you wearing now?

Alyssa: OMG that was a terrible segway

Sam: A motorized, stand-up scooter used by tourists in San Fran?

Alyssa: Segue* You're such a nerd.

Sam: Sorry—I've never had phone sex before, or whatever this is called. Let me try again *Ahem*

Alyssa: ...did I mention what a nerd you are?

Sam: That skirt you wore tonight made your ass look fantastic

I couldn't stop looking at your breasts in that blouse

And the glimpses of your black bra was complete torture

Your calves made my heart skip in those heels

I only have one question

Alyssa: What's that?

Sam: What color thong were you wearing tonight?

That's the only part I didn't get to see.

Alyssa: I wasn't wearing a thong

Alyssa: I wasn't wearing anything under my skirt, in fact

Sam: What?

Alyssa: You read that right

I couldn't text anymore—I needed to hear her voice. I called, and she answered immediately.

"Wait a minute," I said, jumping into the conversation without preamble. "You weren't wearing any underwear all night?"

"Mm-hmm," she said seductively.

"And I had no idea!"

"My dirty little secret," she said. "I almost never wear them with skirts."

"I'm going to have to check from now on."

"Well, if you insist."

"So...are you wearing any right now?" I asked, my voice slightly trembling.

"No, ma'am."

I swallowed hard. My blood pressure rose.

"Are you wearing...pants?"

"No, ma'am."

A heartbeat started throbbing in my clit.

"Are you wearing a shirt?"

"No, ma'am." Her voice was low and sultry.

"A bra?" I asked, trying to keep my voice steady.

"Again, no, ma'am."

The arousal between my thighs was intensifying.

"That is...incredibly hot."

My phone dinged in my ear. A text message had arrived. I glanced quickly. Photo message from Alyssa.

"Did you send me a picture?"

"Yes..." Her voice had lost some of its calm control.

I quickly opened the message. Alyssa lay on her back on her bed, naked. The picture showed the bottom swells of her breasts, just below her nipples. It showed the flat of her stomach, with her arm across her belly and her hand between her legs. The photograph showed nothing elicit or pornographic, but merely hinted at them. The placement of her hand covered her groin, and her breasts showed only cleavage. It was artistic in a seductive and sultry way. But somehow, the missing pieces made it even more erotic. My imagination was filling in the blanks from memory with zealous detail.

A soft, high moan from the phone's speaker brought me back to the present. I brought my phone back to my ear.

"Are you touching yourself, baby?" I asked, my voice low.

"Yes..." Alyssa's voice was high and strained.

"Can you feel my tongue on you?"

"Yes..."

I stopped to listen to her breathing for a moment or two. The sound of her pleasure, so close and yet so far away, was both exhilarating and torturous.

"I'm touching your breast. I'm squeezing your nipple between my fingers. Can you feel it?"

I could hear her move. "Hold on, I have to hold my phone with my shoulder..." More sounds of movement. "Oh god. Sam...I can feel it."

"Does it feel good?" I was concentrating on keeping my voice low but it was becoming more and more difficult.

"Oh! Sam! Keep licking me. Don't stop!"

"I'm licking you, baby. You taste so fucking good."

"Oh god. Sam, please, keep going."

"Can I go inside you?"

"Yes. Now. Please!"

"One finger or two?"

"Two. Oh god, I can't wait. Tell me when."

"Okay, you ready? There. Oh god, you're so wet."

Alyssa made a sound—a primal, toe-curling sound that hardened my nipples and tightened my clit.

"I'm sliding in and out of you. Faster. Faster. Come on, baby. Come for me, Alyssa."

"Oh fuck! Say my name again."

"Alyssa, I want to hear you. Please, Alyssa, I *need* to hear you."

Her voice rose in pitch and volume, each exclamation of pleasure driving me insane. She kept climbing and climbing— panting and gasping and moaning. Without warning, she went completely silent. *Is she holding her breath? Did the call disconnect?* Three, four, five heartbeats of silence passed, and I kept listening intently.

As quickly as she had stopped, she restarted—this time with an intensity that could be nothing other than her climax. Like the finale at a fireworks show, there was no mistaking these sounds for anything but orgasm. In my mind, I could see her stomach muscles tightening, could see her head and neck lift from the pillow. I felt her clenching around my fingers with each orgasmic pulse. The sweet scent of her hair, the warm smell of her sweat, and the delightfully feminine musk of her arousal filled my nostrils. A glowing, glistening sheen of sweat covered her breasts and stomach. I could picture that perfectly landscaped blond hair between her legs, and my fingers buried just below it, riding each wave of her climax to completion.

As she wound down, I marveled at how good even phone sex was with her. *Fuck, if it's like this, maybe long distance would work until I settle my affairs in Denver.*

She had fallen silent again, this time for a very different reason. I envisioned her limbs akimbo and slack with her hands resting on her lower stomach, her halo of golden blond waves surrounding her face on the pillow. Her eyes were shut, and her face was turned slightly to the side with her phone between her ear and the pillow. The comforter and sheet were bunched at her feet, kicked aside in her fit of passion.

I decided to fill the silence. "Alyssa, you are so incredible. I could listen to your ecstasy forever. And knowing that I get to share in it is beyond words for me. I am honored and humbled to know that a goddess of your caliber has chosen this mere mortal to share in your taste of heaven."

I paused briefly and could hear the slow, rhythmic breathing of sleep. This sweet angel fell asleep on the phone with me, naked and exhausted. I couldn't help but smile. I decided to take the chance to air out some thoughts.

"You know, I really thought my ex was 'the one.' Obviously, or I wouldn't have asked her to marry me. But my feelings for her were like a slow burn. It was a friendship that developed into lovers and, eventually, into its own form of love. It was comfortable but it wasn't exciting. It wasn't passionate and it certainly wasn't…whatever this is. I want you. I need you. I crave you down into the marrow of my bones. You are the drug I cannot live without. I think about you. I dream about you. I miss you terribly, and I love absolutely everything about you." *Oops, did I just say the L word?* The thought of giving my heart away again so soon after enduring the heartbreak Sophia caused was terrifying. And yet, my growing love for Alyssa was real, undeniable, and inevitable. It felt like I had been waiting for this woman to come into my life and fill the void in my heart.

"And if you'll have me, I want to show you every day how much you mean to me. Sleep sweet, gorgeous girl. I can't wait to see you in the morning." I waited a half minute or so, listening to her sleepy breathing to see if she'd wake or respond. When she didn't, I ended the call.

I set my phone on the nightstand and settled in to sleep. But, in some strange way, having my phone all the way over there felt like Alyssa was also too far away. I picked my phone back up and fell asleep holding it in my hand.

I woke early to the buzz-buzz of my cell phone ringing under my pillow. As consciousness invaded and my brain cleared, I remembered last night—the dinner, the conversation with Manz, and listening to Alyssa pleasure herself to sleep. I quickly clawed under the pillow to find my phone, anxious to see her name on the screen. My heart fell when I saw Sophia's name there instead.

I angrily answered. Without saying a greeting, I said firmly, "Stop calling."

"Samantha, I need to talk to you." Her elegant voice was syrupy sweet and turned my stomach to acid.

"There's nothing to say. We're done. It's over. Goodbye." I hung up the call and set the phone, screen facedown, on the bed. I flopped my face back into the pillow and let out an exasperated sigh.

My phone began buzz-buzzing again. I looked at the screen—Sophia. I sent her to voice mail and turned my phone off. Hell of a way to start the morning.

Once dressed, I left the bedroom and was surprised to hear voices downstairs. *What time is it? Did I sleep in?* I could smell coffee, bacon, and something sweet—vanilla, maybe? I rounded the corner into the kitchen and found Manz cradling a cup of coffee at the counter while Jen flipped something in a skillet.

"Well, good morning, sleepyhead. I didn't think it was anatomically possible for you to sleep in." Manz set down her mug to pour one for me. "I had to feed the animals myself. The audacity of this houseguest, I tell ya."

"What time is it?" I asked, my voice still gravelly with sleep.

"Almost eight," Jen said without looking up from the skillet. "We didn't want to wake you, but this one"—she pointed the spatula over her shoulder at her wife—"was getting 'hangry.' And no one needs to see that, trust me."

I peeked over Jen's shoulder into the pan. French toast. It smelled absolutely divine.

"This is just about ready, so grab a plate," Jen instructed, checking the underside of the slice.

With plates piled high, we settled into our chairs around the table.

"I made it with Hawaiian bread. They make it in sliced loaves now, so I had to try it. I hope it's not too sweet."

She had dusted the French toast lightly with powdered sugar. I moaned audibly as the bite melted in my mouth.

"Jen, it doesn't even need syrup. It's fucking heavenly," I said once I'd swallowed my bite.

"Babe, it really is," Manz agreed. "I might have a new favorite breakfast." She then turned her attention to me. "So what are your plans for today? I assume we won't be seeing you for dinner tonight, hmm?" She waggled her eyebrows at me suggestively.

"I'll head over there midmorning again," I said between bites. "Hey, your French toast reminds me. Is that French bakery still open in town? I should stop in and grab some croissants or something for Alyssa and Marilee."

"Cousteau's," Jen said helpfully. "Get some of their sourdough. It's amazing."

"Great idea," I said. "Sourdough BLTs are the best."

"Even better," Manz added. "Have a BLAST'R."

"What's a blaster?"

"Bacon, lettuce, avocado, sourdough, tomato and ranch dressing." Manz kissed her fingertips like a French chef. "Très bien!"

"Awesome. I can bring them lunch!"

I borrowed Jen's car keys and headed to Cousteau's Pâtisserie. The line was out the door, which oddly made me happy—the business was thriving, so their food must still be fantastic. I soaked up the autumn morning sunshine as I people-watched. Tourists and locals mingled, sipping coffees and eating scones and croissants at small tables.

Once at the register, I requested a dozen croissants and a sliced loaf of sourdough. I paid the cashier and thanked her as she returned my debit card to me. I turned to leave, my hands full of purchases, when a voice stopped me dead in my tracks.

"There you are! I'm so glad I found you." Sophia stood before me, beaming and elegant, a ridiculously expensive purse hooked over her forearm. "Here, there's an empty table over here. Follow me." She capitalized on my moment of shock and took the pastry box of croissants from me to the table. Like a zombie, I followed her, my eyes wide and my mouth agape.

"What are you doing here?" I stammered, a thousand questions in my mind at once. "How did you find me? Why are you here?"

"Sit, please," she commanded. I remained standing.

"Sophia," I said, more urgently this time. "What the fuck are you doing here?" My voice was loud, and heads turned in our direction.

"Samantha," she said, her tone reprimanding. "Please sit down. You're making a scene."

I begrudgingly sat opposite her, the loaf of sourdough in my lap.

"What are you doing here?" I growled again.

"Well, you aren't taking my calls and aren't responding to my texts, so I had to talk to you somehow." Her voice was sickeningly sweet again. "You can't avoid me forever, you know." She was trying for a weird, flirty tone that made my stomach hurt.

"How did you find me?" I was so confused.

"Easy. I still have access to your 'Find My Phone' feature— not that I needed it. I mean, where else would you go?" *Fuck, I completely forgot about that. Mental Note: Change all passwords and revoke all of Sophia's account privileges. Immediately.*

Sophia continued, "And I certainly couldn't go to Manz's house." She laughed sardonically. "That bitch would bury me, depending on what shit you told her."

"What *shit* I told her? You mean the truth?" I asked incredulously.

"Whatever." She flapped her hand at me dismissively. "The truth is always up for interpretation."

"Interpretation?" I echoed. "Sophia, I saw it with my own eyes! This isn't some fucked-up rumor that got out of hand. I caught you red-handed!" I couldn't believe what I was hearing. I rubbed my face with my hand and ran my fingers through my hair. I let my elbows rest on the café table.

"Listen." Her voice became quiet, like she was trying to calm an irrational child. "It's not like that. It is nothing. A blip on the radar. A bad dream." She waved her hand as if to shoo away a pesky fly. "We can easily move past all of this." She reached and took my hand, trapping it between hers.

I tried to wriggle my hand free, but she held it steady.

"Let go of me. I don't ever want to touch you ever again," I snarled.

"Stop, Sam." My name dripped from her tongue like oil. "You're making a scene again. Just hear me out."

I balled my hand into a fist. At least if she was going to touch me, I wanted to give her as little surface area as possible.

"Talk fast. Your timer is ticking. And when your time is up, I *will* make a scene if you don't let me go."

She continued holding my fist with both hands, rubbing her thumb over the bumps of my flexed knuckles.

"I made a mistake. He meant nothing. It wasn't even good sex."

"Oh god." I winced. "I don't want to hear about that."

"He's out of the picture entirely now. Gone forever. And it made me realize the immense mistake I made. You can understand that, right? With the wedding coming up, I need to be sure. I needed to *know* that choosing to be gay is really what I want and—"

I interrupted, trying again to pull my fist away unsuccessfully. "Choosing to be gay? What the fuck, Sophia? To see if being gay is what you 'want'? When did being gay become a choice? Because, for me, I guarantee it isn't a choice. And if you're choosing to be gay for the novelty of it, maybe that should tell you something."

"Okay, okay, okay, calm down." *Word to the wise: Don't ever tell an upset woman to "calm down." It has quite the opposite effect.* "Wrong word choice, okay? Shit. You're in a mood."

I couldn't believe the audacity of this woman. "Hold the fuck on a second. You cheated on me, got caught, followed me three states away, and have the guts to tell me that I'm in a mood? You're fucking right I am. Let me name a few..."

"Sam, you're getting loud again," she cautioned, still clasping my fist with both hands.

"How about...angry? Irate? Hurt? How about confused? Regretful? Annoyed? Indignant? Resentful? Betrayed? Or maybe furious? Those are just a few of the moods I'm currently experiencing, Sophia." I spat her name like a bitter taste on my tongue.

"Now that you've shown your verbal lexicon skills, can we get back to the topic at hand, please?" There it was. Her sarcastic tone. I much preferred that to the saccharine sweet tone she had earlier.

"Say what you have to say. Your time is almost up," I said through clenched teeth.

"Fine. I'll get to the point. Who lives down the road from Manz?"

"What?" The sudden topic pivot caught me completely by surprise.

"You've been spending all day at a ranch down the road from Manz's house. What were you doing there?" Her tone was lurid and suggestive, as though she suspected she'd somehow gained the upper hand with this knowledge.

I leaned closer to her and whispered, "None of your goddamned business."

"You had a little sleepover there the other night. You're fucking someone there, huh?" Her voice had turned sinister.

"Your time's up," I said flatly, yanking on my fist to free it, without success.

"You fucking hypocrite. You judge me, curse at me, yell at me, when you're doing the exact same fucking thing, aren't you? She cute? She good in bed? Do you think of me when you fuck her?" Her voice dripped with venom now.

Movement drew her attention to the large glass window next to us. I looked too and saw Alyssa staring wide-eyed, her eyes darting between Sophia and me—Sophia's hands still wrapped around my fist, the box of croissants on the table. I watched as her lips—those beautiful, sensual lips—mouthed the word "Sophia." Her eyes instantly welled with tears. She nodded twice, turned on her heel, and walked quickly away.

"Let go of me!" I roared and yanked my hand free at last.

"Is that her?" Sophia sneered. "At least she's beautiful. But then again, you were always weak around a pretty face."

"Shut your filthy mouth," I said loudly, standing to leave. Heads of other diners turned to look at me, but I didn't care. "Get what you want from the house. I'm putting it on the market. You have four days to be out."

"You can't kick me out of my own house, Samantha," she said coolly.

"Wanna fucking bet?" I said. "It's *my* name on the title, not yours. I bought it before we met, remember? I'll split the profit with you because you paid into the mortgage too—not because I give two shits about your future, but because I want nothing to do with you ever again." Spittle flew from my mouth. I didn't care. I needed to get to Alyssa. I needed out of this bakery. I needed away from Sophia. I needed to escape.

I turned to walk out of the bakery doors, and Sophia grabbed my arm to stop me.

"Don't touch me!" I yelled, stopping all conversations in the bakery. I forcefully pulled my arm from her grip. Everyone watched us now.

"You always were a child, my little Peter Pan. I'm glad I found a *real* man to satisfy my needs." Her smile was sinister.

"Fuck you." I turned and walked out of Cousteau's Pâtisserie.

CHAPTER TWENTY-NINE

Alyssa

My nails easily punctured holes through the top of the thin, white paper bag from the pharmacy. Momma's pills rattled in their bottles as I jogged back to the truck, my vision swimming with tears.

You're such an idiot. All the signs were there. You just didn't want to admit it. It was all too fucking good to be true, anyway. This is why you were single for so long. And this is why you'll stay single from now on. You're not meant for love. It just hurts too fucking much.

I unlocked the truck with my remote fob and opened the door. The handle slipped from my hand, and the door closed again. *What the hell?* Through the blur of my tears, I saw someone step between me and the driver's door. I blinked hard, sending a large tear rolling from each eye. I dashed them away and reached for the door handle again.

"Whatever you're selling, I don't want it. Please move. I have to go," I choked out, my voice thick with tears.

"Not so fast, Alyssa. Is that any way to treat the love of your life?" I recognized the polished male voice.

I sighed and rolled my eyes. *I don't have the energy for this right now.* "Tom, please move. I need to leave," I said.

"Aww, c'mon, you need to smile more. You're so pretty when you smile. Wait, are you crying? Did your *fiancée* make you cry?" He sneered through the word.

"Tom, I don't have time for this today. Please let me go." Fresh tears flowed down my face.

"Wait, did she hurt you?" He roughly grabbed my chin and turned my face from side to side. "What did she do to you?"

I pushed his hand away. "Nothing, Tom. You're the only one that hurts people."

"Watch your mouth." He pointed his finger in my face. His eyes blazed with anger. "That little faggot," he snarled. "If she ever lays a hand on you, I swear to god—"

"You swear what, Tom? That you'll backhand her into the kitchen sink? That you'll push her backward into the bathtub so that her ears ring for three days? Or maybe you'll teach her to wear long sleeves in the summer to cover the bruises. What will you do, Tom?"

"You've got a real mouth on you, Alyssa, you know that? You don't know when to—"

"Fuck off, Tom." I was on seriously dangerous ground, but after what I saw at the bakery, I didn't fucking care. It was worth the risk of Tom's wrath to let this monster out of the cage in my chest. I continued, "You don't get to tell me what to do anymore."

There it was. That was the big, red danger button that I knew better than to push, and I'd just slammed my fist into it. I could feel his rage building. I flashed back to the times before when I'd dared to hit that button, and the consequences I endured for it. The air between us snapped and sizzled with his angry electricity. The vein on his forehead bulged, and the muscle at his jaw flexed repeatedly.

"How dare you..." He clamped his enormous hand on my upper arm.

"Let go," I said firmly through clenched teeth, staring into his cold, dark eyes.

He didn't release me. He just stared at me, daring me to resist him, and tightened his grip on my arm. My fingers began to tingle.

"You heard what she said," Sam's voice, loud and authoritative, appeared out of nowhere by my side. "Let her go."

"Sam, leave. This doesn't concern you," I said quietly without breaking eye contact with Tom.

"You heard what she said," Tom said, echoing what Sam had said to him. "Leave now, if you know what's good for you."

"C'mon, big man, afraid to dance with someone your own size?" Sam flexed to her full height of five foot nine, which was still several inches shorter than Tom. It might have been comical on a different day.

"Break it up." An authoritative female voice approached from the opposite side.

Tom's hand released his grip, and I felt the warm rush of blood returning to my arm.

"Officer Chapel, great to see you." He slapped on his charismatic smile, full of perfectly white teeth, and extended his hand to the approaching cop.

"Oh, Mr. Kentfield, I didn't recognize you. Everything okay here?" Officer Chapel shook his proffered hand.

"Sure, sure, everything's fine. Isn't it, girls?" He turned his wolf's grin to Sam and me.

"Alyssa was just leaving," Sam said firmly. Her words forced Tom to step out of my way to save face with the police officer.

"No, *we* were just leaving. Get in, Sam. It's time to go," I said as I climbed into the driver's seat. She complied. Tom followed the truck with his eyes, his stare cold and full of rage, until we drove out of sight.

We drove in silence for several moments, broken only by the occasional sniffling of my nose.

"You shouldn't have challenged Tom like that. He doesn't forgive, and he doesn't forget," I said, staring straight ahead, trying to put miles between us and Tom as quickly as possible.

"He doesn't scare me," she replied quietly.

"He should," I snapped. "He's dangerous." I took a deep breath. My voice got quiet. "Trust me."

"I'd say it takes a pretty weak man to put hands on a woman."

I grunted in agreement before continuing.

"Sophia's pretty," I said. "She looks very…" I struggled to find the right word. "Posh. I can see why you're with her."

"I'm not *with* her," Sam replied. "I'm with you. Did Tom hurt you?"

I rubbed my arm where he had squeezed it. "No, I'm fine." Honestly, it burned, and I was certain it would bruise. But I wasn't hurt. Not physically, anyway, and not by Tom.

"What did he say to you?" she asked.

"It doesn't matter," I said, tears threatening to spill again.

"It matters to me," she said, reaching over to hold my hand.

"Don't," I said, quickly pulling my hand away. "I saw…I know now…so please don't touch me."

"That wasn't what you think," she said, her voice calm and quiet. "She came here to win me back, but I said no."

"It's okay, Sam." I sniffled. "You should go to her. She clearly loves you."

"She doesn't love me. And I don't want to be with her," she said. "I want to be with you."

"That's not what I saw," I said quickly. "Besides, I'm not on the market anymore anyway."

Sam looked taken aback. "What does that mean?"

"It means you're free to hold hands in French cafés whenever you like with whoever you like…just so long as you understand that it will no longer be with me."

Sam's eyes got huge. "No, Alyssa. Don't do that."

"It's fine. Go back to Denver. Go marry Sophia and live happily ever after. I won't interfere anymore. You had your fun vacation fling but now it's over, and you can return to your real life. You'll forget all about me. And vice versa."

"Alyssa, listen to me," she pleaded as she put her hand over mine. I shot her a withering look, and she withdrew it again. "She's been texting and calling but I don't respond. I don't ever want to see her again. I didn't even know she was here until she surprised me in Cousteau's. I wasn't holding her hand—she wouldn't let me go."

I raised a skeptical eyebrow at her.

"I swear! I promise. That's all over now. I don't want her. I want you. Only you…" Her voice trailed off. I imagined Sophia's voice saying so many of those same things to Sam only moments before. They sounded cheap and hollow, and I didn't want to hear any more.

I stopped the truck in Manz and Jen's driveway but kept it in gear. I wasn't staying.

"Please, Sam, don't make this any harder. Just go. It was fun while it lasted, and I'm eternally grateful for your help with Momma and the horses. But it's done now, so it's time to say goodbye." I stared forward out of the windshield.

"Alyssa, please believe me," Sam begged.

"Sam, get out of my truck." My voice sounded much firmer than I actually felt. She got out, closed the door, and I drove away without looking back.

CHAPTER THIRTY

Sam

I stood in Manz's driveway, completely bewildered by this day. Woke in a haze after amazing phone sex with my monogamous girlfriend, rattled by a call from Sophia, a delicious breakfast with Jen and Manz, accosted by Sophia unexpectedly in Cousteau's, spotted holding hands with Sophia by Alyssa, confronted Tom for putting his hands aggressively on Alyssa, a fight interrupted by a cop, and dropped off here, with my adrenaline raging, newly single, and my heart broken. How in the world did all of this even happen? How had this day gone so incredibly wrong?

I stood there in the driveway, waiting to see Alyssa's truck return. I willed the steering wheel to turn, the brakes to be applied, and the crunch of tires on the gravel drive. I sent messages through the universe to her of my sincerity and fidelity. I willed her to return, fall into my arms, and tell me she changed her mind. None of that happened.

I heard Jen's voice behind me. "Hey there. I thought you were spending the day with Alyssa today?"

She looked into my face and spotted the tears streaked down my face.

"Oh shit." She gently took my arm and guided me to the pair of rockers on the porch. "Come with me, Sam."

Once seated, she said gently, "Talk to me."

Where do I even start?

"I don't…" And then I ran out of words to say.

She waited a few moments and, when I didn't continue, she tried again. "Okay, let's start over. When I'm cooking a new recipe, I start with Step One. So, Step One: You borrowed my car to go get sourdough bread. I'm assuming you didn't make it there because you don't have bread…or my car."

The realization that I forgot Jen's car at Cousteau's brought me out of my daze. I also had no idea where the bread and box of croissants were. It all felt like a lifetime ago.

"I'm so sorry. It's safe, I promise. I fought with Sophia, and Tom was manhandling Alyssa, and it all got very hectic."

"Wait, what? Slow down. When did you talk to Sophia?" she asked.

"In Cousteau's this morning," I said quietly.

"Sophia's here? In California?" Jen's eyes went enormous.

I nodded vacantly, staring out to the driveway.

"Hold on." She dashed into the house, and I could hear her calling Manz's name. She returned with three tumblers of ice and a bottle of whiskey.

"What in the world are you yelling about, babe?" Manz emerged into the porch, pushing her reading glasses to the top of her head. Her mood shifted when she saw me.

"Oh, Sam, why are you here?" Her mood shifted again when she saw expression and the whiskey bottle. "Oh shit. The whiskey's out. This can't be good. Jen, grab another chair, will you?" Manz took the rocker closest to me and perched her small frame on the front edge, holding my hand.

Jen pulled an Adirondack chair closer and began pouring whiskey into the tumblers. "Okay, Sam, start over again. You took my car to Cousteau's for bread. Go piece by piece. What happened?"

"I got the bread and croissants and then Sophia was there, out of nowhere, pulling me to a table to talk."

"Hold the motherfuckin' phone a minute," Manz exclaimed. "Sophia was in Cousteau's? Today?"

Jen and I nodded.

"Did you know she had left Denver? Did you know she was coming?" Manz asked.

"No, I had no idea. It all caught me off guard."

"Holy shit. Now I understand the need for whiskey," Manz said, taking a sip.

"I thought you'd want to hear this," Jen said.

"You're goddamned right I do. So what did she say?" Manz asked.

"She found me using 'Find My Phone'—pretty smart, actually. I wish I'd thought to turn it off. Mostly, she just repeated the same crap as before—it didn't mean anything, I want you back, we can still get married, blah blah blah," I answered.

Manz scoffed. "And you told her to go screw herself, right?"

Without answering, I looked at Manz. "She asked about Alyssa."

"Are you serious? How did she know?" Jen asked.

"She was watching my location and saw I stayed the night there." I dropped my chin to my chest. Not from embarrassment or guilt...nothing like that. And I wasn't afraid Sophia would harm Alyssa, her property, or her animals. But I hated that Alyssa was being pulled into my drama with Sophia. And I was particularly dreading the next part of the story.

"We were sitting at a table by the window. She had grabbed my hand, and that's when Alyssa walked up and saw us sitting there."

"Oh no," Jen said.

"My god, the look in her face! It was so awful." I scrubbed my face with my palms, trying in vain to rub the memory out of my eyes. "It was disappointment and hurt and all the same things I felt when I walked in on Sophia. Except it was *me* making her feel that way! And she won't listen to me. She won't believe me that there's nothing going on with us. She shut down and shut me out. She said it's over between us and told me to go home to Denver."

"Fuuuuuck." Manz drew the word out.

"So who's Tom?" Jen asked attentively.

"Tom Kentfield, Alyssa's ex-boyfriend and complete asshat," I said.

"Tom Kentfield? As in Kentfield and Associates, the defense attorneys? Thomas Kentfield's oldest son?" Manz asked.

I shrugged.

"Tall, like over six foot? Looks like he should be an Abercrombie model? Total ditz for a girlfriend? I met her at a Bar Association function once. Candy or something like that?"

"Yeah, that's him. Her name's Cecile—he called her CiCi or Ceece or something like that."

"Shit, his family is loaded. And he's following in his daddy's slimy footsteps. They have no ethics in court—they're just there for the billable hours. They're a very powerful family around here. Anyway, how does Tom come into the picture?"

"So, once I was able to finally get away from Sophia, I chased Alyssa to her truck to talk to her. But when I got there, Tom had hold of her. He is a total douche, and I'm about ninety-nine percent sure he has roughed her up in the past. He had her by the arm and wasn't letting her get into her truck to leave. It got majorly heated, and I..." I rubbed the back of my neck with my hand. "I kinda challenged him to a fight."

"You what?" Manz leapt out of her rocking chair, sending it swinging wildly on the porch. "A duel for a lady's hand! How fucking romantic. So, what happened? You knocked his sparkly white teeth out or what?" She started air-sparring, throwing wild punches at an invisible face.

"No," I said. "The cops arrived and broke it up."

"The cops broke it up?" Manz exclaimed. "Oh my god, this story keeps getting better and better!" She sat back down on the rocker's seat edge.

"I'm so glad you're enjoying the plot twists of my completely terrible day," I said sarcastically. "I'm happy to serve as a source of entertainment for you."

"Oh, get over yourself," she said. "And get back to the story."

"That's about it," I said. "She told me she's done with 'us,' dropped me off, and drove away."

"Damn," Manz said. "I'm sorry, Sammy." She ran her fingers through my hair and pulled me into a hug. I was still in disbelief about all the day had held. The floodgates opened and, like I had done so many times in recent days, I cried big, ugly, sobbing tears.

"God, I want to sock his fucking lights out!" I burst out suddenly. "What did she ever see in that scumbag?" I finished my whiskey, which refilled magically in my hand. My face scrunched up in that "whiskey face" as my lungs lit on fire.

They didn't answer—there was nothing to say. So I relapsed back into crying.

"Tom and Sophia should hook up. They'd be fucking perfect together. Two narcissists battling over mirror time and brand names." I slammed down the contents of the whiskey glass in one large swallow, which Jen quickly refilled. My chest burned from the whiskey, distracting me momentarily from my thoughts.

"How can Alyssa just walk away from this? From what we've started building? It's so beautiful. It's the best I've ever had, and if Tom the Douchebag is any indication, it might be the best she's had too. I can't believe she is quitting on this before it's even had a chance to start."

I had too many feelings. Too many emotions were simultaneously fighting for supremacy. I feared my heart might tear at the seams, bursting with unshed tears and shattered dreams. My mind flashed back to last night, confessing my feelings into Alyssa's sleeping ear on the phone. I finished the third glass and reveled in the burn again. I sat thinking for a moment, studying the ice cubes in my tumbler.

"You know what? Fuck Tom." I shook the glass at Jen, the ice clinking around satisfyingly. "Fuck that guy and his fancy clothes and pretty-boy face and ridiculously perfect teeth."

My tongue was getting thick. Jen and Manz shared a look. Manz added another finger of whiskey to my glass. "I can't even tell you what an asshole he is. How could anyone hurt Alyssa? It's like kicking a puppy. Who does that? Who would kick a puppy? Puppies are cute."

Why am I talking about puppies?

"Wait. Am I an asshole too?" Jen and Manz still didn't respond. *Am I speaking out loud? Can they hear me? Why aren't they talking to me? And why isn't my tongue working right?*

"Tom's an asshole for hurting her, so I must be an asshole too. I hurt Alyssa, and now she hates me." I wiped the snot from my nose on the back of my hand. *Eww, that was gross.* I wiped my hand on my shirt. *Better.*

I raised my glass. "Cheers to the assholes! May we know them. May we love them. May we be them." I finished the glass. It didn't burn anymore. "Manz, I think my lips are numb."

"Yeah?" she replied, stifling a giggle, "I bet they are."

"Yup, numb-numby-numb." I bit my lip, marveling in the sensation. "Oh my gosh! Guys, know what?"

"What, Sammy?" Manz asked, chuckling quietly. *What's so funny? Why's she trying not to laugh? I don't get it.*

"Guys...she is a lesbian virgin," I said.

"What?" Manz scrunched up her eyebrows. It looked so funny—I wanted to pinch the little fold between her eyes, but it disappeared before my arm would cooperate.

"Well, she *was*...she's not anymore!" I laughed at my own joke.

"We figured that, Sam," Manz said flatly.

"Yeah, she told me I was her first. She'd never been, you know..." I whispered loudly behind my hand, "...*all the way* with a woman before me. Crazy, right?"

They nodded but said nothing.

"I took her V-card! Can you believe it? She's way too hot to have a V-card anymore, lesbian or otherwise. I didn't know though, promise. She told me afterward. Would I have...you know, taken her lesbianic virginity...if I'd known before?" I asked myself. I answered myself with a shrug. "I dunno. Maybe." I laughed that weird raspberry laugh that vibrates your lips. "Pfft! Who am I kidding? *Of course* I would have. She's a goddamned goddess of sexiness. That's what she is."

"I have a question though," Manz added. "Does the carpet match the drapes?"

My brain flashed to that immaculately tailored blond landing strip, leading like a flashing neon arrow to paradise.

"Yes, yes ma'am, they do." I pointed at Manz.

Why am I pointing?

"I mean, truth bomb here…but Sophia in bed was like…" I paused to think for a minute. "Walmart cereal."

"What the fuck, Sam? That makes no sense. Break it down for us, oh wise one," Manz said.

"Tastes all right and fills you up, but it'll never be really satisfying."

Manz rolled her eyes. "You are a ridiculous human being."

Jen laughed. "So what does Alyssa taste like?"

Manz's elbow to Jen's ribs elicited a grunt. "What? I was talking about cereal!"

"Sure you were," Manz said sarcastically.

"You know when you work hard outside all day. You've got dirt under your nails, and your muscles are sore. You've got blisters on your hands, maybe a little sunburnt, and feel incredibly hot and sweaty. You fall into a chair and crack open an ice-cold beer and survey your completed work. That's what sex with Alyssa is—leaves you completely satisfied, pleasantly exhausted, and—"

Manz interrupted, "And muscle cramps in your fingers and forearms!" All three of us dissolved into laughter.

"It's funny 'cause it's true," I said, wiping a laughter tear from the corner of my eye.

I looked into my tumbler again.

Someone drank my drink.

"Jen, someone drank my drink."

"I see that," Jen replied simply, filling it again.

"She's really fucking good in bed, guys." I finished the glass. "Like, really, really good." *My mouth tastes sweet. Alyssa's lips are sweet too. I want to kiss her again soon. I want to kiss her forever.*

"Do you think she'll marry me someday?"

And the world went dark.

I opened my blurry eyes to see a tall glass of water and three Advil on the nightstand by my face. *Where am I? What time is it? What happened? How did I get in this bed?* I lifted my heavy head, and the pillowcase stuck to my cheek. There was an enormous drool spot on the pillow.

I sat up against the headboard and immediately regretted it—my head began pounding viciously. As I drank down the Advil, I realized I was in Manz and Jen's spare bedroom. Of course I was. Where else would I be? I was wearing my T-shirt and boy short underwear but no bra or pants. The wall clock said it was seven thirty. But was it seven thirty a.m. or seven thirty p.m.? I couldn't tell—the light was that weird in-between of dusk or dawn, and I didn't know which. I looked around for my phone, and I finally spotted it on the far side of the nightstand. Seven thirty in the evening.

I started backtracking. The last thing I remembered was talking with Jen and Manz on the porch. And lots and lots of whiskey. Like opening a floodgate, all of the events preceding the porch conversation rushed back in: Sophia, Alyssa, and Tom. I rubbed my eyes and tried to lower my blood pressure, which had suddenly started to jackhammer in my temple.

I must have been on the porch with Jen and Manz at about…I don't know…nine thirty a.m.? Ten at the latest? So what happened for those missing ten hours?

I grunted as I laid my pounding head back against the headboard. I ran both hands through my hair and pulled lightly. It released some of the tension in my head, but certainly not all of it. I let my arms flop back down onto my stomach. Their rough landing woke up my bladder, which suddenly demanded my complete attention. I spun my legs over the side of the mattress a little too quickly. My stomach lurched as the room continued to spin after my body had stopped. Okay…not quite sober yet. Stupid whiskey. Why does it have to be so delicious in my times of crisis?

After sliding my jeans back on and tending to my bathroom needs, I headed downstairs slowly. Very, very slowly. I found Manz at the dining room table, her laptop open, her reading glasses on, and files and paperwork strewn everywhere.

I licked my finger and stuck it in her ear...for old time's sake. She nearly jumped out of her skin and swatted at my hand. Once she realized it was not a bug, she swatted me again, this time connecting sharply with my arm.

"Asshole," she playfully growled at me, drying her ear with one fingertip. "Did you get your beauty rest, princess?"

"Something like that," I said groggily. "Thanks for the water and Advil."

"Don't thank me," she said, returning to her paperwork. "Thank your bestie in there who's frying everything in the house to help with your inevitable hangover."

"Oh, hey, Sam!" Jen called from the kitchen. *Why is she so loud?*

"Who should I thank for taking off my pants?" I asked. "And my bra?"

"That pleasure was all mine," she said, planting a juicy, noisy kiss on my cheek. "You really have fantastic tits, by the way. They fit so nicely in my hand." She made a U shape with her hand in the air and stared at it adoringly before loudly honking my imaginary breast twice.

"Shut up, jerk," I said.

She continued chuckling at herself. "Seriously though, how much do you remember?"

"Um..." I rubbed my chin with my thumb and forefinger. "I think I made some inappropriate disclosures about my sex life?"

Manz continued laughing quietly. "That's for sure. That's it? Nothing else?" She raised her eyebrows questioningly.

"Oh god, how much more is there?" My voice was filled with fear and dread.

Before she could answer, Jen entered the room with two steaming platters of food.

"Uh, okay, change of plans," she said, looking at Manz's work spread across the table. "Dish up in the kitchen, and we'll eat at the couch." She turned on her heel and went back into the kitchen. We followed obediently.

Once settled on the couch and love seat with plates across our knees, I asked again, "So, what crazy things did Whiskey Sam do or say?"

Manz sighed dramatically. "I love Whiskey Sam. She brings my heart so much joy. All the singing and dancing…"

"And vivid descriptions of your sex life," Jen added.

"Oh, and don't forget the helpful reenactments! 'Her leg was like this, and mine was like this.'" Manz began twisting herself into various pretzel configurations.

"My favorite part was when she belted out Mariah Carey's 'Without You' at the top of her lungs, using the TV remote as a microphone," Jen said, cutting her chicken fried steak. "I thought she was going to fall off the coffee table, but she managed all right."

"Harry Nilsson sang it before Mariah," Manz said.

"Yeah, but Mariah sang it better," Jen said.

"You just like Mariah's boobs," Manz countered.

Jen shrugged and pecked a kiss on her lips. She picked up the TV remote and put it between them. In unison, they began singing, "I can't live if living is without you! I can't live, I can't give anymore!"

"Very touching, guys," I said skeptically, beginning to doubt how much of this story was authentic.

"I loved it when she raided the freezer and ate Rocky Road right out of the container with a wooden mixing spoon." Jen laughed. "She even offered us bites to share."

"Now *that* I can believe," I said miserably. "Rocky Road is delicious." I took a bite of chicken fried steak with a little buttery garlic mashed potato on top. "Speaking of delicious, this is fantastic, Jen. Thank you."

"We have fried empanadas with dulce de leche filling for dessert," she added.

"Jesus, Manz, how are you not five hundred pounds, eating like this every day?" I took another bite of mashed potatoes and savored the creaminess on my tongue.

"Easy," Manz replied. "Sex. Lots and lots and *lots* of sex."

"And you say I'm the ridiculous human being."

"It's pure cardio, Sammy. Pure cardio."

CHAPTER THIRTY-ONE

Alyssa

"Hey, Momma." I dropped the truck keys on the counter.

"Hey, baby," she said, muting the *Frasier* rerun on the TV. "Did you make it to the pharmacy?"

"Yes, ma'am." I dropped the shredded white pharmacy bag onto the coffee table and flopped onto the couch.

Momma's eyes zeroed in on my body language and read me only like a mom can do.

"What happened?" She curled her knees up into the chair and turned to face me.

"I had a run-in with Tom." I let my head fall back against the couch.

Momma didn't say anything, letting me take my time to tell my story.

"I was leaving the pharmacy, and he wouldn't let me leave." I looked at a cobweb in a corner of the ceiling. "I hate him. I hate him so much."

Momma fiddled with a snagged thread on her chair.

"What did I ever see in him, Momma? Why didn't you shake me by the shoulders and make me come to my senses about what a complete asshole he is?" I froze as I realized my language. "Sorry, Momma. I'm just..." I took a deep breath. "It was a rough morning."

"You know it doesn't work that way," she said, ignoring my curse word and absently twirling the string on her fingertip. "You had to figure it out for yourself. You had to grow from it and learn what you're worth. If I'd barged in and told you he's controlling, you would have been forced to defend him. You put the pieces together in your own time, and we were here to help you when you were ready."

We. That word wrenched my heart.

"Do today's events need a police report?" She probed gently when I didn't elaborate.

I scoffed. "No, not that bad. Besides, the police were there. Officer Chapel? I didn't know her."

"Oh, yes. Lindsay. I know her father." She looked at me meaningfully, continuing when I didn't elaborate. "What else happened today? This feels bigger than a spat with Tom in a parking lot."

"I saw Sam holding her ex's hand in Cousteau's this morning." I swallowed my tears.

"Sam? Like, Sam that's been coming by this week?"

I nodded.

She looked at the muted TV. "That doesn't seem like her."

"I know."

"No, I mean, are you sure it's not a misunderstanding?"

I sighed. "She says it is, that her ex grabbed her hand, and there's nothing going on with them. But that sure isn't what it looked like to me."

Momma still looked at the muted TV, clearly thinking through what I'd said. "I can't see Sam doing that. Has she tried to call?"

"No."

"Will you answer when she does?" She returned her gaze to me.

"I don't know…" My voice trailed off as my throat closed with unshed tears.

"Might be worth giving her a chance to explain," Momma said, twirling the fabric string around her finger again.

"So she can say what? What would make it all better? What would rewind time to be like it was? What can make me unsee…" My voice finally broke. I sniffled. "What I saw." I let my face fall into my hands, my elbows on my knees.

"Baby…" Momma cooed and came to sit by me on the couch. Her warm hand rubbed my back. "If you believe what you saw, then I believe it too." She wrapped her arms around me, and I leaned into her embrace, my face still in my hands.

"This is why I don't let anyone in. It hurts too much."

"No one knows that better than me, baby," she murmured into my hair. "But even with the heartbreak of losing your dad so young, I still wouldn't change a thing."

I looked up at her.

"It's true. I'll endure the pain of his loss for the rest of my life, just for the few moments of happiness I get from my memories of him. The way he smelled. The sound of his laugh. The way every animal on this property came running to spend time with him. How he could make anything he touched grow. And the deep, all-encompassing love he had for you. I wouldn't trade any of that for a lifetime free of pain. Not one, single moment." She kissed my hair. "Hold on to those moments, and don't close yourself off. Trust me on that one too. I've tried—it doesn't work."

I chuckled.

Momma was in bed, and I was thinking about an early bedtime for myself too. My body was tight and aching with tension. My eyes burned from hours of crying. And I was utterly exhausted from the gamut of emotions the day had unleashed on me. I decided on a cup of hot tea when my cell phone rang. I checked the clock—a little after eight p.m.

Sam.

I took a deep, steadying breath and answered. But when it came time to say, "Hello," my throat closed entirely. I couldn't speak.

After a moment's silence, Sam's warm, deep voice came through the speaker. "Can I come see you?"

I cleared my throat, but my voice still cracked when I started to speak. "I don't know if that's a good idea."

"Just to talk? You don't even have to talk, just listen."

I silently debated for a moment. "Okay," I conceded, my voice barely above a whisper.

"See you in ten."

Exactly ten minutes later, I heard Sam's soles crunching the gravel of the darkened driveway. I couldn't see her yet—too dark—and she hadn't broken into the half circle of yellow light from the porch yet. I sat on the top step of the porch with a crocheted blanket thrown over my shoulders. I didn't want her to come inside the house. Too vulnerable. Too intimate. Too many hidden dangers and potential new memories to make in there. I resolved to stay on the porch.

Sam approached quietly and sat beside me on the top step. She playfully knocked my shoulder with hers and, when I didn't respond, straightened her posture again.

"How are you?" Her expression was concerned and a little bit pleading.

"You said I don't have to talk, I can just listen." My tone was frostier than I intended, but maybe that was for the best.

She nodded quietly and looked at her interlocked fingers. Her elbows rested on her parted knees, and her shoulders slouched heavy with invisible burden.

"I've talked to Sophia twice since I left Denver. Both times, I told her to stop calling and texting. She called…" She looked off into the distance, thinking. "…about three times a day and sent about twice as many texts. I deleted all but the first one. It said all the same bullshit as she said right after I caught her cheating on me."

Her voice hitched slightly, but she continued, "I went to Cousteau's Pâtisserie today to buy croissants and sliced sourdough to make you and Marilee some BLTs for lunch. But when I was finished in line, Sophia appeared out of nowhere and took my croissant box to the table by the window.

"In hindsight, I wish I'd let her keep the damned croissants and just walked out. All of this could have been avoided. But, I didn't do that, and I'll have to live with that regret.

"She had stalked me using the location service on my cell phone. She grabbed my hand and wouldn't let go. I kept telling her to let me go, but she wouldn't. I got loud. She got nasty. And when we reached our boiling point, you saw us at the window.

"I know that's not how it looked to you." She ran her fingers through her thick, dark hair. "But I swear on everything, that's what happened. I finally got away from her and ran to find you, and that's when I saw Tom grabbing your arm."

"I don't want to talk about that." My voice was firm and uncompromising. I unconsciously rubbed my arm under the blanket, still sore from Tom's forceful grip.

"I'm sorry. I understand." After a pause and a deep breath, she continued, "I'm not asking you to believe me. I understand that you saw what you saw, and you believe what you believe.

"But what I am asking is two simple things. And please hear me out. I'm leaving tomorrow morning. I am going back to Denver."

"What?" My heart seized in a sickening spasm of…what? Sadness? Fear? I wasn't sure. I could feel the blood drain from my face. I couldn't believe what I was hearing, confirmation of my worst fear. She was leaving. It really was over, and I'd never see her again.

"Please, keep an open mind. I'm *not* returning to Sophia, despite how I'm sure that looks. I just have some…" She seemed to be looking for the right word. "…loose ends to tie up." *Is that a smirk on her lips? This doesn't feel like an appropriate time at all.*

"After I leave, here's the two things I want you to do." She turned her body on the stair to face me, her knees a small but respectful distance from my thigh. "First, I want you to keep an open mind. Again, I'm not asking you to believe me. But I am asking that you believe there's a *possibility* that nothing nefarious happened today."

"Okay, and second?" I said in as noncommittal of a tone as I could muster.

"And second," she said as she leaned forward. I could smell her cologne—warm and woodsy. I could feel her body heat. She was too close but also not close enough, and my heart was incredibly confused. It pounded forcefully at my temple. "Please hear me when I say that I have been—and will continue to be—monogamous with you until you tell me it is absolutely, irrevocably, and undeniably over. But please don't decide now. Give it a little time before you make that decision, okay?"

I didn't say anything. My brain was still scrambling for traction due to her closeness.

"Oh, and one more thing." She stood and brushed the butt pockets of her jeans free of any debris from the stairs. "I'd like to text you now and then. Not harassing and annoying like Sophia has been to me, I hope. And if I am being that way, tell me to stop, and I will. But, if it's okay with you, I'd like to check in with you now and then."

Again, I didn't answer. I didn't know what to say. Too many things were tumbling through my brain. Too many feelings and emotions, bouncing off one another and making a mess. My words were paralyzed by fear of heartbreak, and I was confused because I was no longer sure which was causing the heartbreak—being with her or *not* being with her.

"Give your momma my love." She reached the bottom of the stairs and began to walk away. She stopped and turned back to me, a warm, happy smile on her lips. "My heart is yours and only yours, Alyssa. I've known since the moment I met you that this—what we have—is something special. I'll wait for you as long as it takes. Good night, beautiful." She smiled one last time and stuffed her hands deep into her pockets. She turned and began walking away into the darkness.

My vision blurred with tears threatening to fall. I didn't know if I wanted to run into the house crying, throw myself into her arms, or just keep sitting here until the sun rose. I hugged the blanket tighter around my shoulders, frozen with indecision. *What should I do?*

A quiet, motherly whisper came from behind me through the screen door. "Don't let her leave like that. Go to her."

I turned to see Momma peeking around the edge of the doorframe. "I thought you were asleep," I whisper-yelled at her.

She shooed her hand at me. "Go! Now!"

I still don't know if I stood up due to years of parental obedience or if it was truly what I wanted to do. Either way, the result was the same. I walked down the stairs and into the driveway. Sam hadn't heard me—she continued walking away down the darkened driveway.

"Sam," I said quietly.

She froze, her hands still in her pockets. I watched her shoulders rise and fall as she took another deep breath before slowly turning around to face me. She spotted me hugging the blanket around my shoulders and tilted her face up to the sky. *Is she resisting tears? Thanking someone in the heavens?* I wasn't sure.

She walked halfway back to me and stopped, biting that bottom lip again. *Is she inviting me to meet her halfway? Well played. I accept.*

I walked toward her and stopped about three feet from her. Any closer, and I simply didn't trust myself.

"I'm fine with you texting me, but I probably won't respond." *My voice sounds stronger than I expected.* "I'll keep an open mind but, honestly, I don't know what I believe, and I'm extremely hurt." *Shit, my voice wavered on that last word.* "Especially after we…" *I can't finish. It hurts too much.*

"I know." Her gaze was intense and mournful, and her green eyes were glinting in the porch lights. *Absolutely gorgeous.*

"But, in case I never see you again…" I gripped the blanket harder and tried to find my courage. *Fuck, am I really going to do this? I have to.* I closed the distance between us in three short steps. *I have to kiss her one last time.* I took her face in my hands and pressed my lips to hers. Tears streamed down my face as I raised up onto tiptoes to reach her mouth more fully. She seemed shocked at first, stunned and still. After a moment, she roused and placed her hands, warm and strong, on my waist and gently pulled me closer.

Our bodies pressed together, interlocking perfectly. I needed to feel as much of her body with mine as I possibly could, savoring each millimeter of contact. I parted my lips, inviting her to kiss me deeper. She gently bit my lip, and I groaned softly into her mouth. Her tongue met mine, and a thrill of goose bumps ran over my skin. The crocheted blanket slid from my shoulders as I snaked my arms around her neck, pulling her closer. Her breath was sweet. It was delicious and exotic, with the spice and warmth of…bourbon? Scotch, maybe? *Perhaps she's not handling this as well as she seems to be either.*

I poured all of my emotions into that kiss. With all of my fear, all of my pain, all of my passion, I kissed her, pulling every bit of strength from her that I could. *This is our last kiss, and I need to commit every moment, every feeling, every emotion to memory.* I worked my lips against hers, enjoying her sensual lips and masterful tongue. *I simply cannot get enough of this. Of her. I don't know if I can let her go.*

The kiss—or maybe me—kept trying to spiral out of control, tempting me with cravings for Sam's naked, sweat-slicked skin against mine. I wanted her thigh between my legs, waking my primal urge, and the feel of my hips grinding against her, my breath hitching as climax approached. I wanted to taste her skin, taste her musky arousal, and pull her swollen clit into my mouth. I wanted my body to flood with electricity as wave after wave of pleasure was drawn from me by her knowing caress.

I can't—I absolutely cannot allow her into the house. This kiss stays here, tame and controlled, because I lack the willpower otherwise. Desires pulled me in opposing directions—my need for self-preservation and emotional protection versus my intense longing to drown myself in the ecstasy of her embrace.

Far from satisfied, I put my hands on her chest and attempted to buy some distance. I tried to break the kiss but my lips refused to cooperate. *I need more. I'm not ready to let her go.* With one last slow, deep, loving caress of her tongue and press of my lips, I broke away, tears flowing unabated down my face.

"Goodbye, Sam." Before I could reconsider, I turned and walked away.

CHAPTER THIRTY-TWO

Sam

"Call or text when you land, okay?" Jen's hug was tight and heartfelt.

I hugged her back with equal enthusiasm. "I will."

"Hey, save some for me, greedy bitches." Manz wormed between us. She hopped up to wrap her short legs around my waist and nearly snapped my neck with the intensity of her hug.

"Okay, now what are you supposed to do when you see the Queen of all Cunts?" Manz asked, dropping her tiny frame back onto her feet.

"Kick her in the ovaries and tell her it's from you." I bent to lift my duffel from the sidewalk.

"And?"

"And tell her she is the filthiest goddamned slut to ever walk the planet, and you hope she dies slowly of syphilis." I turned to Jen. "Do people even die of syphilis anymore?"

Jen shrugged. "Fuck if I know."

"God, I can't wait to hear if she's at the house when you get there." Manz began shadow-boxing an imaginary foe. "I hope you clobber that bitch."

"Does she seriously think I'm going to beat up Sophia?" I asked Jen. "It's like she doesn't even know me."

"Let her have her fantasies."

"Oh my god, if Romeo is there, you can beat him up too!" Manz began fighting two imaginary foes simultaneously, forcing us to take a precautionary step back to avoid her ninja kicks and wild punches.

"You are insane, sis," I said, pulling her into another hug once the battle ended.

"Love you. Mean it." She released our hug and moved to wrap an arm affectionately around Jen's waist.

"Love you too."

The house looked dark when the Uber driver pulled up to the curb in front of the house. *Please don't let her be here. Please don't let THEM be here.* After a few quick selections, I put my cell phone in my breast pocket of my button-up shirt. I took a steadying breath and unlocked the front door.

Not so lucky—a male and female voice were talking quietly in the kitchen. All of Sophia's things were exactly where they were when I left. Absolutely nothing had been packed.

"Sophia," I said loudly, waiting at the door to prevent seeing anything I didn't need or want to see. I dropped my duffel on the entryway tile.

"Fuck!" Sophia's voice came from the kitchen.

"It's fine. I already know he's here. Is everyone decent?"

"Um, just…one minute. Stay there."

I rolled my eyes to the ceiling in annoyance. A moment later, Sophia rounded the corner, wearing a new black negligee and a flowing silk robe with Asian designs.

"Hi, baby, I'm so glad you're home." She stepped forward to hug and kiss me hello.

I put my palm out to stop her. "Are you delusional? Get away from me." My voice dripped venom. She stopped just short of my hand, a look of irritation on her face.

"I'm just here to get a few things, and I'll be gone. The house goes on the market tomorrow, so you'd better start packing. The agent says it'll sell fast in this market. A couple days at most."

"Oh, I'm not moving."

I looked at her, confused. "How do you figure? It's my house."

"What's the listing price?"

When I told her, she said, "So half of that is what I owe you?"

My eyebrows rose incredulously. "You're gonna buy me out? With what money?"

"I have my ways."

"Fine. Your boy-toy's money will spend the same as anyone else's. How soon can you get me the money?" I thought for a moment. "In cash or cashier's check. I will have the sheriff evict your ass for anything less."

"Is tomorrow morning soon enough?" She tried to appear nonchalant, examining the cuticles of her immaculately manicured nails.

"Perfect. Now, if you'll excuse me, I need to grab my things."

She stepped aside, adding as an afterthought, "You might want to wait to pack anything from the kitchen or dining room, though. My guest is *sans vêtements*."

I nearly gagged as she used our term—our lovemaking joke from our trip to Paris—to describe her naked lover in the other room. It was an intentional stab, without a doubt, aimed directly at my heart.

"Manz is right. You really are the Queen of the Cunts, Sophia."

"And she is a loudmouth brat with no tits."

"Better to have no tits than no soul like you." I looked her squarely in the eye. "At least she could buy tits if she wanted. But you're shit out of luck in the soul department."

I moved toward the staircase to get the last few items I wanted from the second floor. Sophia grabbed my wrist, which I quickly twisted out of her grasp.

"Don't fucking touch me."

"You're my fiancée. I'll touch whatever I want." Her voice was commanding and elegant, traits that I'd found attractive once but now repulsed me.

"I am not your fiancée. I will never marry you." I threw up my hands in exasperation. "I don't even want to be in the same room as you!"

"Does Alyssa know you're engaged to be married?"

I froze. *Did she just say "Alyssa"?*

"What did you say?" I growled through clenched teeth.

"I said," she repeated with exaggerated slowness. "Does… Alyssa…know…you're…engaged? Don't look at me like that. Thirty seconds on Google, and I can know anything about anyone. How's she handling the death of her father? Were they close?" After a moment, she continued, "Unless it's Marilee the Widow you're screwing. But considering that pretty face at the bakery, I'd say it's safe to assume it's Alyssa who's stolen you from me."

I was stunned. Words escaped me. I stood in complete shock, staring into her cold, hateful eyes.

"Well, maybe we'll save that to unpack another day. Seems the pussy's got your tongue, honey." She tapped my nose with her forefinger. "Besides, I have dinner plans to return to. So if you'll excuse me." She turned sharply and walked back to the kitchen, her silken robe flowing behind her.

I stood, looking around this house, these things, this life we'd built together. I quickly realized that, aside from the items I'd previously packed into my duffel and a few important documents I kept in a lockbox, there was nothing here I wanted or couldn't replace. Everything was tainted. Everything had her fingerprints, her memories, her scent on it. And I wanted nothing to do with any of it.

"I'll send my lawyer by at ten a.m. for the buyout amount. Cash or cashier's check only, and don't be late," I called loudly toward the kitchen. "Have it ready or I will evict you."

"Bye, sweetheart," she called sweetly from the dining room.

I closed the door behind me. I didn't bother to lock it.

An hour later, I was happily nestled into clean white sheets and a pile of fluffy pillows at a hotel about a hundred miles west of Denver. My Tacoma pickup truck was parked in the hotel parking lot downstairs. Knowing I could go anywhere by simply picking up the keys on the dresser was liberating. New paths laid out before me in my mind, brimming with potential and dreams to be realized. My imagination swirled with ideas. It was intoxicating.

I pulled out my cell phone and sent a text to my agent, asking him to have the agency lawyer pick up the buyout money for me at ten the next morning. My agent agreed and said he would deposit the money for me like he did my training earnings. Simple and clean—if Sophia didn't pull any more of her bullshit, of course. I also told him I was done with my unexpected sabbatical and ready for more training assignments. His prompt reply said he'd keep me informed.

After a quick text update to Manz about my interaction with Sophia—she was predictably disappointed I didn't actually kick her in the ovaries—she replied that she was completely unsatisfied with my quick rendition of the plot and demanded details. I told her she was in luck—I had recorded the entire interaction on my phone so she could hear it for herself. I sent the video. The screen was black from being in my breast pocket, but the audio was clear as day. That should satisfy her.

Why did I record it? Initially, the idea had struck me in case Sophia or her boy-toy did or said anything I'd want proof of later, like threats or something. Considering I'd intended to evict her, and how things had gotten out of hand at Cousteau's, I anticipated our interaction in Denver would get heated too. But in hindsight, I was glad to have the recording of Sophia stating she would buy out my half in the morning. Not binding or anything, but at least she couldn't deny it.

I reached for the TV remote to scroll through the channels. The memory of Jen and Manz impersonating me—or Whiskey Sam, as I prefer she be known—singing "Without You" into their TV remote popped into my head. God, I loved those women so much. They truly were my family in all senses of the word. And Manz—dear, sweet, obnoxious Manz—the only sister I'd ever known.

The memory of my drunken karaoke inevitably led my mind back around to Alyssa—beautiful, kind, funny, sexy, tender-hearted Alyssa. I missed her terribly—the soft floral scent of her hair, the crisp blue of her eyes, the golden waves of her hair, the funny names of her farm animals. All of it made me smile.

I opened a text box to send her a message but, like before, I didn't know what to say. That damned cursor was mocking my silence again. So, like before, I decided to just keep it simple.

I miss the feel of your small, warm hand in mine.

I honestly didn't expect a response, but I sure hoped for one. I waited, staring at my phone, praying those three dots would appear to tell me she was typing. Unfortunately, after thirty minutes, there was still no response. I had to accept that it wasn't going to happen. At least, not today. Maybe tomorrow.

As it seemed to have become an annoying pattern recently, I woke again to the buzz-buzz of my cell phone. I was relieved to see the text message was from my agent, informing me the buyout monies, in full, had been deposited into my account. I sat in utter shock for a few minutes, rereading the message to be sure I had read it correctly. I logged into my bank account, pleasantly surprised to see a six-figure deposit pending availability.

Huh…The boy-toy coughed up the cash after all. As I considered it a little longer, it began to make sense. If he could spit out a few hundred thousand dollars overnight for Sophia, then he was probably able to finance her expensive tastes in clothes, jewelry, vacations, and champagne that I wouldn't.

And suddenly, like an explosion in my brain, the entire affair made sense. She was never with me for love; she was with me for my Hollywood connections and showbiz paychecks. Average movie animal trainers lived paycheck to paycheck, not typically a lucrative business, but quality animal trainers with reputations for excellence were difficult to find, and the good ones demanded great salaries. Mix in my willingness to travel anywhere at any time and ability to train nearly any animal the scriptwriters needed, and I was never without work. Granted, I couldn't knock out a check overnight to buy a house for my girlfriend, but I did well enough to not want for money. Add in my lack of materialism and simple tastes, and the money tended to sit there, collecting interest. Regardless, it seemed Sophia had found her financial upgrade, and I was merely collateral damage. *So much the better for me.*

I sent a text to my real estate agent, telling her that Sophia had bought me out of the house. I told her to draw up the paperwork to transfer title into her name. She responded promptly and said she would make it happen as soon as possible. I told her I would pay any fees or costs, and she said I would be able to electronically sign most of the documents. Anything needing a "wet" signature or notary could be handled via overnight mail. Perfect. The sooner, the better.

I checked the time—10:48 a.m. *I slept in again. I need these hotel blackout curtains at home!* Then the word struck me—home— and I suddenly realized I didn't have one. Everything I owned was spilling out of my duffel onto the hotel floor or in the truck parked downstairs. A mingle of intimidation and exhilaration filled me. Free and boundless? Or alone and rootless? Maybe a little of both, I conceded. *Time will tell.*

After a scalding hot shower, I dressed and packed my few possessions back into my duffel. I left a ten-dollar bill on the nightstand for the maid and headed to the truck. After entering directions into my cell phone mapping app of my next hotel in Salt Lake City, Utah, another three hundred miles to the west, I settled in for the long drive.

But before popping my cell phone into its dash holder, I opened a text box. The fucking blinking cursor. I closed the message and dropped my hands in my lap. I ran my hand through my hair, staring at the roof liner of the truck.

Some things in my life were clicking into place, reaching their resolutions with no raveling edges. But others were in a complete tailspin, crashing to the ground with black smoke billowing from the engine. And Alyssa's gorgeous curves were painted pinup style on the nose of the plane.

This was solvable. It had to be. Nothing that felt this right, this perfect, could end over a misunderstanding. Especially at the hands of manipulative, cruel Sophia. It would be the final stab to my heart with her perfectly manicured nails, and I couldn't allow it to come to fruition.

On Alyssa's porch, I'd tried so hard to appear light and confident, when inside I was trembling with fear. Would she permanently and irrevocably pull the plug on our relationship, young as it may be? I had been petrified. And, although I'd hoped she would have decided to resume our romance, I knew it was a long shot. I was relieved, however, that she agreed to keep an open mind and not immediately terminate our potential. Still, knowing she was hundreds of miles away, hurting and second-guessing her decision to give herself—heart and body—to me was soul crushing. I wanted to scoop her into my arms and kiss those tumbling tears away from her face while whispering my promises of forever.

But that kiss. That darkened driveway kiss goodbye. My eyes lulled shut at the memory as adrenaline flooded my body again. The intensity and passion in her touch. The salty tingle of her tears on my lips and tongue. The pull of my body to hers. The knee-weakening touch of her tongue against mine. The slippery response between my legs to her touch, her hands, her hungry kisses. The battle to keep my lust for her in check so as not to startle this fragile fawn back into the forest of heartbreak. All of it combined and swirled in my mind, a vortex of want and need, pulling me incessantly back to California.

I reopened the text box, determined to conquer the cursor, and typed.

I could spend the rest of my life savoring the feeling of your incredibly soft lips against mine.

There was, as I expected, no reply. I docked my cell phone into its dashboard holder at last, shook the visions of Alyssa's blanket sliding so seductively from her shoulders as she surrendered to our kiss, and turned on the engine of the truck. *The sooner I leave, the sooner I'll see her again.* Hopefully, anyway.

CHAPTER THIRTY-THREE

Alyssa

Sam: I could spend the rest of my life savoring the feeling of your incredibly soft lips against mine.

I stared at the words, reading them again and again. Butterflies erupted to life in my stomach, some of them, admittedly, fluttering south. "The rest of my life." Did she mean those words with the weight they seemed to imply? Or was it just one of those things you say? But envisioning her kiss, that lip bite that worked as an ignition switch for my desire, was doing nothing to help me forget about her and move on. I scrolled up to read the text before it.

Sam: I miss the feel of your small, warm hand in mine.

Distractedly, I stroked my fingertip against my lips, imagining our kiss in the driveway. The memory merged and blended with our first kiss behind the barn. My fingers tangled in her hair, her hands pulling my hips tight against her, and feeling that I might erupt into orgasm at the slightest pressure between my legs.

My blood pressure began to rise in a very pleasant way. I quickly put my phone away. *No. I can't. I'm torturing myself and, for what?* Nothing good could come from these fantasies, and I forced myself to shelve those thoughts away. Besides, there was an entire ranch to keep afloat. I didn't have time for reminiscing on wishes and never-will-bes.

Once the horse stalls were cleaned, I made my way to the chicken coop, which desperately needed to be raked and fresh straw scattered.

"Sorry, girls," I said, tossing grains and dried mealworms for them. They happily ran to me and began scratching and pecking eagerly for the treats. "I'll clean your coop more often, I promise."

I collected the eggs and ripe orchard fruit and headed back to the house. I was hot, dirty, and probably smelled like the barnyard. I was eager for a cool shower and some lunch.

Back at the house, Momma was on the couch, folding a load of towels.

"Oh, Momma, you don't have to do that. I'll finish that up," I said, pulling off Daddy's old baseball cap and letting my hair out of my ponytail.

"I'm depressed, Alyssa, not an invalid. I'm perfectly capable of folding some towels." She looked up from her folding, and alarm spread across her face. "Alyssa, you get into that kitchen right now and drink some water. You are bright red!"

"Yes, Momma," I said obediently.

I went to the sink and splashed cool water on my face. I wet my hands and rubbed the back of my neck, letting the drops of water make lazy trails over my skin. Without drying, I took two glasses to the fridge and poured iced tea for us.

"Here, Momma." I handed one to her.

"See? You look better already."

I flopped into the nearest chair and let my arms and legs relax, the glass of tea dangling from my fingertips.

"How are you doing?" Momma's eyes were filled with concern.

"Good. Hot. Tired. You?" I dodged what I suspected was her real intention behind the question.

With speed and accuracy I never would have expected from her, Momma whipped a dishtowel at me, delivering a painful snap against my thigh.

"Hey!" I exclaimed in surprise. "You brat! What was that for?"

"You know *exactly* why." She stifled a laugh. "I'll ask again. How are you doing?"

"I'm okay," I lied.

She began twisting the dishtowel again, taking aim at my thigh.

"Okay, okay! Jeez." I paused a moment to collect my thoughts. "I'm confused, honestly. I feel like my brain is going in several directions at the same time."

She nodded with understanding.

"Part of me wants to call her right this very second and tell her to come over and never leave."

"Mm-hmm," she said noncommittally.

"And part of me wants to crawl into my shell and hide, safe from lies, betrayal, heartache, disappointment, and any other pitfalls waiting out there for my poor bruised heart."

Momma stopped folding the towel in her hands. "Understandable, but you can't hide forever, my love."

Tears immediately leapt into my eyes. "Why can't I?" I joked, wiping tears away.

"Because, baby," she said, rubbing my knee. "Your heart is too big and too beautiful to hide from the world. You have such a deep, boundless capacity to love and to be loved."

"Ugh, stop." Tears continued flowing. I wasn't sure if I was talking to her or my tears. "Will I ever go five minutes without crying ever again?"

"Give it time. Don't close the padlock on your heart quite yet." After a moment, she continued, "Have you heard from her?"

"Yes, yesterday and today. Just quick texts." I felt a flush creep into my cheeks. Thankfully, Momma didn't comment on it.

"Mm-hmm," she said, sneaking a glance at me as she resumed folding towels. "Did you reply?"

"No, ma'am."

"Give it time." She added a folded towel to her stack and reached for another. "If it's right, you'll know. Trust your heart, not your brain."

"Yes, ma'am."

Several hours and a delicious lasagna dinner later, I finally fell into bed. I lay languorously sprawled across the bed, a blond starfish reaching for all four corners. Tired muscles, hard work, and too much sun had left my bones begging for rest. Yet, something…something kept drawing me away from sleep and back to consciousness. I couldn't identify it, and it was driving me crazy.

I rolled onto my side, frustrated. Facing the spare pillow on my bed, I suddenly figured it out with crystal clarity. I pulled the pillow to my face and breathed Sam's scent deep into my lungs. The warm forest smell of her cologne. The clean scent of her shampoo. The barely there undertone of her sweat. *No, I'm not going to cry.*

Surprisingly, a very different emotion surfaced instead. Sam's scent, so real and so close, was an aphrodisiac I would never have expected. And yet, there I was, immediately aroused and craving her touch. I let go of the pillow and flopped back over onto my back in frustration.

I need a distraction, or I might have to scratch this itch myself. I unlocked my phone and, lo and behold, what was on my motherfuckin' screen? My text conversation with Sam. *Figures. Fine, universe, you win. I'm listening. You have my undivided attention.* I scrolled to the top of the conversation, lingering on the part where I had teased that I wasn't wearing any underwear.

Fuck. This certainly isn't helping. I absently stroked the gap of belly skin between my tank top and my pajama shorts. I closed my eyes, and Sam's fingertips replaced mine. Instantly, my arousal shot into overdrive, and electricity zinged through my nerves. My brain replayed the similar sensation of Sam's fingers teasing me in the tack room, her body pressed against my back as she torturously teased me through the denim of my jeans.

In my mind, Sam slid her hand under my tank top to cup my breast. My nipple leapt awake, pressing tightly against the fabric of my tank.

"Sam," I breathed out.

Sam's fingers touched my nipple, and a groan escaped my throat. She pinched it, and my knees involuntary spread for her like a reflex. Her other hand teased its way under my shorts to discover I wasn't wearing underwear. She groaned—or I groaned, I wasn't sure—and her fingers played lightly with my recently trimmed strip of short hair.

She pinched my nipple hard, incredibly hard, as her fingertips first touched my clit. I turned my head, pivoting slightly to inhale her smell again. The effect was immediate as the warm, slick evidence of my arousal coated her fingertips.

"Fuck me, Sam," I whispered, trying desperately to imagine the feel of her skin against mine. "Please, Sam."

Still aggressively twisting my nipple, Sam's fingers stroked my clit harder and faster, making it nearly impossible to stay quiet. She released my nipple, and her hand wandered south, over my stomach, past my clit, and plunged two fingers deep inside of me.

"Oh, fuck!" *Shh, Alyssa.*

Stroking hard, stroking fast, Sam's hands deftly coaxed my climax to the surface. It lingered just out of reach, the burn of the muscle in my forearm pulling me out of my fantasy. I needed something more, just a little more, to push me over the edge. Sam began grinding herself against my thigh, reminiscent of the orgasm I'd found against hers.

Oh god, yes.

Sam's pace increased again, sliding fast and hard against my clit while fucking me deep. I could feel the slick of her arousal on my thigh, grinding her enjoyment in time with mine...with my wet fingers, stroking furiously in and out of my depths.

"Fuck me, please. Sam, fuck me!" I commanded, my voice a breathy whisper.

With one final, incredible effort, Sam ground her hips hard into my thigh, tipping me over the edge into ecstasy. I could feel my muscles inside clench hard, squeezing and releasing against her still sliding fingers with incredible power. She finally withdrew so I could bite my knuckle. Still stroking the continuing pulses in my clit, the bite stifled the scream that threatened to erupt from my throat.

The delicious musky scent of a female orgasm coated the fingers beneath my nose, bringing Sam close again in my mind. I saw her thick, dark hair sticking to her forehead with sweat as she held herself up on top of me. Her body rocked as she pleasured herself on my lifted thigh, her eyes closed and her lips parted with enjoyment. Unexpectedly, my second orgasm quickly built and crested, taking me by surprise with the ferocity of the waves of satisfaction, which tensed the muscles of my body. My back arched. My eyes rolled back. My teeth dug deeper into my knuckle. And still, Sam guided wave after wave of my continuing orgasm from my clitoris.

At long last, my arousal abated, and Sam's warm, slick fingers withdrew from my clit to my stomach. I rolled to my side and hugged the spare pillow to my chest. Her cologne washed over me again, so comforting and safe, and the inescapable fatigue of orgasm overcame me.

"Good night, baby."

The room glowed with the rosy, peachy colors of dawn. Another long day of ranch work awaited me. I reached for my phone to see if the farmers' market coordinator had replied to my request for a space in this morning's market. Instead, I found a text from Sam. A flutter bloomed through my chest. *Listen to your heart, not your brain*, Momma had said. *Fine, I'm listening.*

Sam: I love making you smile for the pure pleasure of the sound of your laugh.

Reading it made me smile. Simple as that. I tried to settle into that feeling, resisting the instinct to close my heart and deny her entrance. My brain was ready to lock the iron gates and send her away at spear point. But my heart—my uncooperative, glutton for punishment heart—kept inviting her in with open arms. And, if I'm honest, so did my libido.

I considered replying. But what would I say? "I like your laugh too"? "I love your smile"? Or "I love when you bite your lip"? I wasn't ready for that. I wasn't ready to be so vulnerable. Not yet. Maybe not ever.

My phone dinged with a new email alert. My request for a last-minute table at the farmers' market was approved. Time to get moving—lots of honey, produce, and all of the tables, banners, pop-up tent, and other point-of-sale items to get loaded into the truck before the market opened for the day.

Downstairs, I found Momma on the porch with a cup of coffee. I poured myself a cup and went to join her before diving into work.

"Momma, you're outside again. And no coaxing this time." My smile was enormous and entirely genuine.

"Well, I'd hardly consider the porch five feet from the door as being 'outside' exactly, but it's a start."

I kissed the top of her head and sat in the chair next to hers. "I got a booth for the farmers' market this morning. Will you come help me?" I tried to keep my tone light, but I really hoped she would say yes. Not only because I could use the help, but leaving the house would be another step in her depression recovery.

"Oh, I don't think so. Maybe next time."

I rolled my eyes. "If I never hear those words again," I murmured under my breath.

"And what's that supposed to mean, young lady?"

"It means," I responded, making my voice strong and authoritative. "That you said that to me day after day when Daddy died, until one day, you just stopped responding at all. I lost you for months into that darkness, and I don't ever want to walk that path again."

Her facial expression morphed from defensive to realization to regret. "I hate when you're right, you know that?"

"Yes, ma'am," I said, trying not to smirk.

"Okay," I said, dusting off my hands. "Tables are up, so are the banner and the tablecloths. Vegetables over there, fruit over there, and honey and eggs in the middle. Does it look okay? What are we missing?"

"Nothing, baby," Momma said from her folding chair in the shade, wearing oversized sunglasses like a Hollywood starlet. "It's perfect. Your daddy would be proud."

I walked around the table and knelt at her feet, wrapping her in a hug. "I'm so glad you're here with me, Momma."

"Well, as I live and breathe! Is that you, Marilee?"

We both turned to see Ms. Rhonda standing before our market stall. Trying to save Momma from interaction she might not be ready for, I approached Ms. Rhonda for a hug.

"Ms. Rhonda! So nice to see you. Is Mr. Westbrook here too?"

"Of course. He's over there earning the money while I spend it." She chuckled at herself. "Say, I'm so glad I ran into you. I've been meaning to check in on you and your…lady friend." A flash of discomfort crossed her face as she struggled to land on the appropriate term. "Sam, isn't it?"

I nodded, and she continued, "That scene in Cousteau's was beyond upsetting. I wanted to help, but none of us knew what to do."

I must have looked confused because she placed a tender hand on my forearm. "Oh, honey, you don't know?"

I shook my head. "What scene?"

"That dark-haired woman had ahold of her wrist. She wouldn't let Sam go and was saying such terrible things. Just awful. And Sam was so upset. She kept trying to leave, kept telling her to let go and stop touching her. But that woman wouldn't listen. Oh, and the things that woman said…just disgraceful. Hateful. I don't even want to repeat them." Her look was loaded, obviously hopeful I'd ask for details.

But I couldn't speak. My brain was spinning in a hundred directions at once and landing on nothing concrete. *Is it possible? Did Sam tell me the truth? Was I wrong? Did I jump to conclusions and misinterpret what I saw? Did I throw everything away for nothing?*

Impatient for me to probe for more information, Ms. Rhonda pressed on. "I wanted to intervene but, well, I didn't know what to do. None of us did. Half the town was there, and we all wanted to help Sam but didn't know how."

Ever the gossip, Ms. Rhonda dangled the hook. "That woman talked about you too."

That pulled me from my distraction. "Me?"

"Oh, yes. She asked Sam if she thinks of that awful woman when she's..." She leaned toward me to whisper, "...*fucking* you."

I gasped. I actually gasped. "What?"

Ms. Rhonda nodded apologetically. "Oh, I'm so sorry to tell you this, but since nearly everyone at this market heard it or has heard of it, I'd rather you learn it from a friend." She reached for my hand and held it in both of hers. "Give Sam our love and remember"—she patted my hand before letting it go—"James and I love you no matter who you're..." Ms. Rhonda's voice trailed off.

"Dating?" I said helpfully, my eyebrows raised.

She exhaled a sigh of relief. "Yes! Dating! Oh, honey, it's so good to see you and Marilee running a stall at the market again. Be sure you bring Sam out to our gardens soon."

She air-kissed my cheek and moved off into the thickening market crowds.

I turned to Momma, who was fanning herself like a diva with a large leaf of lettuce and smirking triumphantly.

"Told you so."

CHAPTER THIRTY-FOUR

Sam

After another eight long hours on the highway, I checked into my hotel room in Reno, Nevada. The lights, the casinos, the liquor, the women, the gourmet buffets, the gambling… absolutely none of it held any appeal for me. I wanted a hot shower, room service, and sleep. Tomorrow, I'd be back at Jen and Manz's and, if I could have kept my eyes open, I'd have continued driving the final four hours that night.

Naked and waiting for the shower water to get hot, I sent Alyssa a text.

I want your voice to be the first thing I hear in morning and the last thing I hear each night. I'd listen to you read the telephone book just to hear the sweet tones of your voice.

HA! Take that, mocking cursor! No loss for words tonight! Granted, I'd had eight quiet hours alone in the truck to craft it, but that clearly wasn't the point.

My shower was as scalding hot as I'd hoped, and I emerged steaming and scarlet. I picked up my cell phone to move it from on top of my pajamas when I realized I had a text message waiting. From Alyssa. *She wrote back!*

I hastened to unlock my phone to read the message.

Alyssa: Thank you

That was all. Two words, no punctuation and no emojis. But it was so much more important than that. She voluntarily replied. She'd unlocked the door. It wasn't exactly an olive branch, but I was ecstatic to accept even a single olive leaf. It was progress. It was a tiny crack in her armor.

Do I reply? Do I leave it alone? Should I call? I juggled pros and cons, options and pitfalls, while the water on my skin cooled in the room's air-conditioning. I tossed my phone on the comforter to think it through while I dressed.

A phone call would be too much too fast. It might startle her away. But a lack of response felt...I wasn't sure. It felt like I didn't recognize the weight and scope of her gesture. And I didn't want that either.

Okay, another text then. But what? Fuck, it only took me eight hours to perfectly craft the first one! I threw on my Eagles concert tee and a pair of boy shorts. I turned down the lights and crawled into the sheets. Here goes nothing, I thought as I typed out a reply.

I hope I can see you again soon. I miss you.

Short, sweet, and to the point.

I woke early, excited to hit the highway and eager to check for a text response. There wasn't one, but that neither surprised nor disheartened me. I recognized what she had done, and it was enough. I wasn't looking gift horses in the mouth today. I was simply grateful for the gift.

Duffel loaded, a large black coffee in the cup holder, a belly full of breakfast, and I was ready to hit the road. Traffic permitting, I'd be to Manz's house by one o'clock. I sent her a quick text to that effect. She responded that they'd both be back at work, their staycation for my visit done, but I was welcome to make myself at home. Well, her actual response was much snarkier and had a few expletives interlaced, but you get the drift.

I opened another text box to Alyssa.

I am still yours, heart and soul, body and mind. I remain your faithful girlfriend, if you'll have me.

I docked my phone into its holder and began my drive home. *Home.* I marveled at the word while turning onto the highway. A few weeks ago, "home" had been a two-story in Denver with the woman I loved and planned to marry. Home was Denver, with its scenic vistas and crisp mountain air. But now, all of that had evaporated.

Now, home was no longer a place. Home was a feeling, like it had been so many years ago when my parents died. Home wasn't a where—it was a who. The people who loved me. The people who comforted me. The people who refilled spiritual batteries. Home was Jen and Manz, and maybe, hopefully, someday soon, it could include Alyssa.

CHAPTER THIRTY-FIVE

Alyssa

I lay in bed, pondering the day. Yesterday's farmers' market stall had been a success. Several repeat customers and neighbors stopped by, excited to see our return. We chatted and visited, and even managed to sell some items along the way. Momma had been quiet at first, hiding behind her diva sunglasses in the back of the stall. But before long, she was making sales and interacting with acquaintances. Some customers asked when they would see some of her signature bed quilts and quilted tapestries appearing for sale again in the stall. Would she be taking requests? Could an order be placed now? My heart sang to see it—the next step in her healing, seeing her interacting and committing to the future. Sam would be proud.

Sam. I sighed. *What in the world am I going to do?* Ms. Rhonda's revelation yesterday at the market had been nothing short of jaw-dropping. It was no surprise to me that everyone was gossiping about what had happened—that was to be expected in a small town where everyone's nose was so far up in everyone else's business, they could smell what they'd had for breakfast.

What *was* surprising was that Sophia had loudly declared to everyone that Sam and I were "fucking."

Oh my god, just the memory of Ms. Rhonda telling the story made me want to crawl back under the sheets and die. Well, on the bright side, it saved me the chore of coming out. But still, to have my personal life being discussed so freely, and in such vulgar terms, made my face flush with embarrassment. No, embarrassment was simply not a strong enough word. Complete and total mortification.

But, even still, there was, possibly, maybe, perhaps, the tiniest glimmer of good news nestled in all the bad. Sam had been telling the truth. Ms. Rhonda had nothing to gain by lying to me or twisting the truth. She had come to me as a concerned friend with no guile or motive. I believed Ms. Rhonda, which meant…I now believed Sam.

I nearly jumped out of my skin as my cell phone dinged loudly by my head on the nightstand. I leapt for my phone and was surprised to see Manz's name on the screen and—if I allowed myself to admit it—a little disappointed it wasn't from Sam.

Manz: Hey girlie. Thought you should hear this. We should talk.

Hear this? What was she talking about?

A moment later, my phone dinged again as a video loaded to the screen. I pressed play but the screen was black. Confused, I double-checked to see if everything was working correctly, when a woman's voice, silky and elegant, started talking in the darkness of the video.

Woman: You might want to wait to pack anything from the kitchen or dining room though. My guest is *sans vêtements*.

Her French accent was perfect. My limited French returned—"without clothes." *What is this? Why did Manz send this to me?* Then, clear as a bell and seizing my heart, Sam's voice came on the video.

Sam: Manz is right. You really are the Queen of the Cunts, Sophia.

Sophia. I had figured that elegant voice was hers but now I was certain. I immediately hated her, even though I'd never met her. *Real mature, Alyssa.* Suddenly, I felt guilty for listening to this private discussion. But it was shared with me so I could listen to it, right?

Sophia: And she is a loudmouth brat with no tits. *Ouch.*

Sam: Better to have no tits than no soul like you. *Nice one, Sam!*

Sam: At least she could buy tits if she wanted. But you're shit out of luck in the soul department. *Another point scored for Sam.*

I could hear a struggle on the recording.

Sam: Don't fucking touch me. *Oh shit, did Sophia hurt her? Sam sounds pissed.*

Sophia: You're my fiancée. I'll touch whatever I want.

Sam: I am *not* your fiancée. I will never marry you. I don't even want to be in the same room as you!

Sophia: Does Alyssa know you're engaged to be married? *Oh my god, she knows my name?*

Sam: What did you say?

Sophia: I said does Alyssa know you're engaged? Don't look at me like that. Thirty seconds on Google, and I can know anything about anyone. How's she handling the death of her father? Were they close? Unless it's Marilee the Widow you're screwing. But considering that pretty face at the bakery, I'd say it's safe to assume it's Alyssa who's stolen you from me.

There were a few moments of silence. My heart pounded in my temple.

Sophia: Well, maybe we'll save that to unpack another day. Seems the pussy's got your tongue, honey. Besides, I have dinner plans to return to. So if you'll excuse me.

The recording ended. I sat staring at the screen as it dimmed and then went black. Ms. Rhonda was right—Sophia was a monster. Beautiful, sophisticated, and downright evil.

My heart ached for Sam. Sophia seemed cruel and intentionally hurtful. Logic said she hadn't been that way for their entire relationship, but I could imagine that my accusation that she was still with this cold and sinister woman must have hurt that much more. *So stupid.* I knew better than that. In the short time I'd known Sam, I'd consistently found her to be honest and forthright. I'd never suspected deceit from her—not until the incident at Cousteau's, anyway.

I mentally chastised myself. But what, honestly, did it change? Okay, it was more evidence that Sam was being truthful about what I saw—or thought I saw—but did it *change* anything? I was still terrified to let her—or anyone, for that matter—get close enough to hurt me. Perhaps it was easier to just snap the padlock closed on my heart once and for all. Better to be safe than sorry, right?

Yet Momma's words rang through my head, telling me I have too much love to give and receive to squirrel myself away, destined for a life of solitude. And part of me knew she was right. But the other part of me had some very compelling arguments in regard to protecting my heart.

But the chemistry between Sam and me…it was indescribable. It had been instant and all-encompassing. I didn't believe in love at first sight, but what I felt for Sam had me giving that stance serious second thoughts. Nothing and no one in my life had ever made me feel this way before—and in such a short amount of time.

While it was true that making love with her—oops, I mean having sex—was above and beyond the best of my life, it was too simple to chalk it up to discovering I was, in fact, a lesbian. It was more than that—so much more than that. Not only did sex with a woman make me orbit the ecstasy planet without a rocket, but lesbian sex with Sam, specifically, was utterly out of this world. Let's put it this way—lesbian sex, for me, was like I'd tasted strawberries for the first time after a lifetime of eating nothing but zucchini…terrible phallic pun totally intended. It was glorious and sweet. But sex with Sam was like pairing those strawberries with a thousand-dollar glass of cold champagne. I legitimately doubted I'd ever meet her equal. Not that I intended to find out. If I locked my heart's padlock to exclude Sam, it was locked to exclude everyone.

You know what? Nothing has to be decided right now. Besides, Sam is 1,300 miles away in Denver, so what is there to decide anyway? Somehow, even with Sam in Denver, I had a feeling this decision wouldn't lay dormant for long.

I sent a short text to Manz.

Thank you. Yes, we should talk.

Manz quickly replied, as though she was waiting for me to finish the video.

Manz: Damn right, bitch. Come to dinner. 6pm tonight.

Alyssa: Okay. I'll bring wine.

Manz: Well, if you insist (Winking emoji)

I debated wearing jeans and a tank, but I enjoyed getting dressed up now and then. Especially since so many of my days on the ranch were spent in jeans and a shirt I didn't mind getting manure on. During my career in The City, I wore heels and skirt suits every day. But now, living the country life, I had far fewer opportunities to use the items in the other half of my closet.

I chose a knee-length, formfitting black skirt, black stilettos to match, and a deep, rich teal sleeveless, V-neck blouse, skipping underwear as usual when I wore skirts or dresses. It was a hot autumn evening, so I pulled my hair up into a twist. It felt very nice to look pretty, even if my audience was a pair of married lesbians. After all, I wasn't dressing for them—I was dressing for me. I added perfume to my pulse points, made sure Momma had everything she needed, and headed out the door.

I arrived only ten minutes late, armed with two bottles of wine. Manz swung the door wide, and the aromas of Jen's cooking greeted me as warmly as Manz did.

"Bitch, you look incredible!" She gave me a warm, two-armed hug, which I gladly reciprocated, the wine bottles clinking together behind her back. "Come in, come in. Let's pull those corks. We have much to discuss."

I gave the chef a chaste kiss on the cheek and peeked at her cooking.

"Smells fantastic, Jen. What are we having?"

"I went simple tonight—grilled steaks topped with garlic compound butter and grilled onions, and a charred bell pepper, tomato, and mozzarella salad with an olive oil-balsamic reduction dressing."

"If that qualifies as 'simple,' then my goodness, what does a complicated menu include?" I laughed lightly, accepting the glass of red wine Manz handed to me.

"Ten minutes tops, and we can start eating."

I sat on the barstool where I'd sat the first time I'd come to their home. It made me somehow feel close to Sam while simultaneously magnifying her absence. It made me a little homesick for her, which makes no sense whatsoever, but that's the best description for it.

I absently spun my wineglass on the bar counter, enjoying the playful banter between Manz and Jen. Suddenly, a woman's voice came from the door at the far side of the kitchen.

"Manz, have you seen my phone? I want to text…" Sam's voice trailed off as she rounded the corner and saw me. "Alyssa." Her eyes got comically huge. She shot a look to Manz, who shrugged unapologetically. Then her eyes came back to me.

"Hi." The warm timbre of Sam's voice sent a shiver down my spine. It was velvety and soothing on the jagged edges of my heart.

"Hi," I replied, feeling as shocked as Sam looked. I knew immediately this was Manz's doing.

"You're in luck!" Manz interrupted loudly. "You don't need to text Alyssa because she's *right here*." She gestured to me with both hands. She turned to Jen and said, "What are the odds, huh? It's almost like it was meant to be."

Jen rolled her eyes and shook her head at Manz.

I don't know what came over me, but I had a sudden impulse to torture Sam a little. Taking a cue from Sharon Stone in *Basic Instinct*, I uncrossed, spread, and recrossed my legs, giving Sam a private show of my lack of underwear. Her lips parted, and her eyes got even more enormous. With an exaggerated blink, she recovered and crossed the room to greet me.

"You look great," she said, bracing my elbow as I stood up from the barstool. She lightly kissed my cheek as I gave her a warm hug. The woodsy smell of her enveloped me. Momentarily, my head swam as my fantasy and my memories of our night together flooded back.

"You smell great too," she added a moment later.

"Thanks, you too."

She took the barstool next to me, and Manz delivered a glass of wine to her.

"So, you're back?" I said, awkwardly trying to find a place to start.

"Yes, I drove back as soon as I settled the sale of my house in Denver. I arrived this morning."

My mind flashed to the Tacoma I had seen in the driveway. "I saw a truck in their driveway, but I didn't think anything of it. I never imagined it could be yours, back so soon."

"Well, I had no reason to stay. Everything important to me is here." Her look was weighted and intense, and her innuendo caused a tightening in my chest.

"So did your house sell?" I asked, trying to keep the hope out of my voice.

"Yes. Sophia bought me out of my half." After a moment's thought, she continued, "Well, Sophia spends more money than she saves. I think it was her boyfriend that wrote the check. But either way, it'll be finalized once I can sign the rest of the papers. I've already done the first couple batches electronically. The last batch is being overnighted to me so I can get it notarized."

"That's great news. I'm so happy for you."

"So, what's new with you? How's your momma doing?"

"Really great, actually," I said, taking a sip of wine from my glass before returning to twisting it on the bar top. "I had a stall at the farmers' market yesterday, and she joined me. It's the first time she's left the house in ages. She even took some quilting orders for customers, so that was exciting."

"That's really great news," she added, her eyes sparkling.

I debated telling her what I'd learned from Ms. Rhonda. *Eh, why not? Might as well.*

"Do you remember Ms. Rhonda that you met at the market?" I asked, taking a sip of wine.

"Yes, Mr. Westbrook's wife. Your horse instructor."

"Good memory. Yes, I saw her at the market again. She mentioned you…" My voice trailed off.

"Oh?" Sam looked confused. No, maybe concerned. Maybe both.

"She was at Cousteau's. She saw and heard everything."

Her eyebrows launched skyward. "Everything?"

"Everything," I confirmed, stealing a glance at Jen and Manz, who were unabashedly listening to our conversation. "She confirmed your side of the story. All of it. Plus…" I looked at my fingers twirling my wineglass stem. "…a couple parts you left out."

Now Sam looked very confused. "What parts did I leave out?"

"That Sophia loudly announced to the café that you and I are 'fucking.'" I winced internally even saying the word. From Sophia's vile lips, it tarnished something sweet and beautiful. "Well, more specifically, Sophia asked if you think of her when you're fucking me."

Jen's eyes went enormous, and Manz covered her open mouth with her fingertips.

Sam took a deep breath and looked at the ceiling, running her hand through her hair. "She wasn't being quiet, but I didn't think anyone could hear her, either. I'm so sorry, Alyssa. That wasn't her information to blast in the café. I wish I could have prevented it. If she outed you, I—"

"Oh, I don't care about that," I interrupted, speaking honestly. "Actually, she might have done me the favor of putting 'us' out in the open." *Oops, did I just refer to "us" as a current thing, not past tense? Maybe she didn't notice.* "I just hate that she used me to hurt you."

I reached over and squeezed her hand. I didn't even know I was going to do it until it was already happening. *Stupid heart… Quit acting independently of my brain. You're not in control here. I am.*

"I'm so relieved she's out of my life. Relationship over, house sold, all my stuff moved out…It's a fantastic feeling."

"I can imagine. That's how I felt when I finally left Tom."

"Dinner's ready!" Jen suddenly shouted.

"Jesus fucking Christ, woman." Manz playfully smacked her arm with the back of her hand. "Can't you see I'm eavesdropping here? You scared the shit out of me."

We all laughed—most of all Jen who it seems had done it on purpose—and made our way to the dining room to eat.

Once we were seated and served, Manz looked to me and asked, "So?"

"So, what?" I was thoroughly confused.

"So, now that Miss What's-Her-Name's story matches Sam's, do you believe her now? Have you forgiven Sam? Should I reserve a U-Haul? When is the wedding? I have trials coming up, and I need scheduling notice if it'll be a winter wedding. I'm available for babysitting on weekends."

"Manz!" Sam reprimanded.

"What?" she whined. "I'm helping."

"No, you're not." Sam's voice was tight with irritation.

"It's fine, Sam. I promise." I chuckled at Manz's balls-to-the-wall, no-holds-barred style. Now that I knew to expect it, I found her blatant honesty to be refreshing. I continued, "Yes, I believe her. Of course I do. And I don't think I have anything to forgive, since it turns out she did nothing wrong. If anything, I need to ask forgiveness from her." I turned my gaze to Sam's deep green eyes. The golden freckles in her irises were hypnotizing.

"I'll just have to find some way for you to make it up to me." Sam smirked a cocky little half-smile.

Oh, you little devil.

"Dinner was delicious yet again, Jen." I kissed her cheek.

"Thank you so much for coming," Jen replied.

"Move! My turn to hug the hottie." Manz pushed her way between Jen and me, giving me another warm hug.

"No," Sam interjected. "It's *my* turn. So please make like a tree and leave."

"Oh my god." Manz rolled her eyes dramatically. "You'll scare her away with your terrible puns."

I laughed lightly and shook my head at their banter.

"Fine. Babe, it seems our presence is no longer welcome." She hooked her hand in Jen's elbow, and they walked into the house together.

Once the door closed behind them, Sam turned her attention to me. That quiet awkwardness from earlier returned. Sam reached up and rubbed her hand over the short hair on the back of her head. *Clearly, she feels it too.*

Suddenly, Sam started twirling long, imaginary hair around her finger and spoke in an unnaturally high, cheerleader voice. "I had a, like, really great time. So, like, when can I see you again and stuff?"

"Just stop," I said, laughing and putting a hand on her forearm. "It's really not a good look for you."

"Dang," she said, feigning disappointment. "I really thought I had a solid future as a femme."

"No, I like you just the way you are."

She took a small step closer. "I like you too. A lot."

That *we're about to kiss* moment came. But something passed over her face, and she took a small step back again. I closed the distance again, putting my palm on her chest and tilted my face up to hers. My fingertips touched the skin in the hollow of her throat in the V of her collared shirt. Her eyelids drifted closed, and she rested her hand over mine.

She took a deep breath and exhaled slowly. With her eyes still closed, she said, "Alyssa, will you go out to dinner with me?"

I scoffed. "What? We just ate."

"No, I mean, not tonight but—" She was suddenly extremely nervous and tripping over her words. "I mean, this week sometime. Will you have dinner with me? I mean, just me."

I was still confused. "Sam, what are you talking about?"

"I'm sorry," she said, stepping backward and removing my hand from her chest. "My brain won't work with you that close. Let me try again?"

"Okay?" I raised one eyebrow.

"Alyssa, I would like to take you on a date—a real date. Are you free tomorrow night?"

"Yes, of course, but what is this, Sam? I'm so confused."

She closed her eyes again. "I want to start over. I want to do it the right way. I want to take you out on an official first date, since we didn't do that the first time."

I cupped her cheek in my hand. "I'd love that."

She smiled.

"Look at me, Sam."

She silently shook her head no, her eyes still closed.

"Why not?"

"Because if I look into those gorgeous baby blues, I won't be able to resist kissing you."

"And who said you aren't allowed to kiss me?" I asked, playfully indignant.

"I do. Like I said, I want to do this the right way, from the top. I want to take you somewhere nice. Somewhere…elegant." She leaned in and gave a feather-soft kiss to my cheek. "Can I pick you up at five?"

"Yes."

"I can't wait."

CHAPTER THIRTY-SIX

Sam

"Oh my fucking god, Sammy! Would you take a Xanax or something? You're driving me absolutely insane." Manz threw her book at me, missing me by a mile.

"Manz, I'm serious. How do I look?" I asked, smoothing down my necktie over my shirtfront and adjusting my belt to perfect center.

"For the seventeen bazillionth time tonight, you look great. You looked great *without* the tie. You look great *with* the tie. Fuck, she'd be perfectly happy if you walked up wearing *only* a bow tie!"

"A bow tie. Yes! Okay, hold on." I sprinted up the stairs.

"Oh, for fuck's sake," Manz said behind me.

A few moments later, I was preening in front of her again, wearing a dark blue satin dress shirt, a blue silk bow tie in a slightly lighter shade, paired with black Oxfords and black dress pants.

"How's this?" I said, double-checking my tuck and buttons.

"Jennifer Marie! Get down here and help this bitch before I throttle her."

"Like you could even reach that high, babe," Jen said, coming down the stairs, wearing her immaculately bleached and starched chef whites. "Whoa, Sam, you look amazing. Dapper as hell, buddy." She approached me, straightened my bow tie, and brushed something from the top of my shoulder.

"You sure?"

"Absolutely."

"Thank you. I gotta go. I don't want to be late."

"You've got time," Jen said soothingly. "Don't forget the flowers in the kitchen."

"Thank you, Jen. You're the best."

She turned to Manz. "See? It's not that hard."

"See? It's not that hard," she mimicked in a shrill voice. "You are both so annoying. Now someone bring me my book. It's over there." She pointed to where it landed after her terrible throw. I picked it up and set it on the coffee table about two inches too far away for her to reach.

She leaned for the book and realized what I'd done. "Why are you still here? Don't you have somewhere—anywhere—else to be? Jen, if she comes home tonight, be sure to lock her out. She sleeps in her truck tonight."

"Have fun tonight," Jen said, ignoring Manz and handing my keys to me as I picked up the bouquet and my overnight bag...just in case.

My tires hit Alyssa's gravel with thirty seconds to spare. Quick teeth check in the mirror, a deep breath, and I headed to the front door.

"Hey, there," Marilee said at the door. "Boy, you sure look sharp. Come on in. I'll let her know you're here."

"Thank you."

I didn't want to pace, so I sat on the couch. But not pacing made me fidget. I tried not to fidget, which made my knee bounce. *Why am I so incredibly nervous? I've kissed her before. I've made love to her before.* But this felt entirely new and special. I wanted it to be perfect. Jen's wise words rang in my head: You're nervous because you care. If you didn't care, it wouldn't matter. But it matters because *she* matters.

My thoughts were interrupted by the sound of stilettos on the hardwood stairs. I stood and turned, the bouquet of roses before me, to see Alyssa coming down the stairs. She took my breath away. She wore a floor-length black evening gown. It had the slightest shimmer, subtly accentuating her curves and the movement of her body. Thin straps left her shoulders and neck exposed, and her hair was pinned up with tendrils of golden curls escaping. She wasn't wearing a bra, and her high, firm breasts defied gravity. But it was the thigh slit up to her hipbone, her tanned and toned leg appearing and disappearing, that made my mouth go dry. Knowing her tendency to skip undergarments while wearing skirts, I anticipated a wardrobe malfunction at any moment. Or maybe I prayed for one.

I met her at the bottom of the stairs and presented her with a bouquet of pure white roses surrounding a single red rose. She buried her face in the flowers, her eyes locked on mine, inhaling their intense scent.

"Thank you. They're beautiful."

"Alyssa, I…I don't know what to say. You are too beautiful for words."

"Not so bad yourself. You look good enough to eat." She bit her lip.

"No, no, no, my little saboteur. We have dinner reservations."

She took another deep inhale of the roses and set them on the table by the couch.

"Momma, would you put these flowers in a vase for me?"

"Sure thing, baby. Have fun tonight."

I opened the door for her, guiding her elbow as she climbed out of my truck.

"Is this Cacciucco?" Her head spun toward me. "How in the world did you get a reservation on such short notice? It's impossible to get in here."

"I happen to know the executive chef and owner," I said mischievously. "She's married to my sister."

"Wait, what?" Her look of surprise was genuine. "Jen owns Cacciucco?"

I nodded.

"Holy shit, I had no idea."

"Well, Jen's so modest, I'm not surprised. She's not a fame monster. Everyone in town knows she's a chef, but it could be at Denny's or something, not the best restaurant in Sausalito." I considered for a moment. "Maybe the best in the North Bay and beyond. She says her food speaks for itself, and word of mouth is all the advertising she needs."

"She's right. It's award winning. I've been dying to try it."

Alyssa stood staring at the tastefully landscaped entrance, the floor-to-ceiling windows, and the unbelievable view of Richardson Bay stretching into the San Francisco Bay. Angel Island and Alcatraz could be seen in the distance, and beyond that, the Bay Bridge.

We were greeted at the door by a young, androgynous woman, with a faux-hawk and maroon necktie over a black dress shirt. She had a stark white napkin draped over her arm, and you could check your teeth in the shine of her shoes.

"Ms. Monroe, what a pleasure to see you again. And Ms. Johansson, I was told to expect you—very honored to meet you. My name is Alex, and I'll be your personal *serveuse* and *sommelier* for the evening. Anything you need, I am at your service. If you'll follow me." Alex spoke with a slight hint of a southern drawl, which she was clearly trying to conceal.

Alex led us through the restaurant with its elegant touches and enormous rock fireplace in the center. I let Alyssa lead the way and noticed the subtle turn of heads as she walked through. The murmur of voices as she passed made me think they believed she was famous but couldn't place her. I couldn't blame them—she had the beauty and grace of a Hollywood star.

Alex led us out of the restaurant and onto an enormous balcony to the only table, adorned with a short clear bowl of floating rose buds, a bottle of red wine—uncorked to let it breathe—and light from several small candles. The view was spectacular, with seagulls darting and floating over the water as sailboats cut through the waves.

I pulled Alyssa's chair out for her, which she took gracefully. She is truly gorgeous, I thought, trying to tear my eyes away so I could take my own seat.

"Before we begin, the executive chef has informed me there are no allergies or dietary restrictions. Is that correct?"

We both nodded. Alyssa's eyes sparkled in the candlelight.

"The chef has prepared a seven-course *menu dégustation*—a tasting menu," she translated helpfully for us, "in honor of your arrival. However, if you would prefer to select from the menu, that is agreeable as well."

I looked to Alyssa to decide for us.

"Everything Jen cooks is fantastic, so I would like to try the menu dégustation." She tried the French pronunciation and failed miserably, bringing a warm smile to my lips.

Alex reacted slightly to Alyssa's casual reference to the executive chef as "Jen" but quickly recovered. Alex looked to me, and I nodded slightly in confirmation.

"Excellent." Alex poured two glasses of red wine, expertly turning the lip of the bottle on the white napkin on her forearm to prevent any drips. "Unless you require a beverage from the bar, I will excuse myself to begin your first course."

"Thank you, no. The wine is perfect," she said, taking an appreciative sip.

I gave a small shake of my head, not taking my eyes off the bombshell sitting across from me, and Alex disappeared back into the restaurant.

"Sam, this is…" Her words trailed off.

I reached across to briefly squeeze her hand. She didn't need to finish. I understood. I'd felt the same way my first time here, and Jen's improvements made it even more impressive than it had been, especially with this magnificent creature sitting across the table from me.

"Jen found Alex when she was just a punk kid, getting into trouble and destined for jail time. Jen gave her a job bussing dishes, and things shifted. Alex started to blossom. And she climbed her way up to be Jen's front of house. Since then, she's gone to sommelier training and just completed the culinary academy at Greystone in Napa." I took a sip of my wine and lowered my voice, even though we were entirely alone on the enormous balcony. "Jen let me in on a secret—the first course is Alex's creation, and we're the guinea pigs. But we can't tell Alex we know. Jen says she'd be mortified if we knew we were trying her food, not Jen's."

Alyssa mimed zipping her lips closed as Alex approached with two small plates.

"Here we have our *amuse-bouche* course—a fresh Dungeness crab cake tucked inside two fried green tomato slices with a house-made remoulade sauce. Enjoy." Alex topped off our wineglasses, wiped the bottle lip with a fresh towel, and quickly disappeared again.

Speared with a piece of twisted bamboo was a tiny sandwich about the size of a half dollar. Two thinly sliced fried green tomatoes flanked the golden-brown crab cake. Tiny but mighty, the flavors exploded in my mouth. The flavors were expertly balanced—sweet versus sour, acidic versus creamy, and crunchy versus soft, with just a hint of heat from the sauce. Absolutely decadent.

Alyssa hummed with pleasure. When Alex returned to the table, she stated, "Tell the chef I give it two thumbs up. Outstanding."

"I agree! I could eat about twelve more of those and call it dinner."

"Me too." Alyssa laughed quietly. Alex quietly disappeared with a barely perceptible smile.

After a moment, Alyssa asked, "So, now that your house is sold, what are your plans?" She was trying to appear nonchalant, but her intense focus gave her away.

"Jen and Manz will let me stay as long as I need, so I'm not in any rush. But if we—" I halted abruptly and didn't finish the sentence. "It'll be around here, wherever I end up. This is home, and I recognize that now."

Alex arrived with chilled carrot ginger soup with a drizzle of sweetened cream, and then quietly disappeared again.

"What about work?" she asked.

"I messaged my agent that I'm ready for more training jobs, so something will come through soon, I'm sure." I grew quiet for a moment, drawing my spoon through the spiral of cream. "I don't know. My dream is to build an equine therapy ranch. Have a herd of a half dozen to a dozen horses of different sizes and temperaments. Take on clients who need what equine therapy offers. It's all still just a dream, but I feel like I'm closer than ever."

"So, explain this to me. How would this work?" Alyssa seemed genuinely curious.

"Well, I'd have a couple horses who were already trained and safe to interact with kids or people with special needs. But I'd also love to have a sort of advanced course, where the clients help train the horses and win those breakthroughs for themselves. Petting and riding a horse is therapeutic, but winning an animal's trust and seeing them accomplish the amazing things you've taught them is another level of achievement." I took a bite of soup, the sweet and spicy combination a delight on my palate. "I have a very specific skill set that saved me from some extremely dark times, and I'd love to share those skills with others who need it."

"Momma remembers every word you said to her about your equine therapy plan." She chuckled quietly. "I think she might be more in love with you than I am."

My eyes shot up to meet hers, and I watched as the blush creep over her face, neck, and chest. I didn't comment on it, just basked in the warmth of it.

"Momma has been researching it. She wants to be a part of it, if you get it off the ground." She grew quiet, playing with her soup. "It's so wonderful to see her invested in things again—the market, the quilting, the equine therapy. She really has come back to me," she said as she brought her eyes up to mine. "And I have you to thank for it."

"Nah," I said humbly as Alex silently cleared our soup bowls and replaced them with a plate of three perfectly seared scallops. "I just showed you both the path. Y'all walked it, not me."

"But I don't think we would have ever found the path if it weren't for your help." That devilish look flashed in her eyes again. "I'll just have to find a way to thank you." She took a luxurious sip of wine before continuing, "That's two things I owe you now."

Something low in my stomach tightened in anticipation.

CHAPTER THIRTY-SEVEN

Alyssa

The scallops melted on my tongue. The lobster ravioli in lemon caper cream sauce was utterly divine. The Wagyu beef steaks with cabernet sauce were beyond decadent. Alex appeared and disappeared silently, bringing course after course of better and better dishes. Our conversation drifted easily from topic to topic, learning about one another—my time in college and subsequent career in The City, her career and some of the famous actors she'd met, and other fairly generic getting-to-know-you topics.

As Alex cleared our steak plates, I slouched back against my chair. "I don't know if I can eat any more."

Sam chuckled. "We still have two more courses."

As if on cue, Alex manifested at my elbow.

"Here we have the cheese course—an aged Brie from Paris on the right, a smoked Gouda from Holland in the middle, and a blue cheese from here in California on the left. There are also toasted baguette rounds and whole roasted garlic cloves. Enjoy."

"Whole roasted garlic cloves? So much for my good-night kiss," Sam teased, smiling and biting her bottom lip.

"You're in luck. I just happen to love garlic." I popped a baguette toast topped with Brie and a roasted garlic clove into my mouth. "Besides, if we both eat garlic, it cancels out."

"I'll have to discuss this course choice with the chef," she said, pulling a playfully angry face. She spread garlic across her toast, added a slice of smoked Gouda, and took a bite. "Mmm, never mind. This is perfect."

Bellies full and plates empty, Alex arrived with the seventh and final course.

"Here we have a New York style cheesecake, topped with a twenty-five-year-old single-barrel bourbon caramel sauce with house-made spiced whipped cream."

"Dear god." My eyes got huge. "I have died and gone to heaven."

After Alex left the table, I stage-whispered to Sam, "Is it poor taste to request a to-go box? If I eat any more, I will no longer fit in this dress."

Sam laughed at me, spearing a bite. "You've got try it, at least."

I loaded my fork, steadying myself for even more food.

"Cheers," she said, holding her cheesecake fork out to me.

"Cheers." I took the bite into my mouth and extended mine to hers. I could feel her lips—those delicious, begging-to-be kissed lips—wrap around the fork and pull, wiping the tines clean. I momentarily forgot to finish my bite, having lost myself in the intimacy of the action. My nipples tensed, free and braless against my evening gown, and aching for her contact. I've never been jealous of a fork before, I thought. My imagination wandered, inviting those lips, those teeth, that orgasm-inducing tongue to all of my most sensitive and aroused places. I was vaguely aware that Sam had said something, but my brain couldn't grasp it.

"Alyssa? Are you okay?" Sam repeated.

I blinked rapidly, refocusing my eyes on Sam.

"Yes, sorry. What did you say?"

"I asked if you liked the dessert." A knowing smile spread across her face, that cocky half-smile that made my knees weak and made my insides tighten in anticipation. "Penny for your thoughts? That look in your eyes was…illicit."

I was suddenly shy. *What the fuck, Alyssa? You are not shy or timid. Ovary up, cowgirl.*

"I was thinking…never mind." I couldn't finish. *Fuck. What is wrong with me?*

Sam's head tilted slightly to one side. "Tell me," she commanded, her gaze intense and unwavering as she slid another sensual bite of cheesecake into her mouth.

I took a steadying, courage-building breath. "I was thinking how lucky that fork is, getting to touch those lips, those teeth, that tongue." I slipped off one stiletto and traced my toe up her pant leg. "I was thinking I want to ride your face until I come in your mouth, my fingers knotted in your hair." I leaned forward on the table, pressing my breasts together and hoping my gown had a little more gap in the neckline than appropriate for a Michelin star restaurant. "I was thinking I want to spread your legs, bury my nails in your ass, and fuck you with my tongue while you orgasm over and over and over."

Sam's mouth drifted open as I spoke, her eyes unblinking. Without breaking her eyes from mine, she raised one finger in the air. "Check, please!"

Driving home, Sam reached over to rest her hand on my thigh. Her thumb lazily stroked the skin of my thigh where the split in my gown exposed my leg.

"I meant to ask," Sam started, stealing a look at me while she drove.

"Yes?" I played softly with the sensitive skin inside her elbow.

"You seem to have a habit of not wearing undergarments when you dress up. I was curious if that applies to formal wear as well."

"Good question. What's your guess?"

"Chastity belt with padlock," she replied.

I laughed aloud. "You're ridiculous."

"I'm right, huh? Solid iron or chain mail?"

I debated briefly how to respond. *Fuck it. Go for it. Be brave.*

"You tell me." I uncrossed my legs and spread my knees slightly. My blood pressure skyrocketed as her hand began to move. Her fingers explored up the thigh split in my dress to my hipbone. Her warm fingertips explored briefly, searching for fabric and finding none. It was getting difficult to breathe. Her fingers found the crease at the top of my thigh and began following it down, reminiscent of her teasing touch in the tack room. An involuntary little groan escaped my lips. Still walking down the crease in my thigh, her fingers at last found my thin, freshly trimmed strip of pubic hair, which was completely unhindered by fabric. Her fingers wandered a little farther until she encountered the hot, slick wet of my arousal.

This time, it was her turn to groan. She seemed to battle with herself, deciding whether to explore more or stop now that she had her answer. I decided to help her out with her decision, spreading my thighs a little farther and slightly lifting my hips into her warm hand.

"Jesus, Alyssa, you're going to make me wreck the truck," she said, her voice strained, but she didn't pull away her hand. Instead, she continued drawing slow, torturous circles through the slick arousal that had escaped my sex.

I relaxed my head, enjoying the delicious warmth of her hand between my legs, simultaneously touching me and *not* touching me. It wouldn't be enough to push me over the edge, but that clearly wasn't the objective here. This was divine torture, and I promised myself she'd pay for it later.

"I'm sorry," she said, withdrawing her hand. "I can't concentrate on driving. It's too..." Her words trailed off as she put both hands on the steering wheel. I watched her knuckles whiten as her grip tightened. I smiled, crossing my legs again and appropriately rearranging my gown.

"Come inside," I said at the base of the steps of my house. I made my voice firm. It wasn't a request.

I grabbed her hand to pull her inside, but her feet didn't move. I turned and looked at her. Her face was a blend of several emotions—desire, fear, indecision. Suddenly, it dawned on me. We needed to see this first date through to its expected conclusion. Sam's chivalry required it.

Still holding her fingers loosely in my hand, I turned to face her. I stood close but maintained a respectful distance from her.

"Let me start over. I'll follow your lead. Or at least I'll try," I said with a self-deprecating laugh. "Okay?"

"Okay." She exhaled a deep sigh of relief.

I cleared my throat to reset.

"Thank you for dinner, Sam. It was truly wonderful. I really enjoyed myself."

"Me too." Her voice was quiet. "Can I see you again?"

Her tone was legitimately nervous, which melted me. This sweet, tender woman…her vulnerability captured my heart. *I wish I could be so vulnerable. She is braver than I am.*

"I'd love that." I stepped closer, the halo of the porch light washing us in warm, yellow light.

"You are unbelievably beautiful tonight," she said. "You make it hard to breathe even looking at you."

"Thank you," I whispered.

She inched closer.

"This dress is…" Her voice trailed off as she placed a cautious hand on my hip. "Incredibly flattering."

"Thank you," I repeated, resting my hand on her wrist at my hip. I ran my hand up her arm to just below her shoulder and let it linger there.

She took a half step forward, still taller than me despite my stiletto heels. I lifted my face to hers. *Let her lead, Alyssa. Let go of the control. Surrender. Submit.*

Her eyes locked on mine as she slid her hand behind my neck, her thumb softly stroking my cheek. I basked in her touch, savoring the silky feel of her skin on mine.

Kiss me, I thought, willing her to do it but knowing I couldn't say it out loud. *Go on, kiss me.* The wait was driving me insane, threatening to overload the circuits in my hammering heart.

Her eyes darted rapidly between my eyes and my lips. I watched as she bit her bottom lip, and I nearly lost my control to wait, to let her advance, to let her kiss me. Even still, a small purr escaped my throat.

The sound seemed to be the permission she needed. Sam's eyes drifted shut, and she closed the distance between her lips and mine. That first touch—that first soft, sensual brush of her lips against mine—sent thrilling volts of electricity down into my stomach.

Let her set the pace, Alyssa. The struggle between my intense desire to pounce on her and take what I wanted was in direct conflict with my want to give this to her, to let her have this moment exactly as she had envisioned it.

The kiss was sweet and gentle. I released my entire soul into it, feeling light and free as I followed her anywhere she wanted to go. I put my hand on the dip of her waist, my other hand still on the muscle of her upper arm, which was flexed and taut as she held my face in her hands.

At the first opening of her lips against mine, I feared my knees would collapse. I invited her in, waiting anxiously for the first tentative touch of her tongue. And when it came, the feeling was powerful and sensual. It truly was like a first kiss, exploratory and new. I caressed her tongue with mine, feeling a heated flush spread over my exposed shoulders. *I could kiss this woman for hours.*

Her kiss became more insistent as she kissed me deeper. Her breath quickened, and mine sped up to match. I wrapped one arm up her back and the other to cradle her jaw in my palm. She gently bit my lip and released it. Seemingly unsatisfied, she bit my lip again, harder this time, and suddenly sweet and sensual was no longer an option. She pulled my hips in tight against hers, my hardened nipples grazing the fabric of my dress to my exquisite delight.

"Is your mom awake?" She spoke the words into my mouth, her lips and tongue still dancing with mine. She began kissing down my throat, nipping my skin lightly with her lips.

"She went to bed hours ago."

"Can I come in?" Her voice husky and low with desire. The warm tip of her tongue licked its way up my throat to my ear.

"I might die if you don't."

I quietly closed the bedroom door behind me. The bathroom light cast only enough light to see, and Sam's lean, muscular silhouette was in the middle of the room, waiting for me.

"I want to see you," she said. "All of you."

I stepped forward a step and slipped one thin strap from my shoulder. She smiled but let me continue. I slipped the second strap off my shoulder as I took another step toward her. Her eyes were hungry, raking my body from head to foot as she watched my every move. I reached under my armpit and slowly unzipped my gown. The fabric slithered and slid down my curves, puddling on the floor at my feet. I took another step forward, stepping out of the fabric, and stood before Sam, naked except for my heels.

I placed my palms on her chest, my face turned up to hers. She kissed me tenderly and placed her hands on the bare skin of my waist. The warmth of her hands sent goose bumps spreading out over my skin. I leaned into her, my nipples brushing against her dress shirt.

"What do you want? Your wish is my command," I said in a low, sultry voice.

Sam's voice was also low and quiet. "I want to give you whatever you want."

I didn't need time to think about it. "Well," I said slowly, trying to not seem too eager. "I've never used any…" I couldn't bring myself to say it. "I have used them by myself, of course, but I've never been comfortable enough with a partner to try anything like that, or to even suggest it."

She started kissing and nibbling my neck and shoulders again, making it difficult to remain standing. I could feel that cocky half-smile against my throat.

"Any what? You're going to have to be more…" She sucked lightly below my ear. "Specific."

"You know exactly what I'm talking about. I want you to fuck me with…um…if you have one."

"With what?" Her tone was coy and teasing. "I want to hear you say it."

"Sam," I said, my voice a little whimper.

She deeply kissed my jugular, teeth skimming my sensitive skin, and my head swam with lust. I could feel her tongue dancing on my skin.

"Alyssa, say it."

I rose up onto tiptoes, pulled her head down to my lips, and whispered, "I want you to fuck me with a strap-on, if you have one."

As I released her head, her devilish grin was spread from ear to ear.

"Lie on that bed and don't move, okay?"

I agreed, and she left the room.

I removed my heels, and I heard the front door open. I lay on the bed, and I heard her truck unlock. I adjusted the pillows behind my head, arranging my hair, and heard her truck door slam. *Is she leaving? She'd better not be leaving!* But within moments, I heard the front door open and close again, and I was relieved to hear her footsteps on the stairs.

She came back into the room, dropping a bag on the floor, and quietly closed the door behind herself. I lay, naked and vulnerable, on the bed and watched while she removed her bow tie. She kicked out of her shoes. She unbuttoned her shirt, showing a tight black tank top underneath. I watched every movement with unblinking interest.

"That tank top is incredibly sexy on you," I whispered.

"Thank you." Her eyes locked on mine as she unbuckled her belt and pants button, and slowly lowered the zipper. They fell to the floor and her boy shorts soon followed. Her eyes stayed glued on mine, but mine wandered greedily over every new patch of exposed skin. She lifted the tank, taking her sports bra with it, and stripped both off over her head. My eyes devoured the voluptuous bounce of her breasts as they came free of the elastic band. She stood in front of me, naked at the foot of my bed. She bent and unzipped her bag, making a few selections which she set on the foot of the bed. It was too dark to see, but that was okay. The element of surprise was exciting.

Leaving the items at the foot of the mattress, she crawled toward me, kneeling between my knees. She lowered herself over the top of me, using her strong shoulders to hold herself up. She dipped her head to kiss me softly, and I eagerly kissed her back. I ran my hands up her sides, delighted to see her shiver at my touch.

"I need to feel you. Please," I begged, softly tugging her down with my hands.

She lowered herself down, her body pressed against mine. The sudden warmth of her skin made my toes curl. I wrapped my arms around her, holding her close as she kissed my shoulders, my neck, my jaw, and finally my lips.

I lifted my knees, welcoming the contact of her hips against me. With a soft groan, she pressed herself between my legs. I kissed her deeply, tangling my fingers in the short hair on the back of her head. Slowly—achingly slowly—she began to move her hips. The repeated pressure and release woke my clit, which began to throb with its own heartbeat. The sensation was driving me insane. I wanted to claw her back. I wanted to squirm. I wanted more, more, more. But I exercised my small amount of remaining willpower to let her have this her way.

She slid her hips away, kissing her way over my breasts, down my stomach, and kissed my landing strip. I felt the warm tip of her tongue, licking the soft, freshly shaved skin. She groaned loudly, and the vibrations made my hands clench into fists. The feeling was exquisitely satisfying and torture at the same time. Her tongue pressed and slipped into me, at last making warm, silky wet contact with my aching clit. A gasp escaped my throat, and I reached to grasp my hardened nipple to ease my need for more.

She continued teasing me, building my arousal, while she did something else with the items at the foot of the bed, multitasking surprisingly effectively. My anxiety—or maybe it was excitement—rose as I heard the metallic clink of rings and the whizz of leather straps being pulled through them.

Once she'd finished her setup, she added her fingers to my delicious torture, playing softly with my entrance. The shockwave it sent through my body jolted all the way to my scalp.

"God, you're so wet, baby," she murmured between my legs, the vibrations sending another electric thrill through my body.

"Sam, please, I need you inside me."

With an effortless push, her fingers plunged deep inside of me while her tongue continued its circular laps around my swollen clit. I gasped hard, and my back arched. Her fingers stroked in and out of me, driving me closer and closer to orgasm. My breathing became ragged and quick as my fist gripped the fitted sheet.

As my climax approached, her warm tongue unexpectedly left my clit to kiss her way back up my stomach to my breasts. She continued sliding in and out of me while she sucked and nibbled on first one nipple, then the other, which I released to allow her access. She kissed her way up to my mouth and, in one swift, effortless movement, she rolled me on top of her, my hips straddling her stomach. *Jesus, she is so fucking strong.*

I felt something resting against my ass and, with one quick, exploratory hand, I verified my suspicion. Sam smirked as the look of understanding crossed my face.

"Tell me when," I said, my muscles and voice taut with unspent frustration.

"Go ahead, baby. I'm ready when you are."

Baby. It melts me every time.

I lifted my hips and guided her toy to my entrance. Slowly, I lowered my hips, gasping at the fullness and pressure it delivered.

"You okay?" she said, looking up at me and sliding her hands up my thighs.

"Oh god, yes." I breathed out slowly as I lowered myself the rest of the way, taking her entire length into me. I leaned forward, placing my hands on either side of her head, and began to rock my hips, pulling her in and out of me.

I groaned with each incredible rock of my hips. Surprisingly, Sam began to pant and groan as well.

"Can you feel it?" I asked.

She nodded vigorously. "The strap…it slipped…it's…" She didn't finish—her pleasure was obvious.

She slid her hand farther up my gyrating thigh, dropping her thumb down to my clit.

"Oh, fuck." I gasped as each thrust of my hips pushed her deep inside of me while she simultaneously stroked my clit with her thumb.

My speed increased, finding a pace that was bringing my climax closer, as I pushed her deeper and faster into me. My gasps came faster, mingling with the lower tone of her moans. And still, she stroked and stroked my clit, moving her hips in time with mine, meeting me as I pushed her deeper and deeper into me.

Her breathing was becoming gasps. *Is she going to orgasm with me? She just might be on the brink with me.* Reading my mind, she reached her free hand up to grasp my breast. She kneaded my nipple between her fingertips, harder and harder, until everything changed. A zapping current flooded my body, triangulating between my nipple, my clit, and my vagina. My movements became fever pitched and aggressive, fucking this gorgeous woman between my legs hard as she stroked my clit and mercilessly teased my breast.

I realized, as my head began to swirl, I was holding my breath, and my groans of pleasure had fallen silent. Sam's moans continued unabated as I furiously fucked her, relishing the soft friction of her thumb against my clit versus the slick friction of her toy inside me. My brain couldn't process it all at once—having her deep inside me, the stroking of my clit, and the toying of my nipple, all while looking heartbreakingly sexy as she fought her orgasm until I could join her. Still holding my breath, I began to see flashes of light as the pressure of my orgasm grew.

Suddenly, in an explosion of breath and movement, my orgasm took hold of me, grinding myself hard against Sam's thumb and toy. My insides clenched hard around her as wave after wave of spasm rocked my core. I grabbed her wrist hard, keeping her thumb there, yes *right there*, against my clit as I rode the intense high of my climax.

"Oh, fuck, I'm gonna come!" Sam quickly sat up, her face in my breasts and her arm tight around my ribs as her own climax crested, rocking her hips in unison with mine. Our sweat-slicked bodies melded into one as we continued thrusting and rocking together until we were both satiated. As our bodies slowed to a rest, she continued hugging me, her temple resting on my breasts. Her breathing began to slow, and I softly traced my fingers over the silky soft skin of her back and shoulders. Soon, her arm released its hold on me, and she fell back onto the pillow, utterly spent. I climbed off to lie beside her, touching as much of her skin with my own as I could. I pulled the sheet up over us, my sweat-soaked skin cooling in the night air.

"I love you, Sam." She didn't respond. Her slow rhythmic breathing told me she'd already fallen asleep. Nestled perfectly in the comfort and safety of her arms, I drifted off to heavy, exhausted sleep.

CHAPTER THIRTY-EIGHT

Sam

The sky was barely starting to lighten from the black of night to the blues and lavenders of morning when I woke, confused as to where I was. As the sleep haze cleared from my eyes, I recognized Alyssa's golden waves of hair sharing the pillow I was using. I was wrapped around her, my strap-on still cinched around my hips and probably stabbing her in the back. *Oops, sorry Alyssa. Did I fall asleep so fast that I didn't even remove it? My god. She wore me out!*

I backed my hips away a little and, quietly as I could, removed the strap-on. I debated snuggling back into Alyssa's warm body and trying to sleep again. But knowing my inability to sleep in, I knew I'd just end up waking her earlier than necessary.

I slipped out of bed and covered her gorgeous, naked curves with the comforter. I moved quietly to the bathroom where I relieved my aching bladder and washed my strap-on before putting it away in my bag. I debated how to spend my morning while the delicious creature sleeping beyond the door slept. The memory of the promised but never delivered croissants and sliced sourdough from Cousteau's Pâtisserie flashed in my mind. *If we're doing a do-over, we should do-over that memory as well. Perfect.*

With my overnight bag tucked back into the floorboard of my truck, I drove to Cousteau's. It was nearly seven and the bakery was already open, the early risers beginning to arrive for their caffeine and pastry needs. I paid the cashier thirty dollars in cash, telling her to keep the change.

Back out on the sidewalk, a man's voice called to me from behind.

"Samantha Monroe, is that you?"

I turned in confusion—*I don't know any men here*—and my stomach dropped to see the tall, muscular form of Tom Kentfield only a step or two behind me.

Fuck. Not today. The hair on the back of my neck stood up.

"Hey," I said coolly over my shoulder and continued walking back to my truck.

"Well, that's not a very warm hello." His voice had the sinister sweetness of a movie villain. "Whatcha got there? Croissants, huh?"

He snatched the box from my hands and jogged a few steps ahead of me into the parking lot.

Seriously? What is it with people in this town stealing croissants from me? What a classic schoolyard bully move. Figures.

Learning from my last experience, I immediately turned on my heel to go back into Cousteau's to buy a second box of croissants. *Plus, I'll have witnesses. I do not trust this asshole.*

"Hey, hey, hey, hold up. C'mon, I'm kidding. Here's your box back."

I stopped to see him holding the white pastry box out to me. Suspecting a trick, I didn't immediately reach for it.

"Here. Seriously, you can have it."

I took the box and continued walking to my truck without saying anything.

"Hey, don't walk away from me. Just stop and talk to me for a minute."

Without turning around, I said, "No, thank you. I need to go. Have a good day."

"I said…" His enormous hand grabbed my upper arm. Hard. Really hard. Something popped inside my arm. His tone dropped into a snarl. "Don't fucking walk away from me."

I spun into his grip, meeting him nose-to-nose. Well, not quite nose-to-nose since he had several inches of height over me, but anyway.

"Let go of me *now*." I growled the words through clenched teeth.

"Not on your life," he growled back. "I have a few things to say to you first."

"I'm not interested. Let go." My fingers were starting to lose feeling, and I feared I'd drop the box of croissants.

"She's not gay, you know. She likes dick. *My* dick. And soon, she'll come to her senses and come back to me. She's not a fucking dyke like you."

"Fuck you, Tom. Let go."

He laughed a dark, foreboding laugh. "Oh my god. You think you love her, don't you? Little pervert. What, you think you're a man? You think you'll ever be man enough for her? You think you can satisfy her like I do? You fucking queers are all the same."

He let go of my arm and kicked my hip, sending me and the pastry box flying. I was able to stay standing after a few stumbling steps, but the croissants scattered across the pavement of the parking lot.

Time slowed as I debated my next move. Run to the café? Run to the truck? Turn and challenge him? Scream? None of them seemed like viable options. I opted to try to simply get into the truck and leave as quickly as I could.

"Fucking douche," I said under my breath as I took the truck keys from my pocket. *Three more steps to safety. Just three more steps.* I unlocked the truck with my key fob.

"Fucking faggot."

The back of my skull exploded with white-hot pain. I felt the keys slip from my fingers, and the world went black.

CHAPTER THIRTY-NINE

Alyssa

The smell of freshly brewed coffee pulled me from sleep. I stretched to the four corners of the bed, luxuriating in the feeling of cool sheets on my naked skin.

Naked skin? Why am I naked?

Deliciously arousing memories of riding Sam's hips while we orgasmed together put a huge smile across my face.

Wait. Where is Sam? Ahh, yes. That must be the reason for the coffee smell. I pulled on a clean tank top and comfy shorts—no underwear would be a treat for Sam to discover later, I decided—and headed downstairs. To my surprise, Momma was in the kitchen, not Sam.

"Where's Sam?" I asked through a yawn, covering my gaping mouth with my fingertips.

Momma looked confused. "Sam? I haven't seen her since yesterday."

"Huh." It was my turn to look confused. "Maybe she's out feeding or visiting the animals."

I filled two coffee mugs, slipped on my boots, and headed to the horse corral. Hickory heard me coming and nickered loudly from his stall. I opened all three stalls and gave each horse some pets and scratches before tossing leaves of hay out into the pasture. No sign of Sam.

I made my way to the chickens. I released my hens to a flurry of fluffed feathers and excited clucking. I tossed grains and feed out for their breakfast and checked their water supply. All good, but still no Sam.

The pigs were also hungry, so I delivered their breakfast with some belly scratches. I peeked beyond the pig enclosure to the orchard and beehives. Sam wasn't there either.

I returned to the house, still carrying two mugs of coffee—one mostly empty and one lukewarm. Momma was stirring scrambled eggs in a skillet while crispy bacon sat ready on a plate.

"She's not out with the animals."

Momma turned to face me, spatula in hand. "Maybe she went into town? Or back to her friends' house? Is her truck here?"

"I didn't even think to check." I backtracked to the front door. "Her truck isn't here."

"Yeah, she must have gone into town or something," she said, returning to the skillet. "She'll be back soon." She transferred the eggs onto two plates. "Did she leave a note? Or send you a text?"

"Oh my god," I said, frustrated with myself. "I came downstairs so fast, I didn't even look."

I trotted up the stairs, checking the nightstand and my cell phone. Nothing. I called her cell phone. After a half dozen rings, her voice mail answered.

"This is Sam Monroe. Leave a message. Or better yet, just text me."

I chuckled at her outgoing message before leaving mine. "Hey, it's Alyssa. We're awake now, and Momma made breakfast. I can't wait to see you, baby."

I hung up and headed back down the stairs. Momma was seated at the table with our plates but hadn't started eating yet. Her attention was on me, waiting for an update.

I held up my darkened phone. "Nothing."

"I wouldn't worry about it. That girl is head over heels for you, baby. She's got her reasons. Now," she said, pushing out my chair with her toe, "come sit and eat."

Breakfast came and went with no sign from Sam. Lunch and ranch chores were completed and still nothing. I pulled out my cell phone to check for the twenty-seventh time in the last hour. Still nothing. I opened a text box to Sam.

I miss you. Call me please. I'm getting worried.

By the time dinner rolled around, my mind began traveling down darker paths. *She split, plain and simple. She left the entire state of Colorado to come here after catching Sophia cheating on her. And now, she's done it to me. She freaked out after the intensity of last night—our date and our amazing lovemaking afterward. Or maybe my whispered words of love. So fucking stupid. I could kick myself. It was too much too fast, and she abandoned ship.*

Fuck, Alyssa, you're such a goddamned fool. You let your guard down, thinking this would be different. Thinking you'd be safe. Thinking this one—this woman—would be special. And here I am, alone and hurting again. Nothing is different. Nothing is special. Same shit, different day.

It's not worth it. It's not worth the heartbreak and pain I keep going through. I tried—I really did try. I let her back in, and now I'm right back where I started. I'm done with love.

And just like that, the iron gates surrounding my heart slammed shut again.

I woke the second morning with still no word from Sam. To say my heart was shattered was too simple of a description. I felt betrayed. I felt unworthy and unlovable. I was broken and irreparable. No one would ever love me. I clearly wasn't worthy of true, reciprocal love. But that didn't matter anyway, because no one was going to get close enough to try ever again.

Momma tried to talk to me, to give me hope and to keep me open to reasonable explanations. But it'd been two days without a text, without a phone call, without showing her face or giving me an explanation for her disappearance. As time stretched on, hour by hour, the demise of our budding relationship became harder and harder to deny.

Momma suggested I ask Manz and Jen for info about Sam, but I resisted. Why? So they could confirm what I already knew? Or worse, force them to lie to me on her behalf? No, I wouldn't do that. This was between Sam and me, not Manz and Jen. I didn't want or need their excuses or platitudes. I knew where the lines were drawn. They were her friends, and I recognized where their loyalties would fall. Plus, if they had anything they wanted to tell me, there was nothing stopping either of them from reaching out to me. So I decided to save all of us the awkwardness and leave them out of it entirely. Easier that way. And less painful for me.

On the third morning with still nothing from Sam, Jen, or Manz, I came to a decision. I stuffed it all into the dark recesses of my mind and turned my back on it—on us. It was time to walk away. Time to move forward. Time to move on and forget Sam ever existed.

I took a deep breath, steeled my nerves, and moved on with life. My single, loveless life.

CHAPTER FORTY

Alyssa

My phone buzzed in the butt pocket of my jeans as I cleaned out Hickory's stall. I paused to check the caller ID: Manz.

Great. Here we go. This is the phone call where they tell me Sam panicked and bolted, doing Sam's dirty work of breaking up with me. No more wondering. Time to rip off the Band-Aid, once and for all. I took a steadying breath and answered the call.

"Hey, Manz." My voice sounded resigned.

"Alyssa? Hey, girl. It's about Sam."

I ran through the fourth-floor elevator doors as soon as they cracked open. My running footsteps echoed through the hallways of the intensive care unit. My brain spiraled in twelve directions simultaneously with Manz's words. *Sam's in the hospital. Beaten. Found unconscious. Coma. Brain injury. Broken bones. Unconscious for three days.*

"Hey! There's no running in here," a male nurse yelled at me from the nurses' station.

I didn't care. I kept running, watching the room numbers drop one by one until I reached Room 417 at last. My boots skidded to a stop as several faces turned in my direction from inside the room.

I looked quickly at the bed. *This must be the wrong room. Sam's not here.* I leaned back to check the room number: 417. I looked back into the room. *But that's not Sam. That can't be my beautiful Sam. It just can't be.*

"Alyssa." Jen's familiar voice broke through my confusion. "Come here, sweetheart. Follow me."

She gently took my arm and led me to the side of the bed. Sam's face—if that was in fact her—was utterly unrecognizable with swelling and the purple-black bruising blooming across her eyes and nose like morbid flowers. Three butterfly strips of gauze tape crossed the bridge of her nose. Clean, white gauze wrapped around the top of her head, plastering her short, dark hair to her forehead. Tubes and wires ran in every direction. Monitors and screens beeped and dropped liquids into long, snaking tubes from bags hung on a metal pole. Oxygen flowed to her nose, and the lowered neckline of her hospital gown showed more sticky pads on her chest. Her eyes were grotesquely swollen and closed, and except for the rhythmic rise and fall of her chest, she was eerily motionless.

I wasn't sure if I stood there for one minute or one hour, tears flowing down my face in torrents. My fixated stare at Sam was finally broken by the warm, comforting hand of Jen, who guided my inanimate body down into a chair beside the hospital bed. I reached for Sam's hand, which had a plastic sensor taped into place over her index finger. Her hand was warm and soft but disconcertingly limp. A fresh wave of tears flooded over me.

Oh god, no. This can't be my Sam. She has blood crusted in her ear. Her eyes are closed. Is she okay? What are all these wires and tubes for? I need to clean the blood out of her ear. There's blood on her scalp at her temple too. Why is there so much blood? And why hasn't anyone cleaned it?

"Does anyone have a tissue?" My voice was shockingly loud in the quiet room as I realized there were several people in the room I did not know, including one with a gun and badge on her belt. *Is Sam under arrest? Is that why there's a cop here? Hasn't she been through enough already?*

Manz handed me a box of tissues from the computer desk, and I took one. Instead of wiping my weeping eyes and nose, I began to tenderly wipe away the dried blood from the valleys of Sam's ear.

"Honey, leave that," Manz said, stalling my hand.

"No!" I snapped. "Sam is clean and perfect and wonderful. I have to clean it for her. Sam would want it cleaned." At the sharp bark of my voice, Manz let go of my hand, and I resumed gently cleaning the delicate anatomy of her ear.

A pretty young nurse entered the room, with a smile. "This must be Alyssa we've been waiting for. My name is Tiffany, and I'm Samantha's nurse."

"Sam," Manz interrupted. "She prefers to be called Sam."

"Perfect. Thank you." Nurse Tiffany nodded agreeably and erased the last few letters from Sam's name on the whiteboard on the wall. "Since everyone is here now, I can give you a little update, if you'd like?"

Encouraged by our eager looks and quiet nods, she continued, "Sam is stable now and has been brought back out of the sedation we had her under while we monitored her. She's sleeping now and pretty heavily medicated to help her rest."

"What are her injuries?" I asked through my tears, never taking my eyes from Sam's closed, purple eyelids.

"She suffered a moderate contusion to the brain when she was hit in the back of the head. She also suffered an abrasion to the forehead when she hit the pavement. The contusion caused some swelling on the brain initially, so we kept her sedated in case surgery was needed. Thankfully, we were able to control it through medications so we didn't need to operate—at least, not on her skull. She also suffered a broken nose, which we repaired."

The officer at the back of the room interjected, "We think her nose broke when she hit the door of the truck or when she hit the pavement. It's hard to tell in the video."

The video. Jesus fucking Christ...there's video. My stomach churned.

Nurse Tiffany continued, "She also has three broken ribs, which will hurt like crazy for a while but should heal without any issues."

My blood boiled in my veins.

"We'll continue to monitor her for residual effects of the brain injury now that she's conscious—motor function, short- and long-term memory, language, that sort of thing." Nurse Tiffany's smile was bright and encouraging. "But if everything comes back clear, she should be able to go home in a few days."

"Can I wake her? I mean, is it okay to let her know I'm here?" I sniffled.

"Absolutely. In fact, you'll be the first person she's seen that she knows from before the accident, so we're curious to see if she remembers people accurately." Nurse Tiffany began typing into the computer stationed in the ICU room. "Unless you have any other questions, I'll just finish my notes and... There. All done." She clicked the mouse assertively and pushed the keyboard back into place. "If you need anything, just come out to the nurses' station, okay?"

"Thank you," we murmured in unison.

"Sam? Can you hear me?" I gently rubbed Sam's hand and brushed her hair away from her forehead—as much as I could with the bandages pinning it down. "Open your eyes for me, Sam. Wake up for me, okay?"

Sam's eyelids drifted open—well, as far as the swelling would allow. My throat constricted, and a hiccuping sob escaped.

"Baby, it's okay." Sam's usually low voice was gravelly and weak, but it was hers. *Baby... It is her. I know her voice. I know her laugh, her moans, her gentle words. This is my Sam lying here, looking like pain personified. It really is her.*

"What's her name?" Manz asked Sam quietly.

I watched as Sam looked quizzically at Manz.

"What's her name?" Manz repeated, gesturing to me.

"Quit being dumb, jackass," Sam said. *Jackass? Not quite confirmation of recognition, but close.*

The older woman behind me spoke up. "Samantha, language please."

"Sorry, Mom."

Mom. *Oh my god, she recognizes her.* Relief swept over me. I looked to the older couple standing behind me and smiled meekly. Manz's parents…but they were Sam's parents too. I hated meeting them this way, but it seemed like a good sign that I had been allowed into the circle of family without question or pushback. Now if Sam could only…

"Tell me her name," Manz persisted.

"This is Alyssa." She squeezed my hand, substantially weaker than I knew she was capable of. "She is my girlfriend…" She looked at me as I covered my mouth to resist sobbing. "…and I love her."

"I love you too." My voice was a strained whisper. I leaned forward and gave her a small kiss on her cracked lips. Jen hugged Manz a little closer. Someone behind me sniffled.

After a moment, Sam turned and looked at Jen for a long moment, recognition spreading slowly across her face. The tubing under her nose shifted slightly, and though her swollen face didn't allow for much of a smile, it was in fact a smile.

"Hey, Jen."

"Hey, buddy."

"Don't serve garlic to people on first dates anymore."

The room broke into happy, tear-filled laughter.

"I'll be sure to tell the owner," Jen said sheepishly.

"Sorry, guys," Nurse Tiffany said, reentering the room. "I tried to let you guys stay as long as I could, but the boss walked through, so I gotta kick some folks out. Only one at a time in ICU rooms, please."

"Thank you, Tiffany," Manz said, sounding more dignified and mature than I'd ever heard before. "We'll come back and check on you, okay, Sammy?" She turned to me. "Let us know if you or Sam need anything. Anything at all. We'll bring it to you."

"Wait. I'm staying? Y'all are her family, not me. Shouldn't one of you guys stay?" I said, looking from face to face in the room.

"Something tells me," Manz said with a smile, "that she wants you." She gave me a warm, tight hug. *Jeez, Manz gives excellent hugs. Just like Sam.* She stole a look over at Sam. "She's wanted you since the first time you met. We can all see it."

Jen nodded in affirmation.

I quickly turned to Sam's parents. "But I didn't get time to meet you yet," I protested, taking her mom's proffered hand.

"Don't worry, Alyssa," her dad said. He was tall and thin, with skin leathered by years in the sun, and a salt-and-pepper mustache. "Plenty of time for that soon." He kindly kissed my cheek, tickling my face with the bristles of his mustache.

Her mom stepped forward, tiny and petite like Manz. "If my girls love you, then I do too, honey. We can do the getting-to-know-you stuff later." She squeezed my hand, and they turned to leave.

The officer stepped forward and pressed a business card into my hand as she headed out of the room. "I'm Detective Sylvia Perez of the Homicide and Robbery Unit. I'm working this case, but I'm also close, personal friends with Jen, Amanda, and Sam. My *wife* and I both are." Her gaze was significant as she emphasized the word "wife." It felt wonderful to be recognized as a lesbian. To be seen. To be known. To be embraced and welcomed to the club. It was liberating, like the shedding of constricting clothing.

"Please, Officer Perez, before you go," I said. "Can you tell me what happened? This is all so overwhelming."

Officer Perez nodded and gave me a sympathetic look. "Three days ago, an unconscious woman was found badly beaten in a bakery parking lot. She had facial injuries, broken ribs, and bleeding on the brain. Docs put her in a medically induced coma until they could get her stable. The woman had no ID. We pulled the bakery surveillance and ID'd the plates of the Tacoma she was climbing into when she was attacked from behind. A single punch to the back of the skull knocked her unconscious, and the male suspect proceeded to stomp and kick her while she was unconscious. He then took her truck, which we later found burnt out on Hillside Drive in the county limits. By tracing the registered owner of the truck, we were able to identify Sam. And when I discovered Roger and Gwen were her adoptive parents, I immediately notified Manz of what happened."

She continued, "When you get a chance, I need to talk with you about..." She glanced at Sam, who was drifting off to sleep again. "This. Specifically, Tom Kentfield."

"Tom Kentfield?" My stomach dropped, and my blood ran like ice water through my veins. My mind spiraled, trying to connect the injured woman in the hospital bed to my bigot asshole ex. "What about Tom? Wait...did he do this? Tell me. Did he do this to her?" I was getting loud again but I didn't care.

"Yes, ma'am." Her eyes were warm and soft. "I believe, with your statement, we will be able to secure a conviction against him."

I nodded in thought, the wheels in my brain scrambling for traction. "Absolutely. Anything you need."

"I should also tell you that a bakery employee heard a male voice say, 'Fucking faggot,' so we're charging the assault as a hate crime."

My blood boiled in my veins. *A hate crime? Against my beautiful Sam?* My temple pulsed with rage. "Fucking asshole."

"And the statute of limitations isn't up yet for certain other..." Her voice faltered. "Other...offenses that we suspect you may be able to help us with. Felonies from your past together. Nothing you did wrong, Ms. Johansson, I promise you. But, if I'm not overstepping my place here, I suspect you were also victim to acts of violence by Mr. Kentfield in the past. And I suspect it's all related. We'd like to add those charges against him, if you're willing to cooperate."

If I'd reported him, could this have been prevented? Would Sam be lying in a hospital bed in pain and attached to machines if I'd been brave enough to come forward back then? I couldn't travel that path right now. I simply agreed and said I'd call.

Soon, the hospital room was empty except for the two of us and the beeps and blips of all the machinery. I sat back down into the chair beside Sam's bed, tucking her sleeping hand into mine.

"Come here." Sam's voice was groggy with sleep and pain meds.

"I'm here, sweetheart."

"No, come here," she said, tapping the hospital bed beside her.

"And lie next to you on the bed? No way. I'm too scared I'll hurt you or disconnect something."

"It's fine. All my tubes and wires are on that side. Your warmth will feel good on my ribs. Please? I'll sleep better, knowing you're right here with me."

I relented and gingerly crawled into the bed with her, curling my body against her side with my head resting on her shoulder. She smelled like the coppery tang of blood and antiseptic, but I didn't care. *She is here. She is mine. And I'll never let her go again.* I gently wrapped my arm around her waist, and she fell asleep immediately.

"Sorry to wake you." A different nurse was softly tapping my shoulder. "I just need to check her real quick."

"I'm sorry," I said groggily. I couldn't believe how deeply I'd fallen asleep. The adrenaline crash of my morning had taken its toll. "Do you need me to get up? Or leave?"

"No, no, no. Nothing like that. I just need to reach around you, if that's okay." She reached over me and checked the sticky leads on Sam's chest, listened to her breathing through the stethoscope, and checked her various bandages and gauzes.

Once she left, I settled back against Sam's shoulder. Sam let out a little groan.

"What happened? Did I hurt you?"

"No, it feels good to have you near me." She spoke with her eyes closed.

I snuggled a little closer, adding a little flirty lilt to my voice. "Oh, so that was a happy sound?"

"Mm-hmm."

"Do you need anything? Food? Meds? Anything?" I softly rubbed her stomach with my hand.

"Some water?"

"There's some ice chips here. Is that okay?" I reached behind me for the cup.

She eagerly opened her mouth for me, her dry lips looking cracked and painful. I spooned a few ice chips onto her tongue. She moaned again with happiness.

Once she had her fill of ice chips, I pulled my lip gloss from the pocket of my jeans.

"Here, you need this." I unscrewed the applicator wand from the tube and spread glittery pink gloss on her lips.

With her eyes still closed, she rubbed her lips together gratefully. "Mmm, strawberry. I taste like you."

"Let me see." I gently turned her chin and placed a small, featherlight kiss on her chapped lips. "No way. I like kissing you way better than I like kissing myself." I rested my head back on her chest.

My head bounced slightly with her chuckle, which made her laugh harder. "Oh my god! It hurts. Don't make me laugh." She braced her free hand against her ribs. Lifting her arm exposed an enormous, hand-shaped bruise. I recognized that handprint— I'd had several identical bruises in my past with Tom.

Keeping the mood light, I said, "I'm so sorry. I didn't think it was *that* funny."

"I just pictured our first sleepover, and your head bouncing on my belly when I laughed while you slept, and I couldn't help it."

"You are such a nerd. And Frosted Strawberry is definitely your color," I said, smiling at how she could make herself laugh over the most ridiculous things. "God, I missed you so much. I thought..." My throat closed on me.

"Thought what?" she asked, her eyes still closed.

"Nothing. We can talk about that later."

"I'm a captive audience. Might as well tell me now."

I took a breath to gather my thoughts. "I thought...I thought..." Emotion was seeping into my voice.

"Take your time, sweetheart."

I decided to spit it out before I lost my courage. "I thought I'd scared you away."

"What? How would you scare me away?"

"With…you know…Maybe I scared you by asking you to use your…toy. And I know, sometimes, I can be kind of assertive. Sexually, I mean. Or maybe…um…" My voice trailed off again. I wasn't trying to be coy, I swear. I was completely embarrassed, and my words kept disappearing.

"Maybe what?" she asked, her eyes shut.

"I don't know. Maybe…maybe…" *Spit it out, already.* "Maybe you heard me whisper 'I love you' that night as you fell asleep, and it scared you away. Maybe, after our wonderful date and such intense lovemaking and orgasming together, whispering my feelings for you was just too much for you to handle. So you ran away from me."

Her eyes opened for the second time since I entered the room. "I love you too." She leaned toward me, wincing as she did it, to give me a kiss. "I didn't run away, and I wasn't frightened off." She closed her eyes and rolled her face back to the ceiling. "Sorry, I can't open my eyes. It makes me too nauseated."

She breathed through flared nostrils for a few moments before continuing, "I woke up early that morning, like I always do. I can't help it. I'm an early riser. Anyway, I didn't want to wake you or your momma, so I decided to go to Cousteau's to get the croissants I had promised previously. A do-over, you know? I wasn't running away. I wasn't frightened of you. Quite the opposite, actually. I couldn't wait to get back to you. But when he stopped me, I was so afraid I would never get back to you." Her voice broke with emotion at her last few words.

"Shh, sweetheart," I cooed, gently rubbing her belly.

She choked out a hiccuping sob. "I was so scared. I thought he was going to kill me."

"He tried. You're too tough for that."

"Tough?" She scoffed at me. "I ran and got my ass knocked out with one punch." She clumsily pushed tears away with her free hand. "Then he beat the shit out of me while I was out."

"Exactly. He is such a fucking coward and so frightened of you that he had to sucker punch you from behind and attack you while you couldn't defend yourself. He's a fucking coward."

With that she fell quiet again, and her tears ceased.

"You think so?" she asked timidly.

"Absolutely, I do. I know him pretty damned well, remember?" I said sardonically.

She grunted in acknowledgment but didn't say any more.

"I missed you so much, Sam." I continued lovingly rubbing her stomach. "I'm so glad you're okay."

CHAPTER FORTY-ONE

Sam

My eventual move out of the intensive care unit to a normal hospital room meant I could have more than one visitor at a time. I loved watching Alyssa, Mom, and Dad talking for hours while I alternated between conversation and sleep. While they obviously were getting to know each other because of their mutual connection to me, it soon became evident they simply enjoyed each other's company. Their collective love of horses gave them endless fodder for conversation—as well as the bottomless pit of embarrassing childhood stories about yours truly.

Nearly everyone I knew came to visit, some once and most several times apiece. As an orphan, the outpouring of love from the community and my family was a little daunting and overwhelming. I was showered with gifts, balloons, flowers, and food deliveries. Because, as Jen so eloquently said, "Friends don't let friends eat hospital food."

Even Alex, the androgynous second-in-command at Jen's restaurant, came to visit. Granted, it was under the guise of delivering food to me from Jen, but she stayed for an hour, shyly chatting with Alyssa and me of her own choosing. It was endearing to see this young lesbian, still trying to find her style and identity, fumbling her way to answers without asking the questions directly. I wanted to say, "Just ask me, I'll tell you," but of course, I couldn't frighten away this timid fawn with such blatant statements.

I also had multiple visits from officers and detectives, checking to see if I had remembered any new details about the attack. That's what we called it now: The Attack. It was a living, breathing creature that, at times, glared from dark corners and growled in moments of silence. We also discussed the first time I met Tom Kentfield at the farmers' market and our subsequent confrontation at Alyssa's truck.

Manz introduced me to Beth Carter, a tough, no-bullshit prosecutor from Manz's office, with a New Jersey accent. Manz's request to handle the case herself was denied due to her conflict of interest and inability to be unbiased. As a peace offering, the DA let her pick who would prosecute the case instead. Manz chose Beth. And after only a few conversations with her, I had no doubt Manz had chosen the right prosecutor for my case.

Throughout it all, Alyssa was my constant companion. She woke me from nightmares, encouraged me when the physical therapy hurt too much, and warmed my aching ribs with her body while I slept. I'd never be able to thank her enough.

After three more days, an astonishing number of tests, and twice-daily, very painful physical therapy appointments, I was finally cleared for release from the hospital. Alyssa hovered over me like a mother hen, filling my prescriptions, receiving the discharge instructions from the doctor, and insisting on pushing my wheelchair out of the hospital.

I protested that I could walk out. After all, hadn't I earned my release from the hospital by performing so well on their tests and physical therapy sessions? I could walk just fine, thank you very much. But Alyssa and Nurse Tiffany tag-teamed against me, and I knew the battle was lost before it started. In addition, Nurse Tiffany said it was hospital policy, citing the liability if I fell and hurt myself on the way out the door. So, eventually, I succumbed to the ride in the wheelchair. Honestly, I would have agreed to anything if it meant I could leave and sleep in a real bed with no lights, no beeping, and no one waking me every hour with checkups.

There was never a debate where I would stay upon my release. I made it clear I didn't want to leave Alyssa's side. And I could say confidently, the feeling was mutual. Not surprisingly, there were no protests from my friends and family. They knew how I felt without my even saying it.

At long last, Alyssa wheeled me out of the hospital doors. A small entourage stood on the walkway just outside the hospital doors: Nurse Tiffany, Manz and Jen, my parents, Ms. Rhonda and Mr. Westbrook, and even Alyssa's momma. They held balloons and flowers and showered me with hugs and kisses. I couldn't believe it. It was overwhelming and reduced me to tears.

With promises to visit and be visited, I climbed gingerly into Alyssa's truck. And after more goodbyes and thank-yous, we headed back to Alyssa's ranch with Momma in the back seat.

The next few weeks passed in a blur. My daily physical therapy appointments finally dwindled to weekly as my doctors became convinced my motor functions were intact with no impairments or lingering effects. Alyssa kept me on schedule with meds and my physical therapy exercises.

But, admittedly, her toughest task was enforcing my rest order. I confess, I am a terrible patient. With my motor functions working fine, my abrasions and bruises nearly gone, and my broken nose healed, only the sensitivity of my ribs remained to hinder me. I weaned off the pain medications as quickly as I could—probably faster than I should have—because I was anxious to just be normal again. I was desperate to return to activity and working with animals. I missed their gentle souls and creating bonds with them. But Alyssa ensured that my manual labor was kept to a minimum. Being the impatient patient that I am, I still snuck in a chore now and then.

"What's the first step on creating an equine therapy program?" Momma asked one evening as the three of us sat on the porch, sipping glasses of wine in the setting sun.

"I have no idea," I replied honestly.

"Probably have to start setting up a nonprofit or something," Alyssa added.

That word—*nonprofit*—clicked something in my brain.

"Hold on," I said, rising from my chair. "I might have an idea."

I ran up the stairs to Alyssa's room—I mean, *our* room, as she kept reminding me. But my still healing broken ribs painfully reminded me to take it slowly, so I slowed to a more conservative pace.

After a few minutes digging though my duffel bag—I still hadn't unpacked, for no other reason than lack of energy and time—I found what I was looking for tucked into the butt pocket of a pair of dirty jeans. I was afraid it'd been in the truck that Tom Kentfield burned to a crisp or destroyed in the wash, but luckily, it was intact.

Back downstairs, I dialed the number on the business card. Alyssa and her momma watched me with curiosity.

"Hi, can I speak to Jim Cambron please? Oh, hi, Jim. You might not remember me, but my name is Sam Monroe. We flew together a few weeks ago from Denver to SF?"

"Oh, yes, you betcha! The animal trainer, right?" Jimbo said cheerily.

"Yes, exactly, the animal trainer. I've got a favor to ask."

"Anything. After saving me from sitting next to that horrible little starlet on that plane, I owe you big time. Name it."

I wasn't going to mention the embarrassing seat-switch debacle. "Wanna help me start up a nonprofit equine therapy center?"

CHAPTER FORTY-TWO

Alyssa

Holding the bottles of wine with Sam following a few steps behind me with an enormous bowl of honey-walnut-drizzled fruit salad from the ranch, I rang the doorbell. Sam chuckled at me, reaching for the front doorknob.

"Family doesn't ring the doorbell. We walk right in." She pushed open the door and gestured for me to head inside.

Rounding the corner from the kitchen, Sam and Manz's mom, Gwen, met us in the entryway.

"Come in, come in! Here, let me take those." She took the wine bottles and rose up onto her tiptoes to kiss my cheek hello.

"Hi, Mom," Sam said, bending to kiss her mom on the cheek.

"You shouldn't be carrying that," she said, handing the wine bottles back to me and taking the fruit salad bowl from Sam.

"Moooom," Sam whined. "I'm fine. I can carry a bowl, I promise."

Her mom gave her The Look, and Sam got quiet. I chuckled quietly to myself, trying not to be noticed. It was comical to see such a tiny, fiery woman exert motherly control over tall, muscular Sam.

"Even when you're sixty years old, you'll *still* be my child."
Sam's mom looked to me. "I bet your mom's the same way,
right?"

"Oh, yes, ma'am."

"Roger! Sam and Alyssa are here. Come give us a hand."

Roger's tall, lanky, cowboy form rounded the corner.

"Hey-ey-ey!" The word came out in several laughing
syllables. "There's my girls!" He wrapped Sam and me into a
tight hug. *So that's where Manz and Sam get their fantastic hugging
abilities.* He took the wine bottles from me. "Everyone's out
back, and the food's almost ready. Follow me."

Gwen and Roger's redwood back porch was enormous, with
several comfortable seating areas, a table for ten, a barbecue,
and outdoor kitchen area. Jen stood at the barbecue, turning
something with tongs, while Manz lounged under an umbrella
with a glass of white wine. The small table before her had several
drink coasters, chips, salsa, and guacamole. Alex and a young
girl with long, pink-tipped blond hair were splashing each other
in the pool below. Detective Perez and a very pretty Hispanic
woman were cuddled together in the hot tub. Horse corrals and
a picture-perfect red-and-white barn sat in the distance across
an immaculate lawn, surrounded with blooming landscaping.

"Look who's here!" Roger's loud voice boomed across the
yard.

"Perfect timing. The meat's ready," Jen said.

Drinks were poured. Plates were filled. Easy, comfortable
laughter of family and friends filled the air, mingled with the
smells of incredible cooking.

Once everyone was settled around the table with steaming
plates of incredible food, Gwen stood and raised her beer glass.

"Attention everyone. I'd like to make a toast. Everyone at
this table is one of my kids—whether you like it or not." The
table chuckled in easy laughter. "We love you all, and Roger and
I are so blessed to call you family. So raise your glasses!"

We dutifully raised our glasses, and Sam whispered quickly
to me, "Health, wealth, and wisdom."

"What?" I asked, confused.

But before she could reply, Gwen said, "On three...One. Two. Three!"

"Health, wealth, and wisdom!" we said in unison.

I leaned over to Sam for a quick kiss and rested my hand on her thigh.

"I love you, Sam."

"I love you too, baby."

More Titles from Bella Books

Mabel and Everything After – Hannah Safren
978-1-64247-390-2 | 274 pgs | paperback: $17.95 | eBook: $9.99
A law student and a wannabe brewery owner find that the path to a fairy tale happily-ever-after is often the long and scenic route.

To Be With You – TJ O'Shea
978-1-64247-419-0 | 348 pgs | paperback: $19.95 | eBook: $9.99
Sometimes the choice is between loving safely or loving bravely.

I Dare You to Love Me – Lori G. Matthews
978-1-64247-389-6 | 292 pgs | paperback: $18.95 | eBook: $9.99
An enemy-to-lovers romance about daring to follow your heart, even when it's the hardest thing to do.

The Lady Adventurers Club - Karen Frost
978-1-64247-414-5 | 300 pgs | paperback: $18.95 | eBook: $9.99
Four women. One undiscovered Egyptian tomb. One (maybe) angry Egyptian goddess. What could possibly go wrong?

Golden Hour - Kat Jackson
978-1-64247-397-1 | 250 pgs | paperback: $17.95 | eBook: $9.99
Life would be so much easier if Lina were afraid of something basic—like spiders—instead of something significant. Something like real, true, healthy love.

Schuss – E. J. Noyes
978-1-64247-430-5 | 276 pgs | paperback: $17.95 | eBook: $9.99
They're best friends who both want something more, but what if admitting it ruins the best friendship either of them have had?

CPSIA information can be obtained
at www.ICGtesting.com
Printed in the USA
JSHW060736300323
39626JS00004B/4

9 781642 474725